Guilty Pleasures

SAM MARIE

Guilty
Pleasures

Guilty Pleasures by Sam Marie

Published by Sam Marie

www.authorsammarie.com

Cover by Sam Marie.

ISBN: 979-8-9893802-1-3 (ebook)

ISBN: 979-8-9893802-0-6 (paperback)

Printed in USA

First Edition

For my fellow smut lovers,
In my darkest, loneliest moments, books have never failed me. I hope
this one is there for you, too.

<h1 style="text-align:center"><u>Trigger and Content Warnings</u></h1>

Be advised the following stories may contain some triggering terms, situations, etc., that may cause disturbing emotions. Proceed with caution.

- Demon Ascending:
  - CNC, forced sex grey area
  - Claiming
  - Demon/human
- The Witching Hour:
  - Mutual power exchange
  - Witch/unknown species
- The Wolf:
  - CNC
  - Blood
  - Mating
  - Marking
  - Werewolf/human
- The Siren:
  - Enslavement

- o Bondage

- o Rough oral

- o Mermaid/human

- Faerie Delights:

  - o Magical coercion

  - o Forced sex fantasy

  - o Gangbang

  - o Multiple male humans/one fae female

- Dom Daddy:

  - o BDSM

  - o Dominate male/timid female

  - o Exhibitionism

  - o Voyeurism

- The Game:

  - o Blood

  - o Sadism

  - o Self-harm

  - o Knife Play

- o Degradation

- o Bondage

- o Manipulation

- o Electrostimulation

- o Sex work

- My Brother's Bestfriend:

  - o Drug and alcohol use

  - o Forbidden love

- After Dark:

  - o Stalker

  - o Attempted rape

  - o Secret identity

  - o Rough sex

- Eat Me:

  - o Oral sex

  - o Married couple

- Airport Security:

  - o Abuse of power

- Confinement

    - Piercings and toys

    - Male x Female x Male

- The Flight Attendant:

    - Public sex

    - Mile high club

    - Workplace romance

- Record Daddy:

    - Age gap

    - ONS

- Soccer Mom:

    - Public sex

    - Age gap

- The Rockstar & The Actress:

    - Secret identity

    - Manipulation

- A Very Merry Christmas:

    - Married couple

- Sweet romance
- New Years Resolution:
  - ONS
  - Female x Female
- Valentine:
  - CNC
  - Magical coercion
  - Spit-roasting
  - Enslavement
  - Vampire/human
  - Male x Male x Female
- Pride Ride:
  - Workplace romance
  - Toys
  - Male x Male
- Office Daydreams:
  - ONS
  - Creampie

Dark Escapes

Demon Ascending

"**Y**ou're ours now, princess," the grey-skinned demon coos into my ear.

His breath smells so sour I can taste it, but all I can do is look away. My hands are tied above my head with a rope hanging from the rafters of this jaunty, old wooden barn on the outskirts of my kingdom.

The demon princes who have been fighting us for a century finally breached the walls of my father's fortress tonight. Miles away, and I can still hear the cries of my people. I can still smell the burning of flesh and bone.

After taking down my father and capturing me, they brought me here. I can only hope my brother escaped unscathed. Yet, in my heart, I know the demon hoards are raping and murdering everyone within and around the palace walls. Humans don't stand a chance.

"Fuck you," I spit in its face.

The demon's fingers latch around my throat and squeeze tightly as he wipes the spit from his face and rubs it over mine. "The more you fight, the harder you'll break."

"Never. You might as well kill me now," I scream in his face, and he squeezes my neck harder, forcing me to gasp for air.

The demon who has been hiding in the shadows stalks forward. Moonlight shines through an open shutter, making his skin sparkle.

He's darker than the others, glittering like the black pearl sand in my kingdom's harbor, unlike the grey ash that lines the bottom of a fireplace like so many other demons' skin looks.

It's rumored that the depth of a demon's skin tone represents the amount of power it possesses. If that's true, this demon is very powerful.

"We don't plan on killing you, princess." He backhands the demon gripping my throat and shoves him away. The demon behind me automatically backs up as well, and both bow in submission. "I plan on making you my queen," the dark-skinned one says.

A gasp and a huff escape me. A queen? That means I'm not just dealing with a prince of Hell. I'm dealing with a king. They're rare. I've never known or heard of a human in existence coming across one. I imagine any humans who have met one died before the claim could be made.

"Like I said, you might as well kill me now because that will never happen," I say.

"In case I haven't made myself clear enough, you won't have a choice in the matter," the demon snarls.

Before I can retort, one claw slices down the front of my bodice, splitting the dress in two as it falls to the ground and leaves me standing in only my lace undergarments.

"Demon scum," I curse him, spitting at his face, but the demon dodges my attempt to soil him.

He *tsks* at me as he shamelessly admires my body. There's hunger in his eyes. My stomach roils at the disgusting thoughts that are surely going through that demented brain of his.

The demons have been fighting my family for half my life, and never once have I heard of even the lowest level of demon fraternizing with a human—to do so would be an abomination on both sides.

"I didn't plan on letting my generals fuck you, but you must be punished. You need to understand where you fit in this new order."

Fuck me? It hadn't occurred to me that making me his queen meant taking my…

The generals snicker behind him, taking a position on either side of their king. One of them gives me a savage look that says he wants to do more than fuck me, and my stomach turns again. I've never seen a demon up close before tonight. They are truly monstrous.

The king and his generals are more human-looking than most demons I saw earlier this evening. They are a far cry from the winged creatures with teeth as long as my forearm ripping through my soldier's bodies. The main difference from me is their skin tone and the sharply tipped horns on their head. However, it makes them no less monstrous than the horde of creatures they associate with and who are currently rampaging my kingdom.

All three take one step toward me, closing in on all sides.

"Please, don't let them touch me,' I say softly.

The demon king's eyes light up in amusement. He's one step closer to breaking me.

"Why should I not, princess? You look at us like we're monsters. Is that not how you see us? Should we not treat you like the monsters you think we are?"

"You are monsters!" My defiance returns in a fury.

They laugh at me and then shift.

Their limbs lengthen, their eyes darken, and their power surges. I choke on the invisible pressure clogging the air. Power like I've never felt before. No wonder we didn't stand a chance.

The demon king brushes my hair back and lifts my chin with a clawed finger. He's at least six inches taller than before. Red lines his black irises.

"You have not seen monsters yet, princess. I will take you like this or like the handsome male princelings you prefer to look at. That's the only choice you'll receive tonight," he says, venom lacing his tone.

He shifts, becoming more human in appearance. His claws and horns disappear, and his skin loses its shimmer. But his face is the same. His body is the same. He is the most handsome man I have ever laid eyes on. I try to ignore it—the attraction.

"This appearance pleases you deeply. I can feel it. It's disgusting," he says.

"It doesn't matter what you look like. You're still a demon, and I'll never forget that," I retort.

He scratches his chin thoughtfully as he paces in front of me. "Perhaps this is my true form, and the other is one we create to instill fear in our enemies. Ask yourself, what do you really know of our kind? Maybe demons are just magical humans."

His generals chuckle, but a sharp look from the king quiets them.

"You can't trick me. I know what you are, no matter what appearance you take on. You're a demon. You'll never be a man. And I'll never be your queen." A flick of his wrist makes his human disguise melt away. I fight a gag as the smell of burnt flesh pierces my nostrils. "Is that really necessary?" I choke out.

In his natural form—the half-human, half-demon flesh—he approaches me. "I have shown generosity. I have exhibited a willingness to compromise. But there is little time left, princess."

"Bael, ten men approach from the East," one of his generals says, looking out a broken slat in the barn's wall.

"It's time," Bael says.

With another flick of his wrist, a shimmering wall of energy surrounds him and I.

"What are you doing?" I ask.

"I asked you a question, princess." Bael steps forward and runs a clawed finger down the center of my chest.

I shiver as he touches parts of my body no man has ever seen or laid a hand on. His claw leaves a faint red line in its wake, a promise and a threat. "Please don't," I beg.

"If I were a human, would you want me to touch you, princess?" Bael's voice is husky as his hands continue to roam my body, sliding the scraps of my dress off of me.

He brushes a knuckle over the curve of my backside before cupping my butt cheek. "Under all those layers of fabric, you'd never know such a luscious body exists," he says, kissing my collarbone.

I shudder against his smooth, velvety lips. I've dreamed about what a man's lips would feel like, taste like.

"I smell you..." Bael warns, nipping my neck.

I jump against the pricking feeling of his sharp teeth on my delicate skin. He laughs and bites harder. They pierce my skin, spiking my adrenaline. I buck to get loose, knocking my body into the Bael's, but it only increases the sharp pain heating my neck.

An enraged snarl splits through his lips. He yanks the rope above my head, breaking it from the banister. My heels hit the ground just as Bael tosses the rope's end around my shoulders. He wraps it twice, twining my arms behind my back and tying it tightly. A drop of blood on the corner of his lip shines brightly against his dark skin.

"Please," I beg again despite the dryness scratching my throat. Tears well in my eyes as I realize it's my blood on his lips, and it's not likely the last that will be spilled from me tonight.

Bael presses himself against my back and whispers, "One day, you'll beg for me to fuck you, princess. You'll beg me not to leave our bed. But for now, I must make you mine before someone else tries to first."

I would never beg him to fuck me. I don't even know what fucking is. I've dreamed of making love, but it certainly wasn't to a demon. Bael shifts into his human form, the claws and horns misting away as if they never existed, as he turns me to face him.

"This is what you fantasize about. Consider it a mercy that I take on this form," he says softly. The gentle tone is a juxtaposition to his actions.

"No. I don't want it," I say. He embodies the man of my dreams. Yet, every part of me knows exactly who he is underneath. I'd rather face the truth than allow my mind to be deceived. "If you're going to force me, do it in your true form!"

Bael's hand contorts as he morphs back into his demon form fully, embracing the terrifying beast. He spins me back around, tugging me into his chest. His arm traps me as a clawed finger slices through the front of my undergarments. He tugs them off, and my breasts bounce with the movement. His snarls drown out the pounding of my heart.

When he cups my breast, rolling my nipple between the pads of his fingers, I feel something harden against my backside.

"Wh—What is that?" I stutter.

The demon king chuckles. "Do you not know what a cock feels like, princess?"

"No. Not really." I squirm against his front, but it forces that hard rod to dig sharply into my bare buttocks.

"That is my cock you're rubbing against, and it's exciting me."

I gulp. "Oh. I—" I'm at a loss for words and cut off by Bael's dark laughter.

"Have I caught myself a virgin? Tonight could not get any better." He kisses the side of my throat as he grabs my hips and pins my backside to him. "Do you know I've never fucked a human, princess? In a way, I'm a virgin, too. I hear it's one of the most pleasurable sexual experiences in this realm."

"Humans and demons don't fornicate," I argue, but the words are weak and breathless.

He laughs again, sliding his hand over my stomach and dipping it lower. Claw traces lines down my body. "On the contrary, they do it constantly. Someone of my status requires…Someone of your status, though. Hence my lack of experience on the matter."

"You don't have to do this," I whisper.

His hand dips lower, and he sinks a finger into my folds. I cry out as the sensitive area jolts and tingles in response to his touch. The backside of his claw strokes down my middle; the hard, sharp point doesn't pierce me, but the fear of it makes my body burn.

"If you're so repulsed by me, why are you so wet, princess?"

My lip quivers as I fight for a response, but I'm speechless with his hands on me. He moves his fingers, circling the base of my sex lazily. Those wicked-looking claws faintly brush my skin. The feeling is unlike any other. It's putting me in a trance. Time stops as I take one gasping breath.

"You're quite the unexpected conquest, my little queen. Despite your curse words, your cunt is thirsty. Is it my cock you desire, or is the perversion more your thing?" Bael teases.

"I don't like any of this," I say, tensing.

His hand flies up to my neck, choking me as he growls in my ear. "Never lie to me."

"I—I'm not," I manage to say.

Bael laughs and releases me. "Enough of this. Do you know how this works?"

He walks around to face me, unfastening his pants. I watch as he pulls a huge shimmering black penis out. My handmaiden has described men's genitals to me, but this…This is unlike anything I expected.

"Clearly, you have no idea," Bael says, approaching me. He hooks his arm under my right leg and lifts it, exposing my sex. "This is my cock—" he grabs himself, stroking, but releases it "—and it's going in here." He shows me his hand, claws retracting before he shoves two fingers into my sex.

He slides in effortlessly. My inner walls clench around him. *Oh, my gods, those fingers.* He moves them around, in and out, curling and straightening. Not even my own fingers have breached this area.

A little moan escapes me when he shifts his hand to rub his palm on the outside of my sex.

"This is nothing compared to the pleasure I'll give you with my cock, princess. Give yourself to me willingly, and I promise you won't regret it."

A promise? Demons don't make promises nor honor them.

"I don't believe you," I pant.

His fingers continue to stroke me, sliding through my sex, taking turns rubbing the outside and plunging into the inside.

"Everything you know about us is a lie. Do you at least believe that?" he asks, sliding his fingers through my moistening cunt. He moves purposefully, like he knows exactly where and how I want to be touched.

"No," I say.

"My cock is nearly the same as a human. Superior in every way, obviously, but since you've never had one, you'll not know the difference. It will pleasure you immensely, princess," he says gently.

I shake my head defiantly. His penis bobs between us as his hand moves. It's so close to touching me, and Bael notices. He takes hold of himself and positions it at my entry.

"Wait," I cry.

He pauses. "Why be ashamed of your attraction to me, princess? Submit to me, and it will make this far more enjoyable." He glides the head of his penis across my slit.

"Oh gods," I say, as a shiver rolls down my spine.

"Let me show you how good I can make you feel," Bael says, rubbing his shaft through my slit.

My wetness sparkles against against his shimmering black skin. He applies more pressure, thrusting himself through my folds. The tip of his penis pokes my entry but doesn't breach it. I close my eyes, trying not to let my mind see the handsome male demon before me.

Once again, his tip prods at my entry but doesn't enter. My traitorous body shakes violently with the need to push him away and suck him in simultaneously.

"Tell me, princess. Tell me you ache to feel me inside of you."

"I don't," I lie.

"Your smell says differently."

"You don't know that."

Bael laughs knowingly, but his words turn serious. "Others would not be as kind as I. But you must be mine before the end of the raids or another will take you. My promise to you holds true, but for now, this must be done. I'm sorry."

The tip of his cock pushes past my entry. It's so hot and wet. And with my leg held high, my entrance is fully open and displayed for him. I peer down at our sexes through thick lashes and watch as his massive penis disappears into me, and a very full, pleasant feeling washes over me.

"Wh—" My words are cut short as he slams into me.

He fills me completely. The head of his manhood sinks into me and is only stopped by something internal. He nudges against it, making my body squeeze around him. My insides roll around him as he retracts and slams back into me. It's like he's pushing my walls outward, forcing my body to give him more space to explore.

Liquid seeps from my body, slickening the base of his cock every time he pulls out. "I told you. You must be mine. No one else's. Mine," he moans, pumping himself into me faster.

The handsome demon king's face is stern as if he is fighting something, but his hands hold me gently. They caress my body, appreciating the curves and mounds of my womanly features. I hold my breath, willing my body to dry up, to refuse the overwhelming pleasure radiating through my center.

He yanks my other leg up and rips off the restraints binding my arms. Instinctively, I wrap my arms around his muscular shoulders before I fall back. It's the first time I've touched a demon, and his skin is as soft as his velvety cock. His muscles are as firm as they look. And his body is warm, nearly unbearably so, like the infernos of Hell boil within his blood.

My body heats against his. He holds me up and pounds relentlessly into me. Picking up my hips and dropping them down onto his hard rod. The stiff member fucks me thoroughly.

I've never felt anything like this before, and I can't imagine it's always this good. My handmaiden never described it to being like this. It's maddening. It's life-shattering. And with a demon...It's so wrong. But it feels so right. My fingernails dig into his shoulders as my sex tightens around him. Bael's growl fills the silent barn like an animal ravishing its prey.

I am his prey. I am his.

Shit. I am his!

My body betrays me, tightening around his cock as my heart palpitates erratically. Bael's fingers pull my head back as his lips slam onto mine. He tastes of rage, anguish, and fire. He is smokey and intoxicating. He makes my head spin in the haziness as magic makes the air sizzle.

"What's going on?" I say, pulling away.

He forces me back into a kiss, and I submit. The air buzzes with energy.

"Mine," he says, thrusting deeply into me.

My sex swells, and my body tenses. He continues railing into me despite the growing pressure. Bael tunnels through my tightening walls, massaging my shaky muscles.

"Bael." His name is a whisper on my breath. A soft plea to stop whatever is happening. I don't know what is happening to me, but my mind is disintegrating. Losing itself to this feeling in my core.

My skin tingles, and Bael smiles. "Mine," he roars and bites my neck.

The demon king's bite burns as he punctures my skin. But then it electrifies me. I combust, feeling the fiery inferno burn through my veins and electrify my sex. My walls suck in his cock, swelling and pulsing against him, milking him of his hot seed.

The magic in the air snaps, making my ears pop like a spell breaking from our sensual binding.

Bael spills himself into me as he licks the side of my bleeding neck. Darkness threatens to overtake me, colorful bubbles of light explode around me, blurring the barn, the other demons, and anything else from my vision.

"My queen," Bael says softly, setting me down on both feet and kissing up the length of my neck. He holds me like a prize he's fought centuries to obtain.

"I'm not a queen," I mumble, my mind still in a haze and my body becoming heavy.

"You are that and more, little queen. Now, we must go." Bael takes my hand, and the world disappears into the darkness.

The Witching Hour

It's nearly midnight, and I have no one to channel my celestial power through. Every succubus in town has found their counterpart tonight, except for me. If I don't participate in the yearly mating ceremony, my powers will weaken. I can't afford to lose any power this year.

I must find a worthy male.

This is why I find myself stumbling into a dusty tavern full of drunkards that smell like horse excretions. The men are not visually appealing, but they are strong and stubborn, which will suit my purpose for them well.

I hike up my skirts and sway my hips, walking between benches full of men guzzling pints of amber beer. Eyes turn and watch me behind the foamy glass rims of their cups.

Approaching the bar counter at the back of the tavern, I plop down on an uneven bar stool, facing the arrangement of men and crossing my legs. The slit in my skirt slides further up my crossed leg, exposing my upper thigh, but I leave it there.

Only prostitutes show this much skin. I don't judge the profession, but I don't particularly love appearing as if I am one.

I'm using one of these men; they will not be using me, and they will certainly not walk away thinking they had. The celestial power that will race through them, using them as a conduit for my power, will feel like the best orgasm they've ever had. If anything, they should be thanking me after.

"I haven't seen you in here before," a strong male voice says behind me.

Taking my time, I spin around on the barstool and flip my hair over my shoulder. "It's my first time. What's a woman got to do to get a drink around here?" I say cutely to the burly bartender.

He crosses his arms, the muscles bulging against the strain of his tattered shirt. "Looks like you've already figured that out." His eyes move down to my ample cleavage—another purposeful display of my womanly form to draw attention.

It's clear the bartender isn't falling for my act, but it doesn't concern me. At least one of the men in this bar tonight will entertain my needs.

I dismiss his comment and say, "I'll have the strongest drink you've got."

"Coming right up, witchling," he smirks.

"Keep your voice down," I hiss, but he's already walking away.

My motives are none of his business, and I don't need him outing them. It's no secret tonight is the celestial full moon. Many men sign up to be a succubus's escort for the evening. However, there will always be another group of individuals who celebrate this night with a hunt for my kind.

It's likely a few of those believers are having an evening drink in this very tavern before heading out. I'd rather not make it easy for them or put a damper on my evening. It's best I appear a lonely human woman and nothing more. How the bartender knows I'm not merely a human is beyond me. It normally takes inhuman senses or spelled objects to identify us.

"You're in my bar, sweetheart. I'll say whatever I want to whomever I want." The bartender threatens me as he mixes a drink in front of me.

I stand on the stool's foothold, leaning in so only he can hear me. "The moment you begin to oust me, I'll turn my sights on you. Would you so easily offer yourself in place of one of these drunkards, bartender?"

He laughs whole-heartedly, bellowing the jovial sound before shouting at the patrons, "Everyone out. I've got to teach a *woman* some manners." He says *woman* with disdain as if he really rather have said witch, but still, he doesn't reveal me.

Everyone's eyebrows shoot up as they eye the bartender and me, grumbling about not finishing their drinks. The bartender's face remains in a serious grimace, and it doesn't take long for the men to shake their heads and follow orders. Without a second thought or one last sip of beer, they stand from their seats and exit in a single file. In less than a minute, the tavern is empty.

I scowl at him. He's not an easy conquest. I much prefer seducing one of those order-following men. "How dare you," I say to him, pushing my stool back from the bar.

Planting one hand on the bar top, he hurdles over the decaying wood plank to stand by my side. His agility and speed catch me off guard. Before I can move away, his hand wraps around my upper arm.

"Release me," I command, pouring magic into my voice.

"Isn't this what you want? You come into my bar looking for a man to use as your conduit, knowing it will drain him. He'll be nothing more than a husk when you are done with him."

"That's not true," I argue.

This man, or slightly more than a man, doesn't know anything about the ceremony, nor me. I've never left a man depleted of his soul. I take what I need and give back what I don't. Leaving them paralyzed or disabled is the act of a novice. I've been doing this for over a hundred years. The men I choose are left feeling sexually satisfied and nothing more. I give them a gift, not a life sentence.

"Prove it," he challenges me.

I laugh in his face, tugging my arm out of his grasp, but I fail and his fingers grip me harder.

"Prove it," he repeats.

Power that isn't mine pricks at my skin, increasing my intrigue.

"With you?" I ask.

He nods.

"Have you slept with a witch?" I ask, my curiosity growing.

How much experience does this bartender have? He's clearly not just a man—humans possess no magical power. I can normally identify preternatural beings.

"I've slept with much worse," he responds.

His eyes begin to glow—a faint yellow rim forms around bright green pupils.

"What are you?" I ask.

"Try me and find out."

His tongue flicks against his upper teeth. He's bating me, but he lowers his hand and steps back to give me a choice. I tilt my head, assessing him. What I failed to notice before is now abundantly clear.

The bartender is fearsome. He has chin-length hair with five days' worth of facial hair. Underneath all that hair, deep scars line the only exposed parts of his body. His eyes gleam with some mysterious force.

He doesn't smell like a werewolf. He's too alive for a vampire. He's too burly for a fairy. It's possible he's of the rarer shifter breeds, but I'm well-versed in many of those. This bartender has me stumped.

My stomach knots with interest in the unexpected beast before me. I sniff, trying to place his ancestry. There's something ancient and powerful inside the male. Someone like this wouldn't offer themselves to me. They are the once-in-a-millennia type of conduit. He could boost my power tenfold.

Witches are happy enough with an easy human man. Other magical beings don't like to risk us using them on this night. It leaves them vulnerable and at our mercy. No being with power would put themselves in such a risky situation.

This offering appeals to me. His power loosens the longer we stand here. I can taste it on my tongue—honey bark and smoke. My knees squeeze together as I feel my body responding to the desire for what he offers—power.

"I smell your arousal, witchling. Are you going to make me beg for it, or are you going to ride me already?' he taunts.

His vulgarity excites me. I can't wait to shut him up.

I slide my hands over his shirt and up his muscular chest, feeling the heat of his body and the firm pounding of his heart under my palms.

He wastes no time, lifting me up by my thighs and setting me on the bar top. He reaches behind his neck, pulling off his shirt in one tug and exposing a scarred, hairy chest.

I follow his lead and slide my skirt up to pool around my waist. The heavy fabric overheats me, making me yearn to sink my tentacles of power into him.

"Touch me, witchling, or you won't be able to refuel your powers." He takes my wrists and guides my hands to his cheeks.

My palms flatten against the bristly hair on his jaw, and I feel the power begin to transfer between us. It's unlike anything I've felt before.

"So quick to offer yourself to me. Are you sure you know what you're doing?" I say.

"More than you know," he says.

My brows furrow. *Who is this beast?* I pry into him, wedging my power into his aura, seeping into the cracks of his very soul.

Then, I see it. There's something inside him that channels power better than my own. I expected it to be strong with him, but part of me questions if the table might turn. I peer up at him in shock, and he's smirking.

It doesn't take more than a taste for me to know this is a bad idea. I release my hold, pulling my power back into me, but he grabs my wrists and forces my palms against his chest. Power surges within him, streaming into my hands, forcing me to take it. My hands shake and tingle as if holding onto a ball of energy that vibrates faster than the speed of magic. It's never this strong. It's never this uncontrollable.

"What are you doing?" I ask, trying to break our connection.

"You can handle it, witchling. Focus," he says.

His words taunt me as power pours from him. I grind my teeth as it surrounds my entire body, heating my skin. A phantom limb caresses the back of my neck, soothing me.

"Good girl," the bartender says softly, running his hands up the insides of my thighs as I shake uncontrollably.

I squeeze my eyes shut. I'm lost in the buzzing energy now flowing between our bodies. It is an intoxicating high. It's so intense I'm seconds away from losing control and being at his mercy. It wants me to give myself over to it, to absorb it at *his* will.

The bartender rips the slit of my skirt, throwing the fabric to the side. The cool tavern air rushes in to stroke my sex. The shocking change in temperature forces a moan of surprise and pleasure out of me. My back arches, and a new tingling stirs at the apex of my thighs as I fight an invisible force with the rest of my body and mind.

"Stop," I say, forcing a command on him, but it has no effect.

He huffs indignantly. "That won't work on me, witchling." He unlaces the front of his pants, letting them slide down slowly. "I grew up around your kind. I know all your cute, dirty little tricks."

He releases my hands, but I'm locked in place. The power is like a handcuff—once it's on, only the person with the key can remove it. And he holds the key.

"Fortunately for you, I tend to like those dirty little tricks," he says, leaning forward and brushing a kiss to my neck.

The tender touch makes me whimper. I'm wound tight as I fight against his control. "What's your agenda with me?" I manage to say.

His hands glide up my inner thighs, stroking so close to my bare sex that a millimeter more would have him touching me. He continues lazy strokes along my tender skin as he takes it upon himself to kiss up and down the length of my neck.

"Answer me," I pant. My arms cramp as the magic wraps around them, squeezing and working its way toward my chest.

"My agenda is your agenda," he says between kisses.

He sucks the lobe of my ear into his mouth, I cry out and his power surges, wrapping around my shoulders, my chest. My upper body is immovable against it.

"I highly doubt that," I say, shaking my head to push him away.

The beast is undeterred. He knows he's found a weak spot. Once again, he sucks on my ear. It shatters me, and his power traps my entire body. Invisible tendrils of magic force my legs apart. My hold on his chest is torn away as my arms are bound behind my back.

He smiles down at me, stepping away to admire his handi-work. "Perfect. Now submit fully, witchling, or I won't give you the power you came here for," he says.

"As if you'd give me any." I only speak because he allows me to speak.

"I plan on giving you more than a worthless human man has to offer."

"Show me your word is binding," I say. There's only one way to bind oneself to their word, and there's no way he'll do it, not with me already in his control. He'd be stupid to make that kind of oath.

He laughs. "You're so pessimistic. What happened to you, witchling, that you can't trust a male?"

A claw shoots out of his finger, slicing the palm of his left hand. It disappears as quickly as it appears.

"What the hell are you?" I say.

He tilts my head back and brings the bleeding wound to my mouth, as he says, "I give my word. My word is binding to you and only you. I offer you power and release under the celestial moon."

His palm flattens across my mouth. Blood pours over my tongue, and I suck it down. The words are clear enough, which means I'll get my power. I'm just not sure if I'll be alive past the night—that much was not promised.

When he releases me, his wound heals. "Now relax, witchling. Tell me the words. Tell me you're mine," he says.

"I'm already bound. You might as well consider me gagged because I'm no one's," I say.

The male slides his pants down, letting them drop to the ground. He steps out of them, his cock bouncing with the movement. He's hard as a rock, yet, he strokes himself as if to ready it.

"If you think a good-looking cock will make me say the words, you're wrong," I say.

He chuckles, stroking himself, happy to let me watch. "I'm in no rush, witchling. I offer you power and release, but it's you who has to accept it. I'm happy to keep you bound and gagged—as you say—as I get myself off to your pretty little cunt," he says, looking down at my exposed sex. His magic pulls my legs apart even further, forcing my ass to the bar's edge.

"You offer…" I mull over his promise. "Fuck," I say.

"Submit, witchling," he says, stepping closer as I teeter on the edge of the bar.

He strokes himself mere inches from my sex. A bead of liquid graces the tip of his cock and he wipes it on my inner thigh. It's so disgusting. Yet, I find myself focusing on the velvety texture of it. My eyes can't break away. His hand latches onto my leg, his fingers digging in as he pumps himself faster. More pre-cum surfaces, and he rewards me, wiping it across my leg.

Each time he brushes against me, he moves closer to my entry. The skin on my legs chills as his arousal dries. He pleasures himself as if he has no care in the world. He shamelessly tightens his grip, letting out a groan of satisfaction. Power and confidence radiate from him.

"Tell me, witch, are you ready to submit?" he asks, jerking his cock so close to my sex that one shift of my hips would push him inside me.

I stare down at him. The smooth length of his cock beckons me, but I continue to fight it. My lower body thirsts, my lips glistening with my own arousal. But I convince myself it's an enchantment, a trick.

He leisurely leans forward to whisper in my ear, "Take what I offer." The tip of his cock pokes my sex.

The touch is like a jolt of electricity to my center. I suck in a breath that doesn't come to me. And then, his lips are on my ear, licking up the outside as his shaft rubs against me.

Feminine energy seeps out of my pores. The male inhales through his nose, running it up the side of my neck. "Delicious. Again," he says, thrusting his hips so his shaft massages my clit.

I quiver. My body takes over, rolling my hips to feel more of him. There's a snap of magic in the air and my arms are released. Instead of pushing him away, I grab his face and slam my lips onto his. He purrs into my mouth as his hands roam my body, appreciating my curves.

"Give it to me," I say, biting his bottom lip.

"Give you what?" His hands pause on my hips.

"Power and release," I say.

"Say you submit," he says.

"No."

He slaps my sex and growls against my mouth. Our teeth clink as we standoff.

"Submit."

"No."

He slaps me again. The sting reverberates through my body. A feral energy swirls between my legs.

"Submit," he says, delivering another debilitating blow.

My back arches as the pain binds me as thoroughly as his magic. "Just do it already!" I say, nearly begging for more.

"Say you submit." He shoves two fingers inside me, and I nearly topple over. He pumps them in and out, forcing my vision to blur.

"Yes," I say.

"Yes—what?"

His hand moves faster, pounding into me. Then, power. He thrusts it into my center so hard, I cry out as my body clenches onto it. It's pure, undiluted power. It's intoxicating. His power is an endless abyss that offers ecstasy unlike any other.

One taste of it and I need more. But then, it's gone. I cry out again as it leaves me, aching and unfulfilled. I feel it there, on the edge of my grasp, but I can't reach it.

"Say it," he growls, withdrawing his fingers.

"Yes, yes. I submit!" I say breathlessly.

"Good girl," he says as he fists his cock and rams it into me.

His power blinds me as it surges over and around us. The air swirls and turns hazy, but I'm overwhelmed by the thrumming energy pulsating through my body and his smooth cock sinking into me.

As his lips find my neck, I'm spellbound. The celestial moon's power is like washing in a cold mountain spring, but the bartender's power is like bathing in the deepest pits of Hell.

Fire and ice consume me. They tear me apart, thread by thread, from the touch of his mouth and the impaling of his cock. Gargled sounds fill the empty tavern. I'm not sure whether it's from me or the beast.

I dig my fingers into his chest, beckoning for more, and he answers my call. The male shoves himself into me, slamming against my thighs while his power swallows me whole.

I surrender fully, plunging into a chasm of infinitesimal power. My body thirstily consumes the offering and shudders as he wrecks me. An aromatic scent fills the air—the smell of our bodies joining. I watch as he enters me, glistening with the proof of my desire.

"Ready?" he asks.

"Ready for what?" I ask breathlessly.

"For the finale."

He responds by thrusting harder, faster. His satin cock pounds into me, slicing through my dewy folds and tight walls with ease. I open myself to him—mind, body, and soul.

He groans, his bright green eyes rolling into the back of his head, and before I can prepare myself for the strength of this finale, I'm catapulted through time itself. Starlight surrounds us. Shockwaves of energy roll down my body, tightening my muscles and tingling my skin as I feel like I'm floating through the universe.

I strain against the feeling as I transcend this world.

And with the same tenacity that built me up, I come crashing down when he pulls out of me. Liquid drips from the tip of his cock, and I slump, exhausted when our skin fully separates, as I watch him step away.

"What was that?" I say.

He smirks, "That's what you get when you fuck a real male."

"Tell me what you are," I say warily.

"I'm your enemies' worst nightmare, witchling," he says as he walks away, leaving me hungry for more. "I'll be seeing you real soon," he adds.

My enemies' worst nightmare, but not my own? Who is this male and what have I got myself into?

The Wolf

It feels like an explosion is going off in my skull, but somehow, I'm still awake. I'm still aware. I feel the excruciating pain, but most of all, I feel her presence.

It's like a million shattered bits of bone are stabbing through the skin surrounding my head. They retract, then puncture the tender lining again. And again.

If I had a brain capable of rational thought, I'd latch onto it, but it disintegrated in the eruption. There are no thoughts to be had anyway, only pain and the growing hunger caused by her scent.

"Kade! Kade!" She shouts, but her words are distant. "Kade!" She shakes my shoulders aggressively.

I shrug her off, pressing my palms into my skull and trying to keep the bone fragments from escaping my head. It feels like I am dying, and the only thing I know is that I'm not ready to die. But I can't be sure as to why.

Cold water slams into my face, spreading goosebumps across my bare flesh and making me shake harder. More water douses my chest, and the smell of raw meat fills my nostrils.

My eyes snap open instinctually. The rich, intoxicating scent hones my senses. Light floods in through my eyes, obscuring the darkness. The brightness sears straight through my iris to my already burning brain. I'm on fire.

"Arrgh," I yell, fighting the intense pressure building in my skull to combat the yearning of my body and its directive to take what it most wants.

"Kade, take a bite. Take a bite!"

The woman shoves a huge chunk of raw, bloody red meat in my face, smothering red liquid over my lips.

The taste of blood and fat overwhelms me. My canines extend, piercing through my gumline as if it is a natural thing to occur. For a moment, the pain dissipates as that other being fighting to emerge gives up its fight for a taste of chunky, lukewarm cow flesh.

I lick my lips, savoring the sweet, rich taste of iron and fat. My head slowly starts to knit back together, each bone fusing into place. I focus on the meat before me, breathing in the intoxicating scent and lapping up the fresh blood around my mouth. The taste of raw meat gives me a slight reprieve from the pain.

I need more, though.

The wolf needs more.

"Take it, Kade. Take it," the woman shouts, shoving the meat against my lips again.

The wolf growls its displeasure at the easy offering. It wants to savor the feast. It wants to make the kill. And I want to take my time, or else I risk losing complete control. She's frustrating us with her commands. It's not her place to be in charge or tell us what to do.

I growl at her again before tearing the meat from her hands and stuffing my nose into it. Once again, the smell and the taste of fresh meat deter any alternative action. This is what we need.

"Fuck. Hurry up, Kade," she curses at me, her tiny shoulders shaking as she rubs her arms.

I sink my teeth into the food and stare at the beautiful woman who gave us this offering. Her heart is pounding frantically in her chest. The plump swells of her fatty breasts do nothing but emphasize how quickly her heart is racing. She's nervous. Scared. The beads of sweat running down her neck distract me. The blood rushing through her veins is fresh, hot, and for the taking. After all, she is offering us flesh. A shudder works down her body, and I lose all sense of self.

My wolf wants her.

Repulsed by the day-old kill in my hands, the wolf throws it aside and crawls to the woman. He licks his lips, cleaning them to avoid tainting the taste of her blood that will soon be on his tongue.

"Don't. Don't, Kade." She scrambles back, tripping over a chair and falling to the ground.

We halt, absorbing the smell of fear growing sticky and thick around us. It sends a chilling thrill down our spine, honing our senses. We need a taste.

She smells so deliciously sweet and salty. Her flesh is pale and untouched. The taste of her skin will be like an aphrodisiac, heightening my desire before indulging in the delicacy waiting beneath her skin.

"Kneel," I demand, halting my crawl and rearing back on my knees to watch her bow down to the wolf.

She drops to her knees, unable to resist the command in my voice. My prey is shivering in fear before me, which only excites me more. A throbbing sensation forms in my groin, telling me there is much I should do with this young feast. But first, a taste.

I grab her by the throat, pulling her body flush against mine. She hangs limp in my grasp, gasping for air as I squeeze the life from her lungs, testing her resiliency.

The pulse below her flesh slows. Her face morphs into a ghostly white, and her mouth forms a perfect O. The soft strands of her fire-red hair brush my claws as they prick the tender skin of her neck. She's all red and white, exactly how I like my prey.

The throbbing in my groin increases exponentially, so I release her throat. I want her blood pumping hard and fast when I tear into her. I want it to spew into my mouth as I suck it down, drinking the life out of that perfect pouty face until she's frozen in this form forever.

She falls to the floor, panting and clutching her neck. My dinner is such a lovely sight. A feast like I've never tasted before.

"Please, Kade. It's me," she begs, batting her thick red eyelashes.

Delicious and weak.

This prey will be a meal unlike any other. She shakes, her heart pounding faster as I lean toward her. My vision is laser-focused on her. There is nothing. There is no one but her.

I yank her up again, pinning her body to mine. I want to feel and savor her before I finish my meal. I lick a bead of sweat running down the side of her neck. My tongue flicks over the delicate vein pulsing there. The life beneath this thin layer of skin is so fragile. It excites me, and I lick the vein again, tasting my salty appetizer.

"Kade, please," my meal whimpers.

The plea of my dying prey makes me chuckle. I drag the points of my canines across its skin, skimming just enough to leave a pink trail of intention behind. It slumps against me as the smell of arousal taints the air.

I strike.

My teeth sink into its neck, and the mouthwatering taste of hot blood fills my mouth. I suck on the puncture wounds, drinking as much savory liquid as possible.

This gives me life. This *is* life.

I pull away to admire my bite and the weeping prey beneath me. Blood slides down the side of its neck in a steady stream. I lick it up, unable to get enough as it works down her neck and across her plump breasts. A euphoric feeling builds between my thighs. Something about this place and this prey is exactly what I always needed. What I always wanted.

My dying meal turns its head. Tears stain its pale cheeks. "I'm sorry," it says.

Curiously, I study the face, the water streaming down it, and the curve of its small, upturned nose. A weak, meager thing. I lick up the side of its cheek, tasting its eyewater. Salty. But not the satisfying kind of salt. This salt is condensed and sharp. It insults my tastebuds. I wipe the foul taste off my tongue using my prey's chin, but my mouth brushes the outside of its mouth.

I stop.

Its mouth is so soft. Softer than its skin. And plump. I want to taste its mouth.

I lap my tongue across the upper and bottom lip. There's the faintest flavor of cherry. I don't prefer it, but I like how it feels. I need to feel more of them. I need more of the sensation it brings to my lower body.

Holding my meal's face steady, I slam my lips against it. I shove my tongue deep into its mouth to taste more of it. Vanilla and cinnamon coat my tongue, and soft lips suck it off. A groan and a growl escape me. The little prey's mouth envelops mine, matching my movements with its tongue.

"Kade," the prey whispers against my lips as it cups my balls.

I look down and see myself restrained by pants. The prey is undeterred and shoves its hand into them, wrapping its tiny hand around my cock, and stroking me. I pull away from its lips to watch its attempts to dissuade me from eating it.

It strokes me vigorously while clutching my balls tightly. The tightness of its hand around my cock makes me harder and leaves me wanting more.

This prey knows how to please.

I shove my pants down and lean back, grabbing it by the neck and shoving those plump lips down on my cock. If the prey aims to please, I will be pleased.

It gags and chokes as I hold its head down and thrust myself into it. Its teeth clamp down at the base of my cock, and my dick throbs harder.

The prey continues to please.

I watch as it sucks me into its mouth, swiping its tongue across the head of my cock and slurping up the beads of my seed. Blood drips from its neck onto my thighs, forcing a tremble of need to spur me into action. I want to roll in its blood, be covered in its life force.

I shove my prey down on my cock, forcing it to take my entire length into its mouth. The heat of its mouth is like shoving my dick into the pits of hell. It burns, and the burn feels good.

My prey pulls back, gasping for air. It pleases me immensely to watch it struggle. I chuckle as I find my voice.

"You're mine, prey," I growl.

In one swift movement, my claws extend and I slice the clothes on its body in half. Its fatty breasts flop out. It becomes imperative that I devour them.

As I reach out to grope them. It kneels before me, bits of cloth hanging from its body and blood dripping down its neck, chest, and stomach like a broken little thing.

"Yummy," I groan, licking up the trail of drying blood between its breasts.

"Kade, come back to me," it says, stilling to my touch.

My cock is throbbing and cold. I need to warm it up. My claws retract to test the prey's lower entry. Its mouth has sharp teeth. While exciting and fun, I'm ready for the soft inner flesh to milk my cock while I take its life.

As I search for the sweet spot that will please my dick, I find the warmth of her entry accompanied by a sticky substance to coat my cock. I plunge three fingers into it. It's slick and hot, just as I like. I wedge my fingers back and forth inside it, sloshing and spreading the wetness across my hand before I release it, slapping the outside of its fleshy cunt in appreciation. My prey whimpers.

I slap its center again, warning the prey to keep quiet, and it groans loudly, reaching for my wrist. I jerk its limb away. It will not have what is mine.

I bring my glistening fingers to my lips, showing the prey I will have what is mine—its body is mine.

The smell of this sticky, clear substance is different than my prey's blood but equally intoxicating. I clean my fingers like I am cleaning meat from a bone while the prey watches and shivers.

The blood flow on its neck slows as its eyes become hooded and its body wavers. That won't do. It's time to devour the hot feast before me fully.

Still kneeling, I lift its leg and eye the hole. It's spread wide, and its center twitches involuntarily when my breath wafts against it. I drive my hungry cock into it, feeling the heat and the juicy walls clench around me.

This is even more satisfying than its mouth. I pump my cock into it, thrusting in and out reverently.

"Kade," it screams, clutching its entry around me.

Its wetness coats my cock, dripping down my balls and thighs as I pound into it. My cock swells, the heat becoming nearly unbearable.

I need its blood again. I need to fill its hole as it fills mine.

I bite its neck, reopening the wound, and blood squirts into my mouth as my cock spurts into its hole.

As the last bit of my seed leaves me, I pull my teeth and cock from my prey. It sags against me, but I don't have the energy to finish eating right now.

I feel the same lull and exhaustion as my prey and fall back onto the floor, taking my feast with me. I'll enjoy it later. For now, the heart can continue to keep this meal alive, and I'll rest until it's time.

The Siren

I've been traveling alone in search of my kin for far too long. The only company I find is from the men lost at sea. But they don't entertain me for long. They aren't built for the water, and the water demands a price from those who weren't born here.

The sea creatures are even more flighty. They travel in pods or stay near their homes. The sharks would be the best company, but they're fickle and moody. I don't particularly care for most of them after one got brave and sliced a tooth down my tail.

I've decided not to trust other lonely travelers, either. Those who travel alone only do so for two reasons: they're lost, or they're searching for something. I'm both, and I'm certainly not trustworthy.

It's a terrible feeling to be both lost and searching. I hope that I'll one day find my kin, but fear lingers in the back of my mind. Maybe there is no one to find because there is no one left.

A ship bobs on the horizon.

I've learned to be wary of ships full of men. Without my pod, I'm in danger of things like fishing nets and spears. Having a pod means having others to watch your back or rescue you.

The ship draws nearer, blocking the setting sun with its massive sails. Long strips of sunlight peer out behind it like a crown. It's much too small to be this far out in the ocean.

There's no land for thousands of miles, and the direction they're sailing has no habitable land anyway. They would need to carry more supplies than this ship can hold if they plan to explore those parts. They'll not find a welcome home. They are better lost at sea, which makes me consider the only real possibility for their presence—they are lost.

I'd be doing them a favor by introducing them to the water. It's a more relaxing way to go than the wild terrain they sail toward.

After all, I would know. I'm heading in the opposite direction, following the scent of my kin as they fled those wild lands in search of a new place to call home. Fat, snobby beasts overwhelmed our shores. They doused the air with their stench and loud mouths.

It became unbearable living there. No longer an island oasis but a treacherous, stinky, sinking Hell hole.

As my kind fled, I became trapped in a sea cave that collapsed under the weight of those beasts. They likely think I'm dead, which is why they haven't left a trail for me to follow.

The ship and I creep closer together. The pace of our advancement is eerily slow, but I relish it. I'll be doing them a favor. Or at least a few of them.

The ship sways eerily as it fights the ocean currents. It wasn't built for these waters. The next storm will likely tear it apart. I near the ship's bow, drawn to the voices of men that come to me like whispers in the wind.

There are more of them than I expected, and it's still light out. I dive underneath the boat, deciding to wait for nightfall so I don't risk capture.

As the sun makes its exit, darkness consumes the ship. Only a few lanterns are lit for those who walk the deck throughout the night. The clear skies and calm waters bless me tonight. They lull the men to sleep early and deeply on the assumption that there are no threats.

When the sounds of their snoring below deck replace the sound of their banter, I emerge from the depthless water. Light footsteps pace along the bow—a guard keeping a keen eye on the darkness above and below.

"Hello, sailor. Where are you going?" I croon.

My voice comes out in a song—beautiful, mystical, and all-consuming. It captures the man's attention. He leans over the bow, looking down into the darkness in search of the voice.

"Who goes there?" he asks. Long tendrils of hair frame his face.

"It's me. Your lover." I paint an image of the woman he desires. I don't need to see her face to know who he misses back home. His aura practically reeks of desperation and longing.

"Mariane?" he asks with furrowed brows.

"Let down your rope," I tell him.

"Mariane? Is that you?"

His confusion is normal.

"Yes. It's me. Help me up! Please. It's cold down here." My song turns frantic—begging for his assistance like his lover is in pain. He obliges me, tossing a rope over the edge of the railing. I wrap it around my waist and say, "Pull me up."

He does. As he does, I turn my fluke into land legs. When I swing them over the ship's railing and plant them firmly on the worn wood, the man stands frozen before me.

"You're not Mariane," he says flatly.

"I'm not. But I'm better. Am I not more beautiful?" I croon, circling him and running a finger over his shoulders. All it takes is my touch.

He shudders and says, "Yes. You are undeniably more beautiful. But—"

"Is my body not more pleasing? Is my hair not more luminous?" I ensnare him with my words as I continue circling.

"Yes. It is." His eyes follow every step I take, consuming the lines of my body hungrily.

He reaches out to touch me. I allow him to run his calloused palm down my naked waist.

"Come with me, sailor." I take his hand and lead him to the edge, ready to plunge back into the water.

He walks blindly, nodding as his eyes never stray from me. "Yes," he says in a daze.

I reach the railing, throwing a leg over the side. "Come on now," I say, pointing at the edge.

He lifts his leg, his hand still in mine, when he's torn from my grasp and thrown backward onto the ship's deck.

"Shit," I say, throwing my other leg over the railing as I attempt to dive back in the water, but broad arms encircle me.

I buck against the giant man's body as he hauls me back onto the deck. How did I not hear him approaching?

"Not today, siren," he says, dragging me backward.

My land legs are less sure and unable to gain footing. They drag against the wood, splinters biting into the bottom of my soles.

"Get under deck in case there are more," he yells at the sailor he saved. Others rush to the man's side, helping him to stand, and staring at me with cautious eyes. "Put the barriers up, now," the man behind me yells another command.

"Yes, Captain Drake." The sailors scramble around on deck, following his order and lifting nets up every side of the boat.

They may have nifty safety measures to protect against my kind coming aboard, but they unknowingly gave me a name. A name is helpful. "Captain Drake, let me go," I sing, pouring lust into my voice as I wrap my fingers around his wrists. I'll figure out how to cut through those ropes and escape.

He refuses to release me, though. His arm tightens around me while his other slaps a hand over my mouth. "You won't be trapping me, siren," Drake says.

The captain drags me into his private quarters, only releasing my mouth to lock the door and bind my wrists with chains. "I'll leave you be. Just let me go," I plead, changing my tone to garner sympathy.

When he finishes binding my wrists in heavy iron shackles, he drops into an old leather chair. "Let you go and have you follow us, plucking my sailors into the sea one by one until there are none left. Don't think me so daft."

Drake spreads his legs and arms, stretching across the chair. He's a massive man. His aura is all-consuming and threatening in nature. Even though he looks utterly relaxed in the chair, I know he can be on his feet and ready to fight in seconds.

I turn to find a place to sit and negotiate. There's nothing but wood floor around me. I'm shackled in the middle of this room—right where he can keep an eye on me, and I can't reach anything that can free me.

He's certainly not stupid.

"I just wanted one night of company, that's all. I wouldn't have harmed him," I explain, sitting on the floor. I cross my land legs, unsure what to do with them. I haven't been on land this long in…Well, I can't remember how long I've been drifting exactly.

Drake stares at me, his eyes moving up my body. He assesses me, but it's not entirely as a threat. While I wouldn't usually target someone like him, there might still be a chance. A man at sea without any woman around gets desperate.

I stretch my legs out in front of me, spreading them. "Do you like what you see, captain?" I ask.

He grunts. "Of course I do. Sirens are the most beautiful creatures on the land or in the sea. But don't think I'm fool enough to follow you into the ocean's depths with the promise of a taste I'll never receive."

"I'm not that cruel. Your most sinful fantasies would come true if you came with me. I have needs, after all," I say.

"I'm sure you do, but they aren't the same needs as a human female."

Drake looks away, picking up a knife on his desk and fiddling with it. Bored as he may look, I know he's still watching me, so I skim a finger up my inner thigh immodestly.

"Stop that," he says without looking at me.

"I said I have needs too. They can be taken care of here or in the water. I promise to be good, and then you can release me. No harm done."

"No chance." He stands as if to leave.

"Come on, captain. How long has it been since you have been with a woman?"

Within seconds, he's in front of me, grabbing my throat and hauling me onto my knees. "You'll not seduce me, siren."

"You want to be seduced. It is a man's greatest desire," I counter. His hand is still around my throat, but I don't fear a lack of oxygen. Like he said—I do not have the same type of needs as a human woman.

Drake leans down, his face inches from mine, as he says, "Not mine."

"I'll prove it to you," I say.

He laughs, but his laugh is cut short when my bound wrists grab his waistband and rip down his pants. His cock bounces free, and before the captain can throw me aside, I wrap my lips around him. I suck him down. My lips hit the base of his stomach, and he gasps.

Captain Drake's hold tightens on my throat as he says threateningly, "Stop, siren." But he doesn't shove me away.

Gagging on his hardening cock, I say, "No."

"If you don't stop, I'll fuck your throat so hard, I'll do permanent damage. You'll beg me to stop, but I won't," he threatens.

But I don't move away. Instead, I twirl my tongue around his cock and slather it in my saliva. The loneliness is gone. I'll make this man give me what I want. If my words can't seduce him, my mouth can.

He growls when I don't stop and it sends a purr to my throat, vibrating around his shaft. I suck on him harder, bobbing my head like the ship on the ocean.

"Have it your way." Drake releases my throat and grabs the back of my head.

I ready myself, opening my mouth as wide as possible as he does what he promised. His cock stiffens to a full erection. The skin stretches taut as it leaves no room for misinterpretation. I've captured the captain's attention now.

His hands brace the sides of my head as he harshly thrusts into my mouth. The tip of his cock pierces the back of my throat, making me gag and spit on him. I breathe through my nose and stick my tongue out to guard his penis against my teeth.

Drake doesn't care if he is choking me or not. He fucks my mouth wildly, his hips swiveling with each push into me, making me pay for trying to take his sailor.

I love it.

I want more of it.

I want him to spill himself inside me.

Drake pulls out of me and grunts. He fists his cock and pulls my face under his shaft. "Suck my balls, siren."

His voice is laced with pleasure, so I do as he says. I suck both balls into my mouth and swirl them around while the captain pumps his cock. Liquid beads at the tip, making me hungry to taste it. I release his balls with a pop and swipe my tongue across his tip. He tastes salty like the ocean. It's delicious.

"I didn't say you could stop," Drake shoves my face under his shaft again.

I lick his taint as he strokes himself, watching as his furious face contorts. I feel his balls tighten against my chin, and Drake pulls me off him by the hair. He tilts my head back and moans as his body tenses.

I open my mouth, ready to taste all of him, but as I suck his cock down my throat, he pulls me off and holds me in place as his cum squirts onto my face. His eyes close as his release spills onto me.

"Look at me," I demand.

If he refuses to let me taste him, he better watch. The captain opens his eyes, watching as his seed covers me. There's so much of it that it shoots into my hair and drips down my neck. He grinds his teeth as the cum slows, then rubs his cock around my lips.

I lick the tip, cleaning him, and he lets me. The captain is so delicious. His eyes close, and his head falls back, but he keeps a firm hold on my hair.

"Mmm, yes," he says quietly as if only to himself.

"Yes, let me have you," I sing.

His eyes snap open and he pulls away, shoving me to the ground.

"Ow," I say. "You could say thank you."

He runs a hand through his hair, the seduction fading. "You're good, siren, but not that good."

"I beg to differ. Give me your cock again and see what happens," I say.

He smirks and I'm taken back by the devilish promise in his grin. "Don't worry, siren. I'm not done with you yet. This is going to be a fun trip," he says.

"You have me for the night, that's all," I say confidently. If I get my pussy around his cock, he'll be as malleable as a jellyfish.

He lifts the chain on my shackles and pulls me forward, forcing me to fall face-first onto the floor.

"I beg to differ," he says with a dark chuckle.

Faerie Delights

Branches slap and scrape my face as I dive into the clearing through the underbrush. My feet hit the ground for a brief moment before they're airborne again, launching me into a sprint. The sound of pounding feet hitting the cold morning soil races behind me like a beating drum. It's all around me, approaching from every side. I'm halfway across the clearing when the first one breaks through the treeline ahead of me.

I pivot, sliding two meters before finding my balance as I turn toward the Forbidden Forest. Grey leafless trees and thorny vines await. If they want to chase me, I won't make it easy.

The sunny day turns gloomy as I near the Forbidden Forest's edge. It sucks the life out of the very air around it. It's a home for monsters and their offspring. The type of beasts told around military campfires and to make disobedient children follow orders. Faerie tales don't deter the hunters behind me. They enter without hesitation.

Running as fast as I can, I weave through the thicket, searching for the densest area. The coppice grows overhead, intertwining as if it's one plant, not a million individual branches, as I run deeper into the forest. It blacks out the sky. I smile, knowing I'm close.

To the average eye, it would look like an escarpment lines this edge of the forest. But to those who know better, it's a wall and a door.

I blast my magic into it, throwing it open to catapult myself through it. I'm panting, sprawled out on the ground, when a deep laugh makes me whip my head around.

"What the—" I say, leaping to my feet.

"Did you really think you could outrun us?" he asks.

His broad shoulders turn to fit through the door. He's a monster of a man—the size and shape of a boulder. Three more men shrug through the invisible entry to my hideout. Each of them dons an emblem on their tunic. The largest man and first to enter bears the mark of a scepter—the leader. The second's is a snake emblem. The third—wings. The last—a dagger. The rest of their ensemble is built to hold weapons of every shape and size. At least three daggers on each man's legs, a broad sword down their backs, and several other unique torture devices.

"If you were smarter, you'd be weary of the Forbidden Forest," I say, taking three steps back from the leader. The men spread out, facing me, as they get into a position. Four on one is entirely unfair, but I have magic on my side.

"The Forbidden Forest isn't nearly as dangerous as you. And you don't see us shying away from you, now do you?" he asks.

I flex my hands, loosening the joints. "No. I don't." I roll my neck as the men unsheath their chosen weapons.

"We can do this the easy way or the hard way. It's your choice," the man with the wing symbol says. He's by far the most handsome of the group. His fair hair and luminous skin practically glow against the dark shades of my hut.

"I'll never choose the easy route, pretty boy," I taunt.

He frowns, but the man with the snake emblem puts a hand on his shoulder. "The hard way is going to be rough. You won't enjoy it, but we will," the snake man growls.

I bare my teeth at them and say, "Try me."

A gruff order from the leader has all three men moving. The man with the dagger emblem is the first to attack. He's quicker than I expected. A knife flings out of his hand. I barely move aside in time before it flies past my cheek. I suck in a breath, spinning on my heel as the fist of the snake man is next to knock me down. My back arches, dodging the hit as the man with the wings tackles me. He knocks the air out of my lungs as we both hit the ground.

I slam my knee upward and am rewarded with a grunt, but he keeps hold of me. He flips us around, pulling me on top of him, pinning my arms against his chest, and wrapping his legs around mine. We struggle, but I don't have enough leverage with my arms pinned beneath me and his legs spreading mine apart. The only option is to release my magic on them. So, I do.

The energy swirls in my core, building for release. I tense, ready to send a blast of power into the leader, when a collar is clamped around my neck. "Agh," I cry out as the collar stifles my magic. It feels like they've cut off a limb. "Where the fuck did you get that?"

The leader kneels before me, eyes roaming my body as I remain trapped by his comrade. "You chose the hard way, remember?" he says.

I spit at him, but the saliva falls to the ground between us. The men chuckle at my meager attempt to fight back.

"Here's the thing, Evelyn," he says, and I shudder. "My men and I like the chase. If you hadn't run, we might not have followed.

But as soon as those pretty doe eyes fled, there was no stopping us."

"Lies. You're a hunter. This is what you do. You have no empathy or compassion for my kind," I snarl, letting the men see my feral side that will rip them to shreds when they least expect it.

The dagger man smiles genuinely as if I made a funny joke. "Thane, we've got ourselves a wild one," he says.

Thane, the leader, replies. "All beasts can be tamed, Wynnstan. Isn't that right, Geoff?" he asks the snake emblem man.

Names are powerful. I smile inwardly at what they are unknowingly revealing. Thane—the scepter. Wynnstan—the dagger. Geoff—the snake. All I need is the winged man's name.

Geoff kneels next to Thane. "I'm going to enjoy breaking this one," he says, biting his bottom lip as his eyes roam my spread legs.

I fight to close them, but the winged ones hold is too tight. He whispers in my ear, "It's okay, sweet one. They always ask for more when we're done. Of course, you won't get it, but you'll always want it."

His words pierce my ears. How many others have been in this position?

"Not again with the pet names, Arden. She's not sweet. Look at her," Wynnstan says.

I smile at the men. Wynnstan thinks I agree with him, but he doesn't know I've been waiting for a name. All I have to do is bide my time.

Thane stands, smacking Wynnstan upside the head and knocking him forward. "In position," he says.

Geoff and Wynnstan get to work. They unsheath weapons and other objects, laying them out in a line. Thane tosses Arden a rope, which he expertly uses to tie my arms behind my back. He forces me onto my stomach, sitting on my back while the other three men converse quietly.

"I'm not going to run. At least let me sit up. You're hurting me," I say to Arden.

My cheek scrapes across the dirt and gravel-covered ground as I speak. Arden uses a knife to pick dirt out from under his nail. He glances at me for a brief moment.

"I learned a long time ago not to trust a faerie's word, sweet one," he says. Thane shoots him a pointed look.

I snarl at the leader but respond to Arden, hoping to appeal to him. If he's giving me a pet name like *sweet one,* he's got a weak spot for me, and I plan to use it. "I swear I won't run. Fae can't lie. If you've captured enough of us, you'll know we cannot lie."

He chuckles. It shakes my body. "Sweet and dangerous—just like I like them," he says, leaning down.

Arden stabs his knife into the ground by my cheek, making me jump as his body lays flat against my back. He runs the tip of his straight nose up the side of my face, inhaling deeply. I shudder, straining against him. My shoulders and wrists ache from the restraint as his body presses them into my back.

"Mm...Smells like flowers"—he licks up the side of my neck—"tastes like sin."

Thane shoves Arden off of me. The absent weight is a relief. I roll over. Even with my arms pinned, I'd rather not give the men my back. I need to see them. Thane hauls me up by my dress, forcing me onto my knees, facing their spread of toys. I suck in a breath, realizing what they have planned.

"This is what you do to your prisoners?" I laugh disbelieving-ly.

"No. This is what we do to female fae who think they can outrun us," Geoff says, picking up a metal object.

I gulp as he approaches. I rack my brain for ways he might use it, but I'm not creative enough to come up with a reasonable conclusion.

Arden slides up next to me. His hands gently rub my back as if to console me. I snarl at him, but he only gets closer, wrapping himself around me in a hug. Wynnstan flips a knife in his hand.

Thane says, "Undress her."

"What—" I begin to protest, but Geoff slices the knife down the center of my dress. He hands the knife to Arden, who shreds the rest so they can peel it from my bound body. "You soulless human vermin," I curse.

Arden shoves my knees apart, making me sway as Geoff drops to his knees in front of me. He positions the metal object underneath me. "What are you doing?" I cry out, fighting their hold.

Thane's massive hand grabs my neck. He squeezes, silencing me. "Geoff is doing you a favor. Unless you're thanking him, I don't want to hear you speak again," he says. I grind my teeth and jerk my head, but Thane keeps hold of me. He lowers his face to mine. I snarl, but he smiles. "Fight all you want. It only makes us harder."

Arden pushes my knees even further apart, as I debate how to make Thane pay for this, forcing me lower to the ground. The metal object pierces the center of my body. Thane holds my head in place, forcing me to stare him in the eyes as the men shove me down onto the cool, sharp object. It slips inside my body, and I whimper. Then I hear a crank and tense. I shake my head, but Thane holds me still.

It cranks again, and intense pressure pushes against my inner walls, stretching me. Another crank and it expands. A third crank, and I cry out as my body clenches painfully.

"One more," Geoff says as another crank enlarges the metal object.

I try to lift myself off the ground, but Arden's fingers dig into my hips, holding me in place as Thane chokes me. My body convulses against their hold. Cool air slips into the opening in my cunt. I've never been opened this far. The sensation chills me to my bones, but the intense pain the men inflict on me heats my skin.

Wynnstan stands next to Thane. He runs a hair through my hair. A gentle touch, like Arden's, but I know it's a lie. He wants to hurt me. "Such a pretty face. I can't wait to ruin it," he says.

Thane smiles beside him and says, "You're going to be a good little toy for us. Aren't you, Evelyn?"

I hate that he knows my name. He only says it to prove a point. I know theirs, but he knows mine. He releases my neck, allowing me to speak. "No promises," I say, spitting at him. This time, it hits home.

Thane wipes my spit from his face, growing angry. He slaps me, then smears the saliva across my face. "Apparently, I'm going to have to teach you," he says as he shrugs out of his tunic and loosens his pants.

Shit.

Arden's lips brush my ear. "Oh, sweet one. You're in for it now," he says.

Thane drops his pants, pulling out his massive cock. My mouth gapes at the size of him. His girth is unreal. Wynnstan smiles devilishly, taking off his clothes as well. His cock is straight as a dagger, thick at the base and pointed at the end. Geoff stands and follows. I gasp.

No wonder he stretched me. Geoff's cock hangs down his leg, wide and long. He notices my shock, and it twitches. My body responds, clenching at the thought of that thing being inside me, but the metal object presses into my center, making me cry out. Arden's hands move to my front, massaging down my abdomen and nearing my sex as the three men fist their cocks.

"Hand me the wooden phallus," Arden says.

Wynnstan retrieves it. Arden kneels in front of me while the other men watch. I'm still perched on the metal object, unable to move. I've assimilated to the size. If I move, I'll feel something, and they'll likely just put me back on it.

"Open your mouth," Arden says, bringing the wooden cock to my mouth.

I whimper but do as he says. He stuffs the wood into my mouth, shoving it to the back of my throat. I gag and choke, but he doesn't remove it. He bashes it against my larynx, making me salivate all over it.

"So good, sweet one," he coos as he pulls it out of my mouth.

I cough, spitting on the ground. The men smile down at me. Arden—proudly. Wynnstan—menacingly. Geoff—lustfully. Thane—arrogantly. I catch my breath and am about to curse them when Arden slides the artificial phallus into my cunt. I don't feel it until it prods the back of my cervix. The metal object keeps it from touching all of me, but the feel of it stabbing the deepest part of my vagina has me bucking. As swift as the wind, Wynnstan shoves my shoulders down, forcing me deeper onto the spreader.

Another cry slips out but is caught in a gargle as Thane grabs the back of my head and bashes his cock into my mouth. He's so girthy I can't even bite down. He thrusts his hips into me as Arden pounds the wooden cock into my other opening. My body is on fire.

Then, everything is gone. One second, I was so full I thought I might be torn apart. The next, my jaw aches and pops, and my pussy relaxes and throbs. I pant, head sagging as I try to catch my breath. My shoulders, neck, and back ache. My entire body feels like it's been beaten.

Arms are hauling me to my feet, lifting me. My head is in a daze, and my vision is blurred. I can't make sense of much before I'm impaled again. A warm rod shoves into my cunt, filling me, massaging me, and pleasuring me. It rocks my body in slow, methodical strokes.

I close my eyes as the gentle touch of hands palm my breasts. They glide over my backside, appreciating my curves. They knead and roll, firm but gentle. The warm, slick press of lips is on my neck. I moan, relaxing against them. Sensibility tells me not to enjoy this. I'm a prisoner to these men, but the steady thrusts of—my eyes pop open—Geoff's cock feels so good.

He smiles, grabbing my face so I can't look away. "Now you see why I stretched you," he says.

Arden speaks behind me, kissing my neck as hands caress my backside. "Suck it, sweet one," Arden says, putting his finger against my lips. I hesitate. "You won't like the other option."

I open and suck on his finger. When he's satisfied, he removes his hand and presses the finger against my backside. "No, please," I whimper, but he sinks it in as Geoff's cock settles into my cunt.

Geoff holds me suspended on his cock as Arden moves his hands. One finger. Then two. He spreads them, stretching me.

"No. None of you can fit back there," I protest.

Thane steps into my view. His semi-hard cock bounces against his leg. "Wynnstan," he says.

Wynnstan walks up to his side, a wicked smile on his face, as he says, "It will be my pleasure."

Arden steps away, Geoff holding me up, my legs on either side of his waist with his cock still inside me, as Wynnstand stands at my back. I breathe in shakily as the tip of Wynnstan's cock prods at my backside. Thane grabs my face, pinching my cheeks again.

"Relax," he orders.

"I can't do it," I say, tears welling as I feel Wynnstan's penis push into me.

It's too much. It feels like he's stabbing me, cutting me open to bleed out. Thane bites my neck. I scream as Wynnstan buries himself in me. I don't know how my body fits both men, but it feels like I absorb them. They melt into my core like they were always meant to be there. And then, they're moving. I don't know where to feel or what to feel. All I know is that the vigorous roll of their hips makes my body burn.

Geoff grunts, stilling inside me. I feel the rush of hot liquid spurt inside me. Geoff shallowly thrusts into me, pushing his seed into the back of cunt.

Thane runs his nose alongside mine as he says, "Arden, you're next."

Geoff pulls out of me, leaving me suspended on Wynnstan, as Arden comes up to fuck me. His soft, gentle touch is long gone when he slams into me. Thane releases my face, letting Arden hold my head with my legs draped over Wynnstan's arms. Arden's hands squeeze my face as he wildly bucks his hips. He roughly takes me. The speed is so much different than the touch I've come to expect from him. "Arden," I say his name, hoping to calm him, but he slaps a hand across my mouth.

"Quiet, sweet one." His beautiful face contorts.

My voice is muffled against his hand, but I try to tell him to slow down, to stop. It's too much. But his thumb and forefinger pinch my nose, cutting off my air. His other hand drops to my clit and rubs it. I try to breathe, but I can't. I need him to stop. My body sizzles. His thumb circles, pressing as harshly as his cock pounds into me. As my vision blurs, my lower body clenches. Arden groans and releases my face. I suck in a breath, and the tension releases from my body as he fills me with his cum.

I'm panting by the time Wynnstan sets me on my knees. "Clean me," he says, forcing his cock into my mouth.

When he's satisfied with my cleaning, he forces me onto my hands and takes me from behind. He's not gentle, but not rough. I'm in a daze, having come so close to these men making me orgasm, but not. Wynnstan cums in me silently, making sure to stuff his cum back into me with his fingers so I don't lose a drop. I fall to the ground, exhausted.

All of my holes ache from being stretched and abused. Thane kneels next to me, moving the hair from my face. "You make such a good little toy, Evelyn. You take our cum so well," he says, running his thumb over my lower lip.

I shift, turning away from him. He tangles a hand in my hair, pulling me up to my knees. Fire races down my spine as he tugs my head back. He drops down beside me, putting a knife to my throat. I tremble as the blade pricks my skin. "Do it," I taunt him.

"Not before you take my cum, *sweet one*," he mocks. Arden chuckles.

Thane twists me, keeping the blade to my neck as he thrusts his dick into me. Each thrust of his hips shoves my neck into the blade. I cry out, straining to push it away, but there's no use. It slices me as Thane continues. His other hand pinches my nipple, working its way down my body possessively.

"Be a good little fuck toy, and I'll let you cum," he says, slapping my pussy as his knife digs in and his cock thrusts upward.

I cry out, my throat constricting. The blade jerks. Warm liquid glides down my chest. I whimper, fear escalating. Thane laughs as he runs a hand across my chest, bringing it up to my face so I can see the blood. Tears slide down my cheeks.

"You look glorious painted in red," he growls, rubbing his bloodied hand across my face.

I tremble, but this time, he tosses the knife to the side. My head falls forward to see the mess. Blood covers my body. Thane's hands slide down it. He uses the blood as a lubricant to rub my clit. I shudder.

"You're a monster," I say. But I'm relieved the knife is no longer at my throat. Now, it's just his hands on me, using my blood in the most disgustingly indulgent form of possession.

Thane's hands are like magic, bringing my body closer and closer to ecstasy. His rigid cock doesn't help. He uses my blood like it's an aphrodisiac. So primal. So blood-thirsty. My body responds to it. The monster inside me bathes in blood. He licks up the side of my neck, tasting me.

"This world is full of monsters, but do not mistake me, Evelyn. I'm not a monster. I'm the fucking king of monsters," he says as he bites me.

My body convulses against the searing pain, the brutality of his words, and the carnal desire that courses through my veins. I inhale as everything tightens in and around me. My mind spirals into a euphoric chasm, unable to comprehend anything beyond this explosive feeling seizing my body. Thane guides me to the metaphysical cliff and pushes me off, letting fear and liberation fuel my release. I transcend as his cum stuffs me.

I wake to an empty hut. The only proof of the four men is the ache they left behind and a note that says: *Until next time, sweet one.*

Carnal Dispositions

Dom Daddy

1

I t's been five months since I last got laid, and it wasn't anything special. In fact, I actively try to forget how terrible it was, and lately, my vibrator simply isn't cutting it. Even my favorite porn star doesn't excite me anymore.

I need a release—a no-strings-attached, raunchy release.

This is the reason why I find myself setting up a profile on the sketchiest dating apps available.

Is it smart to seek out a man who just wants to hook up? Probably not. Does it hurt to look? Definitely not. Does it hurt to talk to them and see what they have to offer? Also, probably not. It's harmless entertainment, after all. I haven't met anyone in person. At least, not yet. I question whether I actually would meet a total stranger with the expectation and sole purpose of hooking up.

I haven't been on these dating sites since I was in college. The idea of meeting a total stranger is both exciting and scary. Honestly, I don't know if I'll follow through with a meetup, but swiping left and right on people's profiles is helping curve my horniness, and it isn't putting me in danger. I'm safe behind the glass screen, for now.

Since I'm looking for sex with no emotional connection, I press the like button on every hot guy I come across. Not all of them will also match me, but I hope there are some good contenders. It takes time for matches to show up—because they have to like you back—and when I'm about to give up, I see a photo of a stylishly dressed man with an emoji covering his face pop up. He sent me a like.

The profile description reads: *Dom looking for a sub. In an open relationship but like to keep things discreet. Serious inquiries only.*

This is one of the sketchier dating apps, but this is also the first profile I've come across with a description matching exactly what I'm looking for.

The fact that the man hides his face is a major red flag—he's most likely a catfish—but I'll take the risk if it means getting exactly what I want.

I swipe right to indicate I accept the match. My heart flutters excitedly. I sincerely hope he's not a catfish. He's got great shoulders, and his style makes me envious. If he has the face to match and the conversation is spicy, I'll be in literal orgasmic heaven.

However, a thread of fear starts to wind around my racing heart as I wonder if he'll like me once we start chatting. I don't know much about the dom-sub culture, but I've seen my fair share of porn, and it's something I wouldn't mind trying. If the mystery man doesn't think my lack of experience is unattractive, this may be my chance for some life-changing sex.

Steeling my nerves, I send the man named Jones a message.

Lily: Hi

Jones: Hey, Sexy! What are you doing right now?

Lily: Um… Just scrolling through the app. Haha

Jones: Okay. Do you want to meet and do something more fun?

I have a faint idea of what something *more fun* entails, but the rational woman in me needs to get to know this guy a little bit before I meet him in person. He could be a serial killer, for all I know. Plus, I need details. It's been a long time since I have touched or been touched. I need to know I'll be safe. I need to know how far this "dom" thing goes and what he's planning on doing with me. On the flip side, my thirsty lady parts don't seem to care much about safety right now as they pulse with excitement.

Lily: Like what?

Jones: I don't like to beat around the bush, metaphorically speaking. I'll beat your bush if you have one. ;) I'm looking for someone to play with. Are you into that?

Lily: Play with...sexually?

Jones: That's right, kitten. Just looking for a sub who knows how to follow orders and wants to come harder than she's ever come before.

His messages make my pussy throb insistently. This is the perfect no-strings-attached scenario I'm looking for. A man who just wants to play, who just wants to focus on the pleasure. I need that. But I still don't know who he is or how this works. His messages seem too good to be true—like he's reading my mind.

Lily: What does a sub do?

Jones: I can show you, but essentially, you let me control you. It's all pleasurable—I promise. I want you to be comfortable. If something doesn't feel right, all you have to do is tell me to stop. We can talk more about it when we meet.

Lily: But I haven't even seen your face. How do I know it's safe?

Laying all my cards on the table might not be the smartest move. Obviously, a serial killer will do everything possible to make me feel safe, and now he knows I'm suspicious. But my vagina is begging me to keep this conversation going because if it is real, this might be all I need to shove my sexual repression aside.

Jones: We can video chat first if that makes you feel better. Plus, we can meet somewhere public. I want you to feel safe. But let me get one thing straight: I'm not looking to wine and dine someone. I have a relationship. While I might treat you to lingerie and late-night cocktails, there will always be the promise of something sexual. I don't waste my time with women who think they'll get more out of me. This is mutually beneficial, but only in terms of sexual satisfaction.

He's being totally transparent about his desires, which leads me to trust him more. I can't explain the feeling; maybe it's intuition, but I feel like he's being honest.

However, safety is still on the back of my mind. The fear that stems from past experiences gone wrong is forever present. Yet, my pussy begs me to accept his video chat proposal. Because if I'm being honest, taking the risk to meet in person will require him to be mega hot, and I have yet to see his face. I'm safe on a video chat, and it will give me time to decide. I'll get to see if he's a real person and get a better idea of how much further I'm willing to go with him.

Lily: That's a good idea. I think I'd feel better if we did a video chat.

Jones: No problem. But…I want you playing with your pussy when you answer the phone. I do things one way—my way. This will give you an idea of how good I'll make you feel, and it will prove to me how good a sub you can be. Understand, kitten?

My lower lips moisten, imagining being on the phone with a strange man and touching myself in front of him.

Good god, I am ridiculously horny now.

I run out of the living room, into my bedroom, lock the door, and get under the covers of my bed. Reaching over, I grab my hot pink vibrator from the bedside drawer, set it beside me, and slip my fingers under the hemline of my pants while I type a response to Jones.

Lily: When would you like to chat?

Jones: Now.

My heart literally stops. My fingers are already rotating small circles around the bundle of nerves at the peak of my vagina, but nothing can prepare me for this. A pulsing ache beats as fast as my heart between my legs, pumping arousal to the area between my thighs and readying me for my call with Jones.

Lily: Okay.

Jones calls me immediately using the video chat function on the dating app. I hit the answer button and hold the camera at the most flattering angle possible when lying against a pillow. It's not the best, but it'll have to do.

When the screen lights up, connecting our video call, Jones' face greets me, and I am far from disappointed. I already knew he had a hot body, but his face is all sharp angles and smooth skin with dark, angry brows. He looks like the epitome of what I imagine a dom should look like. It's going to be very hard for me to resist this man. I gulp as dryness builds in my throat.

"Hi, kitten." He purrs a greeting like it's a sensual promise.

My knees are weak. If I were standing, I'd soon be on the ground, kneeling before him.

"Hi," I respond, shyly. I don't know how to do this. I have no idea what I'm doing. My fingers pause their circling, but my heart races faster as I study every inch of him and wait for the dom to take the lead.

"Are you playing with your pussy like daddy told you to?"

Oh fuck. He's jumping straight into it. I don't know what else to do, except exactly what he tells me.

"Yes," I say, glancing down to where my fingers hesitantly start circling again under the covers.

"Good girl. Tell me, what will it take to get you to meet me, kitten?" he asks while licking his thin lips. They're severe and punishing to behold.

"I don't know," I say, still rubbing circles around my clit while my mind races disbelievingly at the fact that I'm actually masturbating while video chatting with a stranger.

"Do you want daddy to show you how he'll make you feel?"

How is he going to do that over a call? I sure as hell want to find out.

"How are you going to do that?" I ask curiously, sliding a finger between my lower lips and feeling the wetness soaking me down there.

"Can you take orders, kitten?"

"Yes."

"Good. Show daddy you're doing what he said," he demands.

His voice is stoic and uncompromising. He wants to see me rubbing my pussy. This is so erotic, yet so exciting.

"Hold on," I breathe heavily, setting the phone down and tugging my pants and underwear off under the blanket.

I toss the clothes to the side and pull the covers down. The cold bedroom air kisses my wet skin, forcing me to shiver and my nipples to tighten under my camisole. I masturbate often, but I've never responded as quickly as this. I pick up the phone and turn the camera around, showing Jones what he asked to see. My glistening folds and fingers are on full display.

"That's a very pretty pussy," Jones says huskily. "Move the camera closer."

I follow his command, holding the camera closer to my pussy, while keeping the screen turned so I can see his facial expressions.

"Now spread your lips and open up for daddy."

Again, I do as he commands, spreading my lower lips for him and revealing every crevice of my vagina. My entry contracts and expands with the quick beat of my heart.

"Put a finger inside your cunt," he demands, and I do.

A quiet moan escapes on my breath as I watch Jones's lips part before he bites his bottom lip aggressively. He likes watching me, and I like him watching me even more. I pump my finger in and out of my sex. The slick sound of my arousal only increases my desire.

"Stop," Jones growls.

I pause my movements. My breathing hitches as I wait for his next command. I need it like my life depends on it. I hang on to his every word.

"Do you have a mirror?" he asks.

"Yes," I say. My fingers shake as I itch to give my pussy what it craves.

"Stand in front of the mirror and take your clothes off."

I want to groan from the frustration pausing causes me, but Jones knows what he's doing, and I trust that he'll bring me to orgasm, so I turn the camera around and stand in front of the closet mirror, waiting for his directions.

"Take off your clothes."

With only my camisole remaining, I pass the camera between my hands as I remove my top. I'm standing butt-ass naked in front of the mirror. Jones's eyes roam my body, intently studying me. He takes his time absorbing every inch of me.

"Such a beautiful body, kitten. Those tits are fucking amazing. Rub your tits for daddy."

I grab my breast with one hand and massage it, giving daddy a full view of my luscious mounds. They're my favorite body part.

"Pinch your nipple."

I roll my nipple between my thumb and forefinger, causing my pussy to clench harder from its lack of attention. Nothing but air touches me there.

"Harder. Daddy will pinch that nipple much harder, so show me what you can handle, kitten."

Fuck. His words will be my undoing. My body leaks its desire down my inner thigh. I hear it dripping onto the floor below me as I pinch my nipple to nearly unbearable pain levels and have to bite my lip to silence the moan of pleasure that accompanies it.

"Is that a vibrator behind you?" he asks.

"Yes," I say, panting and squirming in hopes that he'll ask me to use it next.

"Get the vibrator. Set up your phone so you can use both hands, and I can see your body. Daddy is going to make you come so you know why you need to meet him."

Yes. I want to come. I need to come.

I scramble to the bed, grab the vibrator, and set up the phone so Jones can see my front and some of my back in the mirror behind me. He smiles unabashedly when I'm done setting up everything for his viewing pleasure. He's proud of me.

"Good girl. Very good. Do you want to see what this does to me, kitten?"

Jones turns his camera around. He's sitting in the driver's seat of his car, and I can see the massive bulge in the front of his dress slacks. His agile fingers unbutton and unzip his slacks. His cock pops out, unbound by underwear. I whimper at the sight of it. When his fingers wrap around the base of his cock, his girth becomes more apparent. My pussy clenches as if I can feel him inside me.

"You like that?" he asks.

"Yes, yes, daddy," I say, licking my lips and imagining his fat cock inside me—inside every part of me. I seriously need to get laid.

"Put the dildo inside your pussy, kitten. Pretend it's daddy's cock fucking that tight cunt."

Jones keeps his camera on his cock. Jacking himself off while I take the vibrator and rub it across my pussy lips, lubricating it for entry.

"Yes, kitten. Put it inside nice and slow."

I do as he instructs, inserting the vibrator slowly. My body feels every inch and groove of it enter me. I watch Jones pump his cock while the vibrator enters me, and my entire body heats ten degrees as I imagine it's daddy's cock going inside me.

"Now take it out and suck your juices off of it."

"Yes, daddy," I preen, happy to comply and make a show of it.

Bringing the pink dildo to my lips, Jones switches his camera to his face so I can watch his reaction as I lick up the base of the pussy juice-soaked dildo and then suck the entire thing into my mouth. I swirl my tongue around the tip of the dildo, and Jones moans as he adjusts himself.

"You are so fucking sexy, kitten. Daddy is very happy with you. Do you want to come now?"

I shake my head desperately, wanting to come and please daddy.

"Turn it on and put it back inside your pussy. I want you to thrust it inside your cunt every time I pump my cock."

Following his directions, I thrust the dildo inside my needy cunt and turn on the vibration. The sudden movement forces my walls to clench, and the feeling intensifies as my muscles clamp around it.

"Not yet, kitten," Jones purrs sweetly as he turns his camera to face his dick again.

With each stroke of his cock, I withdraw and insert the vibrating dildo. Jones increases the pace of his hand, stroking his cock faster as precum beads at the tip of his dick. My mouth waters shamelessly, wanting to lick it off, but the camera separates us, which only fuels that desperate need into the speed of my own hand.

"Touch your clit with your other hand," he groans, pushing his hips up as his hand works on his thick cock.

With one hand pushing the dildo into my pussy and the other working my clit, I pick up a steady rhythm that leaves my body shaking, tightening, and squirming. I'm so close.

"Watch daddy's cock, kitten. When I come, you come," Jones says, his voice laced with a threatening edge that tells me I better come, or he'll be delivering punishment. "Say 'yes, daddy'."

"Yes, daddy," I pant, moving my fingers faster.

"Are you going to meet with daddy and let him show you how much better he can make you feel than that shitty little vibrator?" he asks, pumping his cock even faster.

"Yes, daddy," I respond, matching my pace with his. I throw all caution to the wind, hanging on his every word for my release. When he says come, I'm going to explode.

"Are you going to be a good little girl and let daddy have his way with you?"

"Yes, daddy."

"You're a good girl. Aren't you, kitten? You'll do exactly as daddy says, even when I take your ass."

My entire body shudders, sucking in the vibrator and refusing to release it as the vibrations shoot up my center, and I scream, "Yes, daddy."

"Come," he says.

Jones's cum spurts up in the air and lands on his cock, sliding down his fingers as he pumps out his release. My orgasm slams into me like a wall. Cum rolls down the vibrator, onto my fingers as I tremble through the waves of my release.

When the orgasm lulls, I switch off the vibrator before my sensitive bud re-energizes and begs for round two. Daddy hasn't said I can have another.

"Very good, kitten. Now, was that good, or do you need another one?" Daddy asks, wiping the cum off his cock with a napkin. He could care less that I'm watching him clean up in his car. He's so effortlessly sexy and confident.

My fingers unconsciously slide between my thighs, and I drag a finger through the wet, sticky cum. In response to daddy's question, I bring the cum-soaked finger to my lips and suck on it.

Jones flips the camera around to show me his pleased face. "Very good, kitten. I'm dropping you a pin. Meet me there in one hour. Wear a tight black dress and no underwear."

I nod my head and say, "Yes, daddy."

Dom Daddy

2

J ones dropped me a pin to a fancy bar in West Hollywood, but I bailed. He understood my hesitancy and we ended up talking more so that I would feel comfortable about meeting in person. Finally, he convinced me to meet him for drinks at a local dive bar down the road from my apartment. It's a low-key vibe, which makes me feel like the expectations will also be low-key. Although, I'm doubting anything with this man will be low-key. The orgasm he gave me was earth-shattering.

He says he wants me to feel safe, and meeting in a public place where I can vet him as a normal human being, not a serial killer, is the best way to do that. To his credit, he's also driving across the city to meet me. I have a sneaking suspicion it has more to do with avoiding a run-in with people he knows because come to find out—he's not just in an open relationship; he's married.

His wife knows he likes doing freaky stuff, so she fully supports him messing around with other women. Or so he says. I hope this isn't a complete lie, and I'm actively participating in a cheating scandal. But I'm desperate for a non-committal release, and this man made me come so hard during our video call two days ago.

Every time I masturbate, I think about that moment. Eventually, I concluded that I needed to meet him in person. The idea of a strange man touching my body is nerve-racking, but it's also exciting and makes me wet from the mere thought of it, especially from Jones.

I walk through the door of the dive bar, wave at the bartender, and head to the back patio at the far end of the small joint.

Jones texted me earlier and said to meet him on the patio.

Worry fills my gut as each step brings me closer to the real him. Meeting in person takes me past the safety net of my phone. The anticipation has me in knots. I don't know what to expect. I don't know how I'll feel. But there's no turning back from here. He suggested we meet in the parking lot beside the bar, but I was purposely running late. Truthfully, I was giving myself time for the option to bail.

Jones warned me that my delay would only make him want me more and that he doesn't appreciate tardiness. A man this incessant should give me red flags, but it also makes my knees weak from his sensual arrogance. He knows what he wants, and he takes it. Repercussions be damned. I'm certain there's some punishment involved on my end. Yet, even that feels like a promise I can't wait to cash in on.

As I push through the patio door, I glimpse Jones in person for the first time. He's even more handsome than on video. He leans back against an old iron chair with an ankle propped on his knee. In one hand, he holds a smartphone. In the other, a beer bottle.

I take slow steps forward. He reminds me of a lion—confident and relaxed, but you know he's ready to pounce at any moment. His outfit is effortlessly sophisticated and pairs dangerously with the timeless features of his face. He's wearing a button-down shirt with two buttons unfastened at the top. His hair is long on the top with fades down the sides. A few strands fall into his dark brow, skimming just close enough to his eye to be bothersome, but Jones seems unbothered. He's perfect. He's like sex-walking. The air seems to change around him, running away as if to avoid competing for space and making it even harder to breathe.

I don't understand why someone like him is interested in someone like me.

"Kitten," he coos, looking up at me as I sit in the only other chair at the table, which is directly beside his.

I turn to speak to him and want to say something quirky, but all I can get out is a strangled, "Hi."

"Are you nervous?" he asks, setting his beer down and turning to face me with a smirk that makes my heart jerk.

Our knees brush slightly, and I resist the urge to lean away. This man wants to touch me far more than this. I won't be getting anywhere if our knees touching scares me off. "I'm a little nervous," I admit.

"I can help ease those nerves. Or would you like to ask me some questions first?" he suggests, sliding a hand over my thigh.

He's clearly undeterred by my nerves or beauty—or lack thereof. I wonder how many times he's done this—met people online and fucked them. Although, I suppose his goal isn't just to get me off. He wants to make me his sub—he told me as much.

At his request, I wore a skirt. He also told me not to wear underwear, but that's too foreign for me, so I kept the panties on. These meaningless requests are part of some bigger dom–sub dynamic I'm unfamiliar with. I did a little research, and from what I gathered online, these demands are part of a test. He's seeing how well I can follow orders and what my boundaries might be. Some interesting articles mentioned these tests help the dom weed out dangerous subs—ones who don't know their limits. I guess there is some risk to this relationship when the sub doesn't know their breaking point and a dom doesn't have limits. It's still a bit much for me to wrap my head around.

The skin on his hand is soft yet rough as it grazes my thigh. I'm not sure what he does for work, but it definitely doesn't involve hard labor. Although, that isn't what I care about anyway. Right? We aren't here to make an emotional connection. I'm here to get off.

"I don't have any questions," I say.

"Are you sure about that? Because you insisted we meet somewhere public. Although, I can't say this is very public," he shrugs and leans back in his chair, looking around at the old, dingy, empty patio.

He has a point. "I just wanted to see if you were real and how I felt around you, I guess," I mumble my useless explanation.

"Come here," Jones says, motioning to his lap.

I slowly stand and turn to sit in his lap, but Jones stops me.

"Bend over. Let daddy see that pussy first. Is it dripping for me yet?" he asks, pushing at my lower back and forcing me to bend over. He hisses when he sees my underwear. "I told you not to wear these."

"But I—," I stutter for an explanation and am rewarded with a firm slap to my ass that makes me jump.

Jones pulls my hips back. "You disobey me, kitten. Sit down now," he commands.

I perch on his lap, my ass still stinging as he yanks my back into his chest before prying my legs apart with his own. His arm latches around my center, holding my arms underneath his forearm while his other hand roams my inner thigh. His fingers trail a path from my knee to my center.

"What are you doing?" I ask breathlessly, looking around to ensure no one is coming outside to check on us. Jones has me pinned.

"I'm punishing you," he growls in my ear, then tugs my underwear to the side and slides his fingers through my sex.

A breath rushes out of me from this unfamiliar but devastatingly personal touch. This is happening so fast, and somehow, I'm already soaked. Something about this man triggers my body's response. It's like his scent is an aphrodisiac, making me want to breed, and my body happily obliges.

Jones rubs his entire hand through my folds, spreading me apart and massaging my folds. He twiddles the achy bud of nerves between my legs and then lavishly rolls his knuckles across my labia. His hands are massive compared to mine; they touch every part of my throbbing vagina. Massaging, moving, twisting. He makes me yearn for more, even though I know we shouldn't even be doing this in public.

A whimper passes through my lips as drool pools at the edge of my mouth. Someone could see us, but my hips roll angstily. I couldn't ask him to stop if I wanted to.

"You've been a bad girl, kitten. You don't deserve to get off," he taunts, moving his fingers in a circle at the peak of my sex. The sloshing sound of my arousal grows dauntingly loud on the quiet patio. "But if you beg, daddy, maybe I'll let you."

The image of me begging him, on my knees, and sucking his cock, flits through my dirty mind. I'd love to beg him. Recalling the size of his dick, which I only saw in our first video chat, I feel him grow against my backside.

He feels even larger than the camera made him look. I swivel my hips on top of the full and stiff cock below me and relish in the feeling of it hardening even more against my ass. I dismiss the fact that my pussy is on full display for anyone who walks through the patio door.

"I said beg, not tease," Jones growls and slaps my pussy. Hard.

A sharp sting shoots across my wet lips. I squeeze my knees together, but Jones's legs keep them pried apart.

"Beg," he says, slapping my pussy again.

I stifle a moan as the slap brings a new feeling to my lady parts. The punishment and pain are a new sensation that only teases me more. It's a new and even more exciting feeling that makes my stomach coil in knots of sexual frustration. I need a release.

"Please, daddy. Please forgive me."

"I should shove this cock into that pretty little cunt of yours and show you why next time you won't want to wear panties."

"Yes," I moan, closing my eyes as his fingers find their place against my pussy again.

He pinches my clit and rolls it between his fingers, forcing my body to spasm against the erotic touch. Then, he flicks it, and the sharp sting of pain goes directly to my core. My walls tighten against emptiness, and I tremble while Jones holds me down. A release is so close, yet so far. I need it desperately. I need the penetration.

"I won't wear panties ever again, daddy. I promise," I beg, my voice shaking as his fingers continue their taunting symphony.

"No. You won't. Or I'll do this to you for hours. Bringing you to the brink of orgasm without ever letting you get off," he says firmly, smacking my clit again. "But since this is the first time, I'll give you something you'll never forget, kitten. You'll be calling me day and night for more. You'll be begging on your knees in no time, just as daddy likes." He smacks my clit again.

Everything inside me aches. I feel nauseous from needing an orgasm so badly.

"Please, daddy," I whisper, losing energy to talk as I focus everything on my need to unravel under this man's fingers.

Jones shifts under me, lifting my hips as he unbuckles his pants. In a daze, I let his hands control my body. I look around the small patio and silently thank the gods we're still alone because my loss of control has me doubting I'd stop this from happening even if someone did walk out here.

The tearing of a wrapper catches my attention and I turn my head to see Jones rolling a condom over his cock. The size of him makes my mouth water. He'll never fit inside me all the way, but I'll still try.

"Show daddy how sorry you are," he says, leaning back and letting his cock stand straight up.

Without a second thought, I drop myself onto his dick, sucking every inch of him into my achy cunt. He fills me so fully that it feels both good and bad.

The pain and pleasure make me soaked, ready to suck him in. I lift and drop my hips, fighting through the pain caused by his massive size as my body adjusts. My skirt is the only thing that hides our nasty public act from prying eyes.

The curve of his manhood strokes my inner walls and feeds the desire that has been building for not only the short amount of time I've waited to meet Jones but also from months and months of no sex.

It feels good to fuck again.

I buck my hips on top of him, clenching my walls tighter and moving faster and faster. Taking him deeper and deeper as I slam down onto him. My insatiable need burns hot and heavy. An unquenchable thirst for a man I know nothing about to get me off harder than I've ever gotten off. A man who I long to prove my worthiness to, if only for another chance to have his cock again. That's what I want. That's what I need.

"Your cunt is so tight, kitten. Do you like when daddy fucks you raw?" he groans, placing his hands on my hips and steadying me so he can thrust himself upward.

"I would, but you aren't fucking me raw," I breathe heavily, stilling as his pelvis pounds into me with unharnessed fury.

"We should correct that. I need to feel you," he says.

He lifts me and tears off the condom. Before I can protest, he thrusts his hips into me. I whimper at the intrusion. It feels so much better raw, and it's not just from no barrier—it's from his claiming. He's taking me and going to fill me up with his cum whether I like it or not. But honestly, I fucking love it. I've thrown all caution to the wind. He sent me negative STD test results a couple of days ago anyway.

"I'm going to come in you, and then we're going to leave so I can really fuck you. Do you hear me, kitten? I'm going to take you somewhere, and I won't stop filling that sweet cunt of yours until my cum is dripping down your legs because it can't fit anymore." Daddy growls in my ear as his cock continues punishing me.

His words are like gasoline to a flame, igniting the fire and making me tingle all over.

"Say 'yes, daddy,'" he says as he increases his pace and hits me deeper. All the way to my cervix.

He penetrates my cervix again and again. Hitting that part of me that toys and fingers can never reach or touch just right. My arousal, my desire, my fucking pussy is on overdrive. The sensitivity increases with each movement. And when I think I can't handle it any longer, his relentless thrusts push me over the edge.

"Yes, daddy. Fill me." I explode under his command, bucking against his hips as my juices slide down his cock and shamelessly soil his pants.

Dom Daddy

3

"Get in the back," Jones says, pointing to the backseat door of his Porsche Cayenne.

I do as he says while he tosses my ruined underwear in the street trash can. Jones enters the driver's seat while I buckle myself into the seat belt.

"Where are we going?" I ask, shifting around uncomfortably as my arousal soaks the leather seat under me.

He gives me a look that says he knows exactly what's happening but doesn't address the issue. "To a parking garage. It'll have to do for now."

"Okay," I say, looking out the window as Jones drives us to an undisclosed location.

I didn't exactly do a proper investigation on Jones. The ever-apparent possibility that he might be taking me to a parking garage to skin me alive is starting to creep into the rational thought-processing side of my brain.

"Why don't you entertain me while we drive there?" he suggests.

"How should I do that?"

"Take off your clothes," he says as he merges onto the highway.

"But…People might see?" I say as cars fly past us.

"I doubt they're paying attention. Regardless, I told you to get naked, so unless you want to be punished—and I can ensure this punishment won't be quite as immediately gratifying—you'll do as I say."

"Okay," I say hesitantly, but I can't deny him.

I don't know what punishment entails, but I know getting naked will likely lead to a satisfying end. I undress. He motions for me to hand him my clothes, so I do. Jones puts them in the passenger seat beside him and adjusts the rearview mirror to face me.

"Play with yourself, kitten. I want you so ready to come that when I enter you again, you're squirting all over my cock."

Jones's words ignite the flame of desire within me. The promise of being inside me again is enough to make me come instantly, but I won't tell him that or let myself. I don't want him to withhold my orgasms.

"Okay," I say as I start to play with myself.

"It's 'yes, daddy', or 'yes, sir' to you. Do you understand?" His hands tighten on the steering wheel. The promise of punishment is clear in the whites of his knuckles.

"Yes, daddy," I respond obediently.

"Actually, take this and fuck yourself with it." He tosses an empty plastic bottle at me.

I catch it and hold it up. The rough edges of it make my lower body clench in a new kind of fear. What kind of person uses trash as a fuck toy?

"But—" I protest, but Jones cuts me off.

"This is a small punishment for making me wait two days to see you, meeting you at a shitty bar, wearing underwear, and forgetting how to address me. Do you understand what happens when you don't do what daddy says?" His words are harsh and unyielding.

I gulp down the growing lump in my throat while my pussy quivers. "Yes," I say, bowing my head and eyeing the bottle.

"Stick it in," he says with a growl.

I press the lid of the bottle against my entry. The sharp edges of the lid roughly shove into me, but I keep pushing, and once the cap is inside me, the rest of the bottle slides in smoothly—but only with a good amount of force.

"Not so bad, huh?" Jones says smugly.

I hide a smile and begin to fuck myself with the bottle, realizing I sort of like this punishment. This is as good, if not better, than a dildo. It's wider but has some give.

Traffic slows, and we pull to a stop on the highway while I beat the plastic bottle into my pussy. I'm still stretched from Jones's cock. The bottle fills me with ease but lacks the firmness of his penis. As we creep up next to another SUV, I lay flat on the backseat, trying to hide from onlookers, but the seatbelt digs into my side and forces my back to arch off the leather bench. My hand pauses as I debate grabbing my clothes from the frontseat to cover myself or unbuckling and risking my safety.

"If you stop, I'll make your punishment public, kitten," he warns.

"What do you mean?" I ask, slowly moving the bottle as I press myself onto the leather bench, hoping I can't be seen by other vehicles. The seatbelt buckle makes my side cramp, forcing me to stop and try to get comfortable.

"Did I say you could stop?"

"No, daddy."

"Then continue."

I continue, unbuckling the harness and trusting Jones to drive safely. With the pain in my side gone, I focus on thrusting the bottle faster and pushing my hips into it as I do so. My heart races. Jones puts his hand down his pants now that traffic is at a complete standstill. My eyes jump from the SUV window next to us to Jones's hand.

"Get on your knees, pussy facing me," he says, turning his head to look at me.

I scramble to my knees on the floorboard, arching my back so my pussy is on display for him.

"Keep going," he says.

I reach under myself and insert the head of the bottle again.

"Slower. In and out."

His words are clipped, but I know what he wants. I pull the bottle in and out of my pussy as slowly as possible; the new speed re-ignites my nerves.

"Play with your clit too," he demands, his hand curving over my backside and spreading my butt cheeks.

To work my clit with my other hand, I press my face against the back seat while both hands are under me, fucking my pussy with a bottle and fondling myself with the other. It's the most uncomfortable position I've ever been in, and yet, the most erotic.

I do as he says, moving my hands slowly and feeling an unusual amount of wetness.

"Good girl," he says as he presses a finger against my puckered asshole.

"What are you doing, daddy?" I ask breathlessly but don't stop.

"Don't mind me, kitten. Fuck—" he curses as traffic begins to move and takes his hand away.

His hand leaving my body is like drinking the last sip of water in the desert. I need it back. I need to know what that finger inside my backside feels like.

He told me before that he would take my ass, and the anticipation has my sex clamping down on the plastic bottle so hard that it begins to deflate. The change in shape has new grooves massaging my inner walls as I continue to move the bottle in and out. It's rough on the edges, slicing against me, but I love the pain. The car shifts into movement, rocking my body from side to side, but I keep my knees spread to maintain my balance.

Before I know it, Jones is racing down the highway again, and the pace of my hands increases. I hear Jones tell me something, but I'm lost in pleasure. That coiling, tightening, out-of-body feeling hits me like a ton of bricks, and I'm spewing. My release spurts out of me, onto the middle console where Jones's arm rests.

"Kitten," he says harshly, swerving off the highway on the next exit ramp.

I'm thrown to the floor and still in a daze as Jones pulls to a stop. His door slams as he rounds the car and forcefully opens the back door. The white sleeve of his button-down shirt is soaked in my sticky cum. I struggle to remove the deflated bottle from my pussy, but before I can, Jones is in the back seat, pushing me onto my ass with the bottle still in my pussy.

It sinks impossibly deeper, and I scream as his hand latches around my throat.

"I told you not to come, kitten."

His hand remains in place, not squeezing but holding. I wait for him to deliver my punishment. Is this it? Is this the moment he fucks me to death?

"You're going to suck this cock for a very long time before I let you get off again. Is that understood?"

I clench around the plastic bottle and shift my hips, beginning to ride it, while I lick my lips and say, "Yes, daddy."

Dom Daddy

4

"Deeper," he says.

Jones holds the back of my head as he shoves his cock into my mouth, cutting off my ability to protest. Although I don't want to protest. This is unbearably hot.

His assault on my mouth continues, fucking me on one end as I ride the head of the bottle beneath me. My knees scrape against the floorboard of his SUV, but I relish the tiny bits of pain licking up my body—my knees, my pussy, my mouth.

"You take my cock so well, kitten," Jones purrs.

His voice is an erotic symphony I won't soon forget. I gargle on his cock as I attempt to say, *more daddy*, and somehow, he translates. His hips gyrate, but his hold around my neck remains steady. It's all I can do not throw up as his cock plunges down my throat, cutting off my air and dizzying my vision.

I sink onto the bottle as his pelvis hits my lips, both penetrating as deep into me as they can get. The bottle widens my pussy as his cock spreads my lips to the point that my cheeks might split. If they go any deeper, I swear they'll touch inside me.

Before I can fully comprehend how thoroughly fucked I am, Jones pulls out of me and shoves me down. My back hits the floor at the same time he tugs the bottle from my pussy, leaving me bare and thirsting. His palm comes down on my clit, slapping harshly as an equally unnerving smile lifts the corners of his lips.

"You've been a bad girl. I'm going to teach you a lesson and show you what happens when you misbehave."

Jones's gaze sweeps down my body hungrily, yet possessively. His eyes etch a trail into my skin that feels like a nail scraping down my body. My skin heats with every phantom touch.

"Please, daddy," I say. I don't know what I'm begging for—an orgasm or simply *more.*

His massive hand swoops down, grabbing me by the neck and tugging me up. I hang limp, completely at his mercy. Somehow, I know this is part of the role, and I willingly throw myself into it.

"I'm going to ruin you, kitten," he smiles.

Then he's cupping my breasts, pushing them up in a show of deceitful delight. Jones grips his cock, pumping it aggressively. Pre-cum beads at the tip, and he wipes it across my nipples.

My bodily juices leak onto the base of his car as he marks me, but he doesn't care that I'm making a mess. The door to his SUV remains open, allowing anyone who pulls into the parking lot a clear view of what's going on—how Jones is ruining me, how he's exercising punishment for my disobedience, and how much I'm enjoying it.

I stick my tongue out, inviting him to fuck my mouth again, but he chuckles. "Very good, kitten," he coos as he lunges into the car, placing one foot on the floorboard and his knee on the bench so his cock is level with my face again.

He fists my hair and pulls my head back so far I'm forced to stare at the ceiling. The sharp sting of his hold radiates through me, making my pussy quiver. Jones's cock slaps me in the cheek, the mouth, the other cheek. He praises me, and before I know it, his cum is squirting across my face, leaking hot fluid into my open mouth, onto my eyes, and sullying my hair.

"You look even better with my cum across your face, kitten."

Jones's voice is as alluring as the devil himself. I lick my lips, tasting the sticky, salty substance that marks me. He pinches my cheeks, forcing me to stop. His grip hurts.

"You like being dirty, kitten?" he asks, mouth parting slightly as he leans in and tucks away his cock.

I remain exposed and tainted on the floor below him. To any bystander, I would look like an abused little girl, a cum slut at the mercy of an evil man—which isn't far off. However, I'm far from it. I feel empowered, exhilarated by how turned on this makes me and Jones.

"Yes, daddy," I say.

"Good. You're mine for the weekend, then. I'm going to cover you in cum, not letting you rinse away my proof of pleasure until I've had my fill of you. Do you understand?" Jones emphasizes his point by rubbing his cum across my face, and slapping my cheek, which makes a horrifically sexy wet smacking sound.

"Yes, daddy," I agree.

His answering dark chuckle scrapes across my spine, making me even wetter. But his slow retreat makes my skin cold. Jones closes the car door, leaving me needy and desperate on the floorboards while he settles into the driver's seat.

We make our way to the highway in silence. Only once we reach cruising speed, and I have buckled my seatbelt, does Jones make a call on the Bluetooth speakers.

"Hello," a gruff voice answers.

"It's Jones. Entry for two, half an hour," Jones says.

"Will you be playing or observing?"

"Playing." Jones's eyes flick to me in the rearview, but his face gives away nothing.

What are we playing?

"Will you require a room?" the stranger on the phone asks.

"Yes—two nights. We'll need a bucket of ice and hot wax upon arrival," Jones states.

"Done." The line disconnects.

A bucket of ice and hot wax? Jones has me thoroughly confused and excited.

"Where are we going?" I ask.

His gaze narrows on me as if that is answer enough and says, "You're about to have the best weekend of your life, kitten. Now be a good girl, shut your mouth, lean back, and touch that pretty pussy of mine. I want you begging for my cock by the time we arrive."

I don't question him. If there's anything I'm learning about this dom, it's that doing what he says is bound to lead to an unforgettable orgasm. I spread my legs, opening myself for Jones to watch in the rearview mirror as I slide my fingers through my sex, teasing and exploring myself, but never coming to orgasm as I imagine where he's taking me next.

We pull up to a nondescript building. Jones is clearly familiar with the place because he pulls into the alley beside the building. The only indication that this is a business is the man sitting under an umbrella outside a black door with a red koala painted on the front. It's odd, but no more strange than the short phone call I overheard.

Jones told me to be hungry for his cock when we arrived. After rubbing my clit for thirty minutes, and Jones making me stop every time I got close to coming, I'm more than hungry—I'm starving.

"Stay here." Jones gets out of the car, a confident swagger in his step as he approaches the seated man.

They exchange a few words, and the man disappears into the building. He returns with a black silk robe, which Jones takes from him. Then Jones opens the car door for me.

"Here,"—he motions for me to turn so he can slide the robe over my shoulders—"Follow me."

I do as he says, passing the man who takes Jones's car keys as we enter the black koala door. The hallway is as dark as the painted door. Only a dim light along the floorboards highlights our path into the building.

Whether the air conditioning is cooling my skin, or the danger of this situation is finally dawning on me, I can't be sure. My pussy is still aching from the lack of Jones's touch. This silk robe does nothing but heighten the desire to feel his rough hands and thick cock again.

"This way." Jones places a hand on the small of my back, turning us right. The hallway ends, but he keeps walking toward the wall.

I'm certain we're about to walk through a wall like something out of Harry Potter, when the wall shifts, opening automatically to expose a hidden doorway.

We step into a faintly lit room. The walls are black like every other wall and door in this place. The only color comes from a rich mahogany desk in the middle of the room.

A woman in her mid-fifties sits behind the desk, wearing a black robe like mine. She's flaunting gaudy gold jewelry on her neck, arms, and ears. Her silver pixie cut should clash with the gold. Instead, it appears perfectly curated.

"Jones. Good to see you again. What can I provide you this evening?" Her words are cool despite their familiarity. This is a strictly business type of woman.

Jones leans in, whispering to her. A sprig of jealousy wells inside me at the proximity of his lips. The woman nods in confirmation and opens a drawer, sliding a black box across the desk.

I tilt my head curiously, trying to get a better look, but Jones steps in front of me, retrieves the item inside it, and slides the empty box back to her.

A knowing smile graces the woman's face as she finally looks at me. It makes my stomach turn. But I'm not given much time to consider the situation because Jones is blocking my view of her. He's certainly playing into the mystery of this place.

"Relax, kitten," he says as his hand slides under the robe's opening.

I tense, and Jones arches a questioning brow.

"Relax," he says again.

His fingers slip through my folds, finally touching me, and I melt. He leans forward as if to kiss me, but when I close my eyes, ready to be consumed by him, he slips something inside my pussy.

I'm already stretched from all the fondling, so it enters me easily. The item is small and smooth, but it doesn't come back out. It sits firmly inside of me while also somehow pressing against my clit.

"Follow me," he says.

"Okay," I stutter uneasily, shifting my legs to ensure the object doesn't fall out. There's no possibility of that, though. Even without trying, my body is clenching around anything it can get inside it.

I follow him, feeling the item he inserted shift inside me, rubbing against my inner walls with each step and tickling my clit. It massages me in an entirely new way. Jones stops at another wall—another invisible door, no doubt.

"Don't ask questions, kitten. Just do what I say and enjoy it."

"Yes, daddy," I say. The need in my voice is heady with desirable intoxication. I'm at this man's mercy.

The Game
Temptation

"I 'll get the money by next week. I told you I just need a little bit more time," I say.

"That's what you said last week." A clicking sound echoes in the background.

"I said I'd get you half last week. You'll get the rest next week!"

The debt collector's brutish voice deepens as the clicking stops, and he says, "And where's last week's half? If you don't pay in full plus interest by the end of the weekend, I'll be taking a lot more than your dog."

I suck in a rushed breath.

My dog, *Rosie*.

I miss her.

Fortunately, Rosie is doing just fine. Not only has Vance sent me photos of her kennel, complete with a bed and a full water bowl, but I recently found out he has a soft spot for animals. A friend of a friend told me they saw Vance walking Rosie with his own dogs. Regardless of her treatment, I have no interest in leaving her with him. She's mine, and she's all I have lately. Trying to pay off this never-ending debt has left me in a state of such deep despair that no one wants to be around me anymore. Not that there were many people who wanted to be around me in the first place.

"Fine. In full plus interest. You'll have it Monday morning," I say, knowing full well I won't be able to make that kind of money in one weekend.

The phone line disconnects.

"Fuck!" I curse, digging through my dresser drawers, turning the pockets of clothes inside out in search of forgotten money.

It's hopeless.

I check the time.

The minutes are ticking by, and I only have fifteen to be camera ready. As I frantically strip and change into something more appropriate, I think of ideas to earn extra cash. In my line of work, if a big spender comes across your page, it's a golden opportunity. The payout can cover your bills for a month or longer. However, those people are needles in a haystack. And I haven't had that kind of luck—ever. Plus, the amount of money I need is significantly more than a few rent checks.

A chiming sound comes from my computer speakers, letting me know people are already joining the virtual room that hosts my live stream. They'll only wait so long for me to get started, but I like to give extra time for stragglers to enter the chat before things start to heat up and people take advantage of a free show.

I dim the lights and adjust the bedding, making sure my pillows and decor are out of the way for what I'm about to do.

The scene is set.

Using the remote control, I turn on the camera, and the live stream begins. A large monitor behind my camera displays the thread of conversation. Tips and requests flow in, but as the number climbs on the side of the screen, it's still not nearly enough to cover my debt. At this rate, I'll be spending hours on here.

"Hi, JD12sexybutt," I try not to cringe at the childish user-name, "It's good to see you joining again! Send those requests through with a tip, and I'll be sure to prioritize yours." I continue thanking and encouraging my regular watchers in a soft, sweet voice, as well as welcoming a few of the new ones, hoping one of them is feeling generous. I'm tempted to explain my situation and basically beg for donations, but that might get me kicked offline. Then I'll really be fucked.

After several minutes of entertaining the watchers with my sensual-toned greetings and carefully placed hand strokes, I begin my routine. Reaching into the bin beside my bed, I pull out a massive black dildo, complete with bulging veins and a suction cup base. I slide the tip of the dildo across the lacy fabric covering my chest. Squeezing my tits together, I clamp them around the shaft, moving it up and down, mimicking a real cock fucking my boobs. It's so lame, but people tip more when they think it'll make me remove my clothes faster.

It won't.

"I wish I had a real cock to shove between my tits…Oh…It feels so good. I can't wait to feel it in my cunt. Who wants to see this big thick dildo between my legs next?" I say. Tips light up the screen in response.

They love to see me shoving things into my vagina. Especially massive objects. The bigger, the better. I might have to get creative and fuck a Coke bottle or something tonight. Or just do everything extremely slowly. If I really need to boost my tips, I could actually bring myself to orgasm—not just a fake one, but a full-on squirt on the camera lens orgasm.

I read the comments thread, deciding which request to tackle next. *Lick your tits.* It's reasonable enough.

I unsnap the back of my bra, letting the straps fall down my biceps, catching on my elbows as I hold the material in place with the dildo. "Is this what you want, blueballs69, to see my achy little nipples?" I fight the gag working its way up my throat. The more cliche the sex talk, the more money I make, but it doesn't mean I like doing it. I focus on the dollar sign as I set the dildo aside, letting my bra fall off completely. Approval emojis and comments flow in. But no tips.

Fucking greedy bastards.Give them a peep show and they won't reward you unless you give them more. And more. And more.

As slow as humanly possible in this scenario, I lift my right breast, pinching the nipple before stretching my neck down and swiping my tongue across the peaked tip. Smaller-breasted women don't have the advantage of being able to do this move. It's one very insignificant thing I have over the hundreds of other women online right now, competing for every dollar these online bastards are willing to throw away, but I'll take what I can get.

The tips climb, collecting another sixty dollars.

I repeat the action on my left breast, then go to town, licking and nipping both. Blueballs69 sends me a hundred dollars and a lovely picture of his erect cock. I stifle another gag and say, "Your cock makes me thirsty! I want to suck it, but I only have a dildo," I pout, licking my fake parched lips.

A picture of three more penises fills my comment feed, so I play along and lick the black dildo, taking my time along the shaft, avoiding the tip. I might as well milk these fuckers for all they have if I have to stare at their meager excuses of a dick.

"Who wants to see me deep throat?" I ask sensually.

Comments pour in, but a picture of a stack of hundred-dollar bills catches my attention. That's a first. I lean forward, giving everyone a close-up of my saliva-covered tits as I scroll up the feed to read the request attached to the mound of money. If something is going to excite me, it would be a load of cash.

User203920: Five grand for a private audience. Right now.

This wouldn't be the first time some asshole promised big money but didn't pay upfront. "I'm sorry, user203920, but usually tips are sent with requests. I can't stop my live stream without significant compensation."

He messages back.

User203920: I'm not sending anything until you do what I ask. That's how this works.

I ignore his message and sit back on the bed. A slight tinge of pain pierces my right eyebrow. Irritation and disappointment typically come in two forms—a headache and an extremely dry vagina. The universe would get a kick out of sending me fake opportunities when I most desperately need them. And at an incredibly inopportune moment—like when I'm about to shove a giant fake cock up my middle.

"Mmm…This dildo looks so tasty. I can't wait to have it in all my holes, but first, I better get it really, really wet," I preen, sucking the dildo into my mouth, and stuffing it down my throat as deep as I can. When I pull it out, a thick string of saliva hangs from the tip of the dildo, connecting to my mouth.

More tips pour in as I shove it back in, choking on it, tipping my head back so the viewers can see the tip of the object pressing against my pharynx. A satisfactory smile lifts my lips as I pull the dildo out. That tingling sensation stirs in my panties—a direct result of the climbing dollar amount.

User203920: I'll give you half now and the other half when you join me.

The number on my screen jumps up by twenty-five hundred dollars. *Woah.* Five grand is as much as I could hope to earn tonight. And that's from doing some kinky ass shit for the next couple of hours. If this guy is serious, I could make a lot more. I *need* a lot more.

Private video calls can get weird and too personal, but the promise of another twenty-five hundred has me leaping off the bed. "Unless someone makes me a better offer, I'm going to have to give user203920 a moment of my time. See you all later, babies!"

Pissed-off messages flood the screen—mostly directed at user203920 for taking me away—and I hope it doesn't lose me devoted viewers. "As a parting gift, I'll send you all an exclusive video of me fucking this dildo. I'll be thinking about you…Kisses!" I lean forward, shaking my boobs, while blowing kisses to the camera. I feel like a fucking idiot, but I've long lost my dignity.

Sending out a video for free better be worth it.

I open a new window with user203920. A black screen greets me. No sound. No messages… This is weird. I'm thankful I don't have to look at whoever is on the other side of this video, though. An ugly mutt is a surefire way of drying up my panties.

Finally, a harsh, purely male voice breaks the silence. "I have an offer for you. Are you willing to hear it?" A voice like this guys' is beautiful and terrifying enough to make me question any amount of money attached to it. If he looks anything like he sounds, there's no way he needs to be paying for a private audience with me.

I sit back on the bed, crossing my legs and arms, as I say, "I'm here, aren't I? Where's that other twenty-five hundred?" The payment comes through. "A man of his word—I like that." Finally, something I don't have to pretend to enjoy on camera.

"We'll see how much you like the rest I have to offer. How would you like to make more money than you've made in the last five years?"

I scoff, not even attempting to hide my disbelief. If this is some stupid con or comes with a catch like meeting in person, I'm disconnecting and keeping his money. "And how would I do that?" I lean back against my palms, unabashedly exposing myself and tempting user203920 to lose his temper with me. Something about his voice grates on the edge of my nerves in a captivating caress.

A low, rumbling hum is barely decipherable through the speakers. It chills my skin. "There's a box on your doorstep. Retrieve it. Then we'll begin."

The Game
The Arrangement

This weird, intricately carved square wooden box is straight out of the Middle Ages. It's heavy. At least forty pounds. I heft it up, barely able to wrap my forearms under the length of it. I don't even want to consider how this random person knew my address. The type of money and resources *that* would take are worth a lot more than five grand. I use an alias online. Unless he knows someone close to me, which is far-fetched, there's no way he could easily find that information. Meaning he has connections or fuck-you money or both.

Somehow, that's not reassuring. I shake off a quiver that snakes down my back and wraps around my spine, sticking there like an oily leech. I drop the box on my bed and sit behind it. There are no latches, no handles, nothing to indicate how to open it. "Now what?" I ask the black screen.

"Retrieve a four-legged, straight-back chair. One from your dining table will do," my mysterious benefactor says. His tone holds nothing but ruthless determination, a steely resolve that tells me I'm going to do it and I better not tell him no. He mentioned an offer, but this feels more like trial by fire.

That tight hold around my spine becomes an ache in my neck and a faint ringing in my ears. The man's voice is unrecognizable, yet he knows the exact type of chair that sits at my dining table. Very few people have entered my apartment. Even fewer have entered often enough to remember something so specific. Silently, I do as he says. The weight of the chair becomes heavier the closer I get to the camera lens' frame.

"Very good," he says. "Set the box on your desk and sit in the chair."

It shouldn't come as a surprise he knows yet another thing about the layout of my apartment and the furniture within it, but fear continues to ripple through me as I do what he says and ask, "Now what?"

"Open the box."

I look at the wooden case dumbly, like one last attempt will reveal how to open it. "How am I supposed to do that?"

"Look again," he commands.

I glide my fingers along the edges, searching for a seam. There are none. I trace the deeper grooves and indentations in the carvings. As I do, I notice the slightest, thinnest cuts that form words around the center circle: *Something that can be given, but never taken, with the power to destroy or liberate, whose value is determined by one, and becomes a heavier burden in silence.*

"What the fuck is this supposed to mean?" I say with a bite in my voice. This is the oddest, most insane private chat room experience I have ever partaken in. Part of me just wants the man to tell me to fuck my biggest dildo or piss on myself. The other part is being sucked so far into this alluring trap that sensibility has been thrown out the window and ran down the street.

"The box won't open itself, honey," the man behind the black screen says. Somehow, his term of endearment doesn't feel so endearing. It's mocking. It's cruel.

"Obviously…Look if you want to spend five grand sitting here watching me try to open this unopenable box, you're going to be very disappointed. I don't have anything to give…Whatever the fuck that means," I say, irritation simmering in my tone. Fear is fueling my emotions, but I refuse to give myself over to it. At least I have five grand to take from this freaky fucked up dude. Although, the possibility that I have a bomb or something equally as dangerous in my lap doesn't sit well. Nor does knowing this guy has my address and knows I'm home. If I don't do what he says, what are the repercussions?

He groans. "None of you are very smart it seems. Tell the box a secret, honey."

The term *honey* spits out like venom, sinking into my skin, turning black as it poisons me into submission. No one's words, online or in person, have ever had that sort of impact on me. I'm not cut down easily, but somehow user203920 slices me to the very core.

"Because that was so obvious," I say under my breath as I think of a secret. "This is ridiculous…When I was fifteen, I lost my virginity." Nothing happens.

"I said tell it a secret. A secret isn't common knowledge. Do I need to explain the definition of a secret to you?"

More venom seeps into me.

I roll my eyes. Panic, irritation, confusion. All these emotions in a matter of minutes are doing nothing but giving me a roiling stomachache. In truth, I don't have a lot of secrets. Not any that either matters or at least one person doesn't know. It's sort of liberating telling anonymous people online things I'd never tell anyone face to face. There's only one thing I've never admitted to because it would likely lose me viewers and with that—money. "Okay…Um…I hate doing this cam girl shit," I say quietly.

The box clicks. I half suspect smoke to drift out, but it's much less anti-climactic than it feels when the top of the box lifts a quarter inch.

"Very good," he says.

Without instruction—because I don't need another comment about my intelligence—I remove the top. There are four quadrants inside. Three are enclosed, their tops are smooth with a single round indentation that forms a tiny funnel into the box's contents. The fourth uncovered quadrant holds a large roll of silver duct tape and a black hood.

This could not be creepier.

Before I can ask, he instructs me, "Tape your ankles, knees, and ribcage to the chair."

"What?"

"Do I need to walk you through it?"

A hint of a British accent sneaks through his voice, furthering my intrigue about the mystery man. I'm in bum-fuck Egypt, the countryside, the motherland, the heart of the United States, in a tiny town that hardly ever hears anything but a thick South-ern-American accent. And just like that, I want to hear more of him. I want to know what hides behind the black screen that knows more about me than anyone else, that has money to throw away, and whose voice is as dark and dangerous as a thunderstorm on a spring day and as crisp and refreshing as the cool breeze that follows it.

"I can figure it out. Ankles, knees, and ribcage. Easy enough." I say firmly, hiding the shake in my voice. This isn't my first rodeo with duct tape. Granted, it's definitely the first time doing so with someone who knows where I live and could quite possibly be waiting to come kill me after I tie myself up.

As soon as the unmistakable sound of duct tape ripping off the roll fills the room, ten thousand dollars lights up the tip counter on my screen. A bleating, momentary thrill of relief escapes me.

"You can continue now," he says.

It takes me several moments to register the amount. For what? For taping myself, for giving him a private audience? It's not much work for so much money. Doubt seeps into my bones by the unrealness of these events. But money is physical. Money is real. And fifteen thousand dollars puts me a lot closer to getting Rosie back than I thought I'd get this weekend. All possibility of being skinned alive drifts out of my thoughts as I make quick work of tapping my legs.

"Tighter, honey. There better not be space between your skin and the chair." I wrap the tape tighter. "Good."

His words of admiration speed up my actions. After securing my chest to the chair, I'm sweating from the effort. He made me wrap the tape around four times. There's no possibility of me getting out of this position without a knife or scissors. Which is something I should have thought of grabbing before taping myself to the chair like an idiot thirsty for another dollar.

"Was that tiring?" He chuckles sadistically.

"A little bit…Now what?" I say, catching my breath.

"If you hadn't bound yourself tightly enough, you wouldn't have worked up enough sweat to open the next box. Here's the thing about the box…It only takes what you consider a reward."

"That's a very cryptic clue."

"Think about it," he says curtly.

I regard the funnel. The box only takes what *I* consider a reward…But the reward isn't a popsicle or a good job pat on the back. No. The reward is something more physical, more sacrificial.

I wipe a finger across my brow. I hold it over the upper right box. He didn't say to put on the hood yet. I'm thankful he hasn't. I'd prefer to see what awaits me next. My sweat glides down the funnels narrow hole.

Another click.

I remove the lid. Inside this box is the bane of my existence. It's obvious by now where things are leading—a place I have actively avoided in every type of sexual encounter. Opening *that* box is like opening a door to the pit of hell and beckoning a demon into your soul. I stick to the cliché kinky shit for a reason. If it means I never really enjoy performing on camera, so be it.

"Inner thighs, sides, and traps. Then the hood goes on," he says, abruptly pulling me from my spiraling thoughts.

A shiver runs down my spine as I pick up the pads and put them into place. My movements are slow and careful, as if placing them in the wrong spot or moving them too quickly will result in being shocked without warning. The cords disappear into the box, meaning someone else is controlling the settings on the electrodes. I could rip the pads off with my free hands if things get too intense, but as another ten grand lights up my tip screen, I know there's not much that would convince me to take them off—even if he shocks me on the highest setting and the pain is overwhelming.

"Now the hood."

I lift the silky black fabric to my face, pulling it over my head slowly. The fabric is thin, but there's not a trace of light that sneaks through the weave. My breath hitches as the hood drops down to my shoulders. It's shallow. Hot. Dry.

I swallow the aridness creeping up my throat, threatening to push my anxiety over the edge of sanity. Three deep breaths ground me. "Now what?" I say. This time I can't hide the quiver of fear that slips through my lips.

The sticky pads are cool. With the hood cutting off my vision, their chill seems to spread across my body. I wiggle, trying to release the nervous energy, but the duct tape tugs against my skin as I move. The friction leaves me feeling raw. My breasts are still exposed, my lower body thankfully covered. Something about the growing silence and the inability to see, to move, has my fear rising. I'm bound in a way that fight or flight isn't even an option. This man knows where I live. He knows what motivates me.

Panic seizes me. I grab the hood, ready to peel it off, when he says, "Don't or you get nothing."

"I've done everything you've said so far. What is this about? What do you want? I'm just some girl from the internet. This is some sadistic sick shit. I can handle it when I'm the one coming up with it, but this is next level…" Fear has me babbling. I haven't released the hood, but I also haven't taken it off. I need the money. Even though what he's given me should be mine, I have no doubt this man has a way of taking it back.

"Do you know how many women I've attempted this little test with?"

"What?" It's all I can say as I process his words. Multiple women? A test? What is he testing?

His voice comes out like a purr. "They're all so curious. Just like you. Why would I do this? Why would I be willing to give them so much money? It doesn't add up. What kind of man gets off on this sort thing?" He's mocking them like he mocked me. "Nevertheless, I don't need to explain anything to you, honey. If you can make it to the end, you'll get all the explanation and money you could ever want. But if I'm interrupted or questioned again, I'll take the money back, and little Rosie can rot in her kennel."

A sharp inhale of breath is my only response. My eyes sting as the realization of where this is going settles into me. I'll get my money, but that's not what I fear most now. I'm afraid this man is pushing me into forbidden territory, into a place I both want and don't want to go.

"Now let's get started," he says, as a shock pierces my body.

The Game
Shrouded Desire

I cry out as six shooting pulses of electricity race into me. My shoulders tighten, my sides clench, my thighs shake. Every nerve in my body tenses against the penetrating force of energy that rocks me. It's agonizing. And then it's gone.

My hold on the chair armrests releases and other feelings wash over me. My nails ache from digging into the wood. My back slumps, exhausted. My legs part as much as the duct tape allows. My chest heaves, gulping down air behind the darkness of the hood.

I'm about to curse at the man when another pulse hits me and my body reacts.

It releases.

Another pulse, even more intense. Even more excruciating. My body burns as it fights the oncoming assault.

It releases.

I tense, ready for the next round, but it doesn't come as quickly as the other three. I wait, counting my breaths as they slow. My body quivers. Waiting. Waiting. Sweat glides down my brow. The salt stings my eye as it slips down my face. Chills pepper my skin.

"I've been watching you for a while now. I know what gets you off or what you pretend gets you off," he says. I brace for another shock, but he only laughs. "Where would all the fun be if I let you prepare for it? Those first three were just a taste, honey. You see, I like to watch you panic. You never panic on camera, do you?" I don't respond. "No, you don't. But I plan to make you scream."

"It takes a lot to do that," I say boldly. My mother used to say defiance was my middle name. It seems even when faced with danger, I don't have a lick of sense. But truthfully, I just want to hear that chime again. I just want to feel the high that comes along with it. The confirmation of money well earned.

"Either you like being a little bitch or you're just too stupid to know better," he says.

"Call me stupid again you fuck," I fire back.

He laughs. "I'm not the one bound to a chair, legs sprawled and tits bouncing, begging for more."

"And I am?" I huff indignantly.

"Your panties are soaked. Lie to me one more time and see how far it gets you."

He's right. My panties are sticky against my skin, the wetness cooling as I sit here coming down from the excitement of being bound and shocked. The pain reverberating through me feels like a fantom limb—a missing part of myself that I never knew was such a critical component to living until now. This was a feeling only the chime of money brought me before. I try to mentally deny it, knowing that the edge of darkness is creeping into me one shock at a time.

"Slap yourself. Hard. I want to hear the impact," he says.

"No," I protest. He shocks my thighs. My body fights to pin them together, as if doing so will release the pain that spears outward from the epicenter of the sticky pad to land directly between my legs, wetting my panties even more. The bundle of nerves there pulses and keeps pulsing even when the electricity coursing through my body fizzles out.

"Do it now," he says.

I slap myself so hard my cheekbone stings. It's an attempt to dull the feeling gathering between my legs, to clear the masochistic yearning attempting to undo me. I want it so desperately it's becoming a primal need. And *that* is not something I can handle—the knowledge that this sadist is turning me on in ways I've never allowed before.

"Again."

I do it again, but this time he shocks my sides, forcing me to bend forward as pain ripples through my core. I cry out in agony as the electricity stabs into my sides over and over, causing my abdomen to cramp.

"Again!" This time a chime accompanies his command.

I slap myself, letting the chiming sound carry me into oblivion. The high builds with each sound and jolt. The loud thunk as I blacken my own eye is like a steadily beating drum—a signal of the psychological warfare happening inside of me. The electricity pierces my shoulders, forcing my head back as I scream. Before the shout ends, he shocks my thighs. My hands land on the armrests, squeezing so hard the chair creaks. As it does, my lower body spasms. Clenches. My back arches. A feeling unlike any other rises deep inside me.

Another chime.

Another rush of unexplainable excitement.

Like a flickering flame being fed a gust of wind, my body absorbs the energy and ignites. I give everything to the fear, the pain, the whole fucked up feeling of this. My hips buck as little pulses of electricity beat through my thighs, my sides, my shoulders, timed perfectly to heighten the arousal growing between my legs. A switch flips inside me, accepting the reality of this situation. Accepting how much I enjoy this perversion.

"Cum like an obedient dumb bitch," he says gravely.

I hate him. I hate his terse, offensive language, but they do something to me that leaves me wanting more. Another chime signals more money flowing into my account. Tears well in the corners of my eyes, not from the relief of paying off my debt, but because I am enjoying this. I am so thoroughly intoxicated by this man's lewd mouth and sadistic fuckery. I need more of it. I need more of him.

"Fuck you! I'll do what I want," I say, baiting him.

He shocks me. Either it's on a higher setting or my body's nervous system is on high alert because this one hurts like hell. Tears slide down my cheeks, pooling in my collarbone. I'm so close to throwing myself into the endless darkness. The promise of some sensational, life-altering moment in time is on the cusp and I'm awaiting it like a lamb ready for slaughter. I wait for the next pulse, but it doesn't come. I cry out asking for more, but he laughs, withholding my oncoming climax.

"If you don't cum when I tell you, then you don't cum at all."

"No, please," I beg, the sound is so unfamiliar. I'm whiney. I'm desperate. And worst of all, I'm so damn close.

"Open the next box."

"How?" I say breathlessly.

"Take a wild guess," he says patiently as if he has all the time in the world and not like he has some woman strapped up, panting for an orgasm.

The last box opened with my sweat. This box…I gather tears with my finger, blindly reaching for the next hole, rubbing around the two remaining lids. One of them opens. It's nearly imperceptible, but with touch as my only sense to rely on, I feel it rise ever so slightly. I fumble for the contents, wrapping my hand around the smooth, curved edges of something cold and heavy like metal. The edge comfortably settles against my hand as if the object is made for grabbing on to.

"What is this?" I ask.

He doesn't answer.

I continue exploring the object, running my fingers along the other edge. It's sharper, narrower, cold but dull to the touch. I search for a way to open it, activate it, deciding it must be some type of sex toy—not the typical kind, of course, but surely something meant to penetrate. A small switch catches my attention. I move it and the object jolts as it pops open. A sharp edge digs into my palm as I gently pull back, holding it carefully now. My hand grips the base. I turn the object over, feeling the weight of it, the balance. After what he's subject me to, this one shouldn't come as a surprise.

"Are you kidding me?" I say in disbelief, fear once again rising to the surface.

"Should I insult your intelligence again, honey? I'm not the type to joke around. I'd think you know that by now."

"You're a fucking sadist," I whisper.

He shocks my shoulders. I nearly drop the knife in my lap, fumbling to catch it and nicking my finger in the process. "Shut your dirty whore mouth," he growls.

My lips snap shut as I adjust my grip on the knife, holding it tightly and familiarly. My arousal halts as I dread what might come next—enjoyment or otherwise. He's testing my boundaries. He's seeing how far I'll go, how much I can handle. But all I wonder is how much more this man knows about me.

"What do you want me to do with it?"

"Slide the blade across your inner wrist. Gently now or you might cut yourself."

"Isn't that what you want, though?" I say, bringing the knife to my inner arm, right below the elbow crease. I angle the blade and slide it toward my wrist, cutting the baby hairs, but not piercing the skin.

"That's not what I told you to do," he says. His voice is angry.

I do it again on the other arm. The razor-sharp blade leaves my skin tingling and raw. A third time, I angle the blade, but this time it's along my inner thigh. My head feels light and fuzzy as I scrape it along the delicate skin.

Without anticipating it, the shock catches me off guard. My arm reacts involuntarily, spasming and slicing the knife deep into my leg. I cry out as the buildup of the last twenty minutes slams into me like a brick wall. The nostalgic feeling of a blade cutting through skin, the well of blood pouring from the wound, the adrenaline rush of pure terror, and the uncertainty of safety become a dark indulgence of orgasmic release. The world of sweet words and soft touches obliterates as a higher power enlightens me.

I drop the knife, not caring where it lands or what it cuts on the way down as my body shakes and hot blood rolls down my leg to gather between them. The salty air under my hood chokes me as the high of my orgasm slowly fades. My body feels weightless and a thousand pounds all at once.

"Open the last box." His voice is a steady anchor in the dark.

It takes every last bit of my energy to run a finger over the cut, the touch stinging as I gather my blood. There's so much of it. I lift my hand over the box, finding the last lid.

"Wait," he says.

I'm tempted to reach inside the box, but I do as he says. Thoughts and sensibility are beyond me.

"Remove the hood."

I yank it off in relief, sucking down a breath of fresh air. The cut is not as deep as I imagined, and I'm left somewhat confused as to why thinking it was worse felt better. But the man on the screen distracts me.

"I—" His beauty renders me speechless.

"Very good. You're the only one to make it this far. I look forward to seeing you soon," he says, and then the screen goes dark.

I look down at the remaining box, curiosity is my only companion now. Another chime. One hundred thousand dollars is displayed on the screen. *Holy fuck.* As I open the last box, my fingers tremble, but inside is merely a small black card. The front is blank. I flip it over and in gold lettering is an address, date, and time.

The final text reads: *Welcome to The Game.*

My Brother's Best Friend
1

It's Saturday and I just moved to Los Angeles. My brother, Oliver, Ollie for short, is being a saint and invites me along to his friend's birthday party so I won't be alone on my first weekend in the city.

I'm a little anxious thinking about all the people I've seen in his pictures and heard about in his funny traveling stories but have never met.

First impressions are the most nerve-racking experiences. One wrong word and I might never get an invite again.

Although Ollie will always have my back, he can't control what his friends think of me. I'll have to be on my best behavior, which means watching how much alcohol I consume. I'm known to get a little wild when I drink too much.

Ollie says his friend's party hard, but I have a feeling I party harder. I'll know soon enough either way. Ollie and I are driving to his friend Allison and Freddy's house. From all the information my brother gave me, it sounds like most of the people in attendance are couples.

I check my makeup in the passenger-side mirror to make sure my lipstick hasn't smudged. Everything is in place, just like it was two minutes ago when I last checked.

"Do you have something in your teeth or eye? You keep looking in the mirror," Ollie says as he looks over his shoulder and switches lanes on the highway.

"I'm just checking my lipstick," I say, turning away from him to look out the window and hide the blush creeping up my cheeks.

"You look fine. This group is chill. You don't need to impress anyone." It's the tenth time he's told me to relax today.

"I know," I groan.

He can't understand how I feel. I'm recently single and new to big-city life. Not only am I curvier than the vast majority of Los Angelians, but I'm not the stereotypical perfect-skin fashionista female I see walking down every street either.

I'm just me.

That's always been okay, but I have this bad feeling that people won't like me because I'm not from here and don't fit the standard. I don't dress all crazy and provocative. And I don't have a cool job or hobbies. I'm just a normal girl from the Midwest.

"Tessa, just have a good time. Everyone's pumped to meet you," Ollie says as he takes the next exit.

The GPS says we're five minutes away, and my heart begins to pound frantically. I remind myself to take deep breaths over the next agonizingly slow five minutes.

We arrive at the house, and I'm blown away. As soon as we walk in, a huge floor-to-ceiling window spans the length of the living room, offering an impressive view of the ocean and valley of houses spread across the hills beyond.

A pang of jealousy for the thriving couple jolts my chest, but I gave up the possibility of having a home and a partner to move here. I wanted to be closer to my family, so here I am.

Attending this party is important to my brother, not only to meet his friends but to make up for lost time together. The reminder of why I am here, not only for myself but for my family, spurs my courage to greet Ollie's friends.

One by one, they introduce themselves and hug me. The men and women give me long, tight hugs. This is not something I'm used to when meeting new people, but apparently, LA is a hugging town. Subconsciously, it does make me feel more welcome.

Allie is the birthday girl. She has strange angular features and a tall, lean frame that reminds me of a model. Her personality is as odd and quirky as her looks, but somehow, the two pair nicely into a welcoming package. I immediately like her.

Her partner, Freddy, is just as warm and inviting. They resemble one another, almost appearing as if they are related. It's a little weird, but they say people often date people who look like themselves.

Another couple, Jace and Monica, who are the epitome of California beauty, are present. They give me life-of-the-party vibes, immediately making jokes and handing out drinks when we arrive.

The last people at the house are Greyson and Chance. Greyson is actually the only local-born girl. She has dark skin and hair, and she is arguably the most drop-dead gorgeous woman I've ever laid eyes on. Not to mention, she has a perfect body. Chance's presence is a surprise.

I know Chance. It's been years since I last saw him. I was a kid, barely a teenager, and he was the hot older best friend of my brothers.

Chance has his arm around Greyson like they're dating, but they don't introduce themselves like the other couples. It's odd seeing him again after all these years, and it's surprising that he knows so much about my life. He asks about my move, my parents, and my job—seeming to know the answers already by the direction of his questions. My brother likely updated him before I moved.

"Tess, Chance, you guys want a beer?" Ollie asks, walking toward the kitchen and leaving me alone with Chance.

"Yeah, sure," I say, nervously glancing at the man he is leaving me with.

"Thanks, man," Chance says to Ollie before turning back to me. "What do you think of LA so far? I know it's barely been a week for you, but you must have a first impression?"

His face is so earnest and kind. Yet, at first glance, his sharp nose and cheekbones would have said otherwise. It probably doesn't help that I have to look up to talk him, making the sharp angles of his face stand out.

"Um... I haven't been able to get out much. This is one of the first things I've done. I didn't want to take a ton of time off work, so that and unpacking have been filling most of my time," I explain my lousy excuse for not taking advantage of all this city offers right away.

"Gotcha. That makes sense. When I moved out here, I planned to switch jobs, so I had a month to explore. It was pretty sweet. I got a good introduction to the city. If you ever need someone to show you around, don't hesitate to call me." He gives me a sly wink before my brother returns and hands us both drinks.

"What are you guys talking about?" Ollie asks, glancing between us like he missed some novel conversation.

"Just talking about how my move is going," I say quickly, not mentioning his best friend's offer.

I'm not sure why I don't tell my brother Chance is offering to "show me around," but based on how he is standing between us and never leaving my side—which I secretly appreciate—I don't think my brother would approve.

The rest of the night continues without a hitch. I get to know the women in the group better and am surprised by their receptiveness to become friends with me. Ollie has a great group of friends out here, and they seem to like me. He also wasn't kidding when he said they party hard. They might be at my level or even more so. It eases some of the tension to watch how much I drink.

Everyone is getting drunk quickly and doing various types of drugs. They offer me some, but I decline. I want to make sure my first experience with them goes well, so I'm sticking to one drink per hour, for now. I'll let them get a little wild before I join the fun.

Soon, we all head out to a bar and skating rink to continue the birthday party. I end up in the backseat of an Uber between Ollie and Chance. The sedan is on the smaller side of sedans, and with two tall, broad-shouldered men on either side of me, our thighs and shoulders sit flush against one another.

While I try to pull my shoulders in and squeeze my thighs together, the more room I allow Chance, the more he spreads his own legs. It's like he doesn't notice or care that his entire thigh is pressed solidly against mine. The connection is nerve-racking. I had a crush on Chance when I was younger, and seeing him now rekindles that young schoolgirl feeling.

He's so incredibly handsome. He always has been. He was the older brother's friend who had it all—hot, funny, athletic—but was somehow never locked down with a chick. I was so jealous of the girls I'd see him flirt with in high school, knowing I'd never have a chance.

"Feeling okay, Tess?" Chance asks, placing his hand on my upper thigh and giving it a friendly squeeze.

My body tenses. His hand is massive compared to the width of my leg, and I imagine how a hand that big would feel on other parts of my body. I shift uncomfortably in my seat, shoving the insane thoughts to the side and subtly removing his hand.

"I'm good. I get a little car sick in the back sometimes," I lie.

Greyson turns in the front seat and says, "I totally would have sat back there. I'm sorry, Tessa. Should we pull over and switch?"

I shake my head no and reply, "It's fine. We're almost there."

Great. Now I'll be the girl with problems.

The last thing I want is to appear as high maintenance. I can only hope Chance doesn't touch me like that again. It might be friendly, but it's been a while since a man touched me in a friendly way, and my brain is spinning things into something less cavalier.

The sedan pulls up to the skating rink, and I slide out behind Ollie. Chance was holding his door open for me, but I didn't want to get too close to him again. My thigh is still burning hot from where it connected to his the entire car ride.

It doesn't faze Chance, though. He walks alongside Greyson, her arm looped in his, while I walk with Ollie into the skating rink.

"You want some molly?" Ollie says in a hushed voice. "It might help you relax."

I shoot him a scathing look. If only he knew how unnerving his best friend could be, he might understand the tension. Regardless, it's annoying that he can read me so well. The two beers at the house felt great until we got in the car. Hopefully, Ollie thinks I'm nervous about the night and isn't picking up on my crush.

"A little," I decide, accepting the bag.

I have plenty of experience taking ecstasy. It won't make me stupid or out of control. I didn't realize that's what everyone was taking earlier and suddenly understand why Chance so casually touched me. It's just the molly—it does that to everyone.

I tuck the bag into my jean skirt pocket. After walking in, our group gathers by the skate station, and I tell the attendant my size. While everyone boots up, I sneak into the bathroom and rub some drugs into my gums.

As I exit the bathroom, I nearly run into Chance's chest. He grabs my hand and pulls me into the single bathroom. He locks the door.

"What are you doing?" I exclaim, looking around as if the answer is written on the walls of this tiny room.

"Ollie said you had the E," he says, leaning against the bathroom door.

"Oh, yeah! Here," I say, pulling the bag out of my pocket and handing it to him.

His face lights up like a kid in the candy shop as he takes it. He opens the bag but stops as he looks up at me with his finger halfway dipping in.

"You want to do it together?" he asks, eyes glancing down my body briefly.

I know it's just the molly making him interested in whatever warm body is closest, so I cross my arms over my ample chest, feeling the need to hide my cleavage from his wondering eyes. Ollie will kill him for looking at me like that, and I'd rather not pretend Chance thinks I'm cute when it's really just the love drug.

"I just did some," I say.

"Do some more. With me." He stalks toward me.

I put my hands up to stop him, and they land flat on his chest. The firm mounds of his pectorals spread wide across my fingertips. I want to rake my nails down his chest but stop and pull my hands away before I lose control.

Holy shit, the molly is already hitting.
Touching him feels so good.

"Here. I'll help you," Chance says, sucking the tip of his finger into his mouth to wet it before sticking it into the bag.

He covers his finger in the loose powder and brings it to my lips. At his silent demand, my lips part, and he sticks his finger into my mouth, rubbing the drug under my tongue. As he goes to remove his finger, I swirl my tongue around the tip and suck off the remaining particles.

Chance's eyes narrow and his mouth parts as he watches me suck his finger. It's like we're moving through time at half-speed.

He stands unmoving while I suck my own finger and dip it in the bag. I'm unsure what comes over me or why my body is partaking in this flirtation, but I continue. With a drug-coated fingertip, I mimic his action and stick my finger in his mouth. His tongue swirls around my tip, and I nearly go molten.

The wet feel of his tongue and the erotic sight of this man sucking my finger has my toes curling inward. As I pull my finger from his mouth, he catches my wrist in his hand and tugs me hard against his chest, knocking the breath out of me. The massive hand that squeezed my thigh earlier snakes around my back and squeezes my waist.

Our faces are so close that our breathing mixes, and I can feel my heart beating wildly against his chest. It feels like an eternity as I stare into this strange, yet familiar man's eyes. It's only been a couple of hours in each other's presence, and he already has this intoxicating control over me that will surely be my undoing.

"Tessa? Chance? You guys in there?" Ollie's voice rings out as he knocks on the door.

My brother's voice catapults me from my lust-induced brain fog. I shove away from Chance. His face contorts with an expression of frustration and sorrow, which I don't quite understand, but I ignore him, turning toward the mirror to check my makeup while Chance unlocks the door for my brother.

Ollie shuffles in, and Chance locks the door again.

"Whose got it?" Ollie asks, holding out his hand.

"Here you go, man. We just finished taking some. All yours." Chance hands him the bag.

I turn to face them, crossing my arms like I'm impatient to leave this tiny room, as I wait for Ollie to finish taking the drugs.

"You're looking a little pink there, Tessa. You take too much?" my brother asks, eyeing me suspiciously, as he stuffs the bag into his jean pocket.

"I'm fine. It's hot in here. Let's go," I say, shoving past him. I exit the hotter-than-hell bathroom, not bothering to hold the door for either man. I'm bound to get in trouble with one of them tonight if I don't put some space between us as soon as possible.

My Brother's Best Friend

2

Other party members arrived while we were in the restroom. The new arrivals are a welcome distraction to Chance and Ollie. I need to put as much distance between the hot-blooded man behind me and his equally hot-blooded best friend. My brother would disapprove of me hooking up with his friend.

He hasn't said *stay away* from Chance, but I'm fairly certain it's been said in our unspoken sibling language. I wouldn't appreciate him coming into town and hooking up with my friends, either. Plus, the warning looks he's given Chance over the past several hours seem like caution enough for us to stay away from each other.

While everyone is skating, I head to the bar to get a beer. The molly is hitting me hard, and skating is too much for my system to handle in this state. I want to sit and enjoy this feeling. The chill from the beer in my hands and mouth is helping me roll.

"How are you feeling, killer?" Chance asks.

His deep voice reverberates in my ear, causing me to jump. He laughs deeply and puts his hands on my shoulders to steady me.

"Careful. You about fell off your seat."

His hands linger on my shoulders for far too long, but I resist the temptation they bring to my body. I sit silently and breathe deeply, reminding myself that he is off-limits and there are millions of eligible men in Los Angeles. I will feel a man's touch soon enough, and it won't be my childhood crushes and brother's best friend who is probably only being like this because he's on drugs. I'm looking for every excuse in the book to explain his actions. One of which could be that I'm overthinking everything entirely.

"Everyone is headed back soon. Looks like Ollie's girl showed up, so he booked a hotel room for the night. He didn't want to take her back to crash at Allie and Fred's. You should come back with the rest of us, though," he says, leaning over my shoulders to put his hands on the bar and either side of me.

Chance has effectively trapped me. There's enough space to turn the barstool, though. So, I do. His arms don't move as I spin around, even though my breasts brush against his bicep as I turn. I can't help it with the limited amount of space he's giving me.

"I'll probably just get an Uber home," I say, pulling out my phone and opening the app.

Chance leans in, peering at my phone. "Just so you know, Ubers at this time of night are super expensive. You should just rideshare back to Fred's with us. They have a couple of extra rooms and a couch you could crash on until you sober up or the price goes down."

I glance up at him suspiciously but go back to typing my new address into the app. He's right. I've never paid three figures for a cab in my life, and I wasn't about to start.

"Fuck," I curse under my breath.

"Fuck what?" Chance puts his index finger—the one I recently had in my mouth—on my phone and pushes it into my lap as if to say *pay attention to me*.

"I was just saying fuck. Like fuck, that sucks. They are really expensive," I explain, tucking my phone into my purse.

A devilish grin appears on his face as he says, "I like it when you say fuck. It's cute."

My stomach tightens and coils with nerves. I swallow the lump in my throat and try to speak. "I—I should go home," I stutter.

He looks around before leaning in so far I think he's about to kiss me, but instead, his lips brush my ear. "You should come back with me, not home. Give me a chance, Tessa."

I shudder from the gentle touch of his lips against the curve of my ear. "I can't," I say breathlessly.

The feel of his mouth, even for one millisecond, has my blood boiling. I need to feel skin on skin. I know it's just the drugs talking, but it's becoming hard to make sense of denying these feelings.

This man uses his own name in a pick-up line, and instead of making fun of him, I'm melting under his charm. The drugs are definitely impairing my ability to think rationally. My brother will kill me, or him, or both of us. Well, probably not kill, but he will be pissed. I really don't want to upset him or hurt their friendship. I remind myself one night of pleasure is not worth it.

Chance straightens, his face looking defeated. "Okay. I'll quit being so obvious about how much I want you, but you should still come back with us. It'll be fun—you'll get to bond with everyone and be saving money. It's a win-win," he argues as if his words didn't just shake my entire world.

There's no doubt about Chance wanting me anymore. He just admitted it. Whether it's because the drugs, I can't be sure, but one thing is certain—Chance wants me. *Me!*

I feign a lack of interest in what he's so clearly offering. All I have to do is get through the evening. It's going to be a struggle with the molly rolling in my system, but hopefully, with everyone else around, there will be enough distractions for me to avoid Chance until I can go home.

On the Uber ride back, Chance sits next to me again, but he keeps his thighs and shoulders to himself. He glances over at me several times, but his expression is unreadable. I don't understand why a guy like him is even interested in someone like me. I'm not the typical LA beauty that I am certain he can pull. Yet, his words keep replaying in my ear. *I'll quit being so obvious about how much I want you.*

It's been a long time since I heard anything remotely close to that and it does something strange to my body. Like a dog in heat, all it takes is a glance, and he has me panting. Maybe this is just some childhood crush for him, too. If so, going back to my brother's friend's house and sleeping under the same roof as Chance is a bad idea. There's going to be constant tension.

The bad idea is further confirmed shortly after we arrive. The couples branch off, eager to get in bed with each other. It's clear the molly is hitting hard, and everyone wants to get comfortable.

Freddy and Allie are the first to go back to their room. Monica and Jace are next to leave and take the second spare bedroom. Greyson soon disappears into the last guest bedroom. I secretly wish I knew her better so I could stay in the room with her, but I'm left to share the couch with Chance.

Chance goes to a linen closet, pulling out blankets and a couple of pillows before spreading them out on the chaise lounge part of the couch. He stacks the two pillows and doubles the blankets before settling in to the smaller side of the couch. His feet hang off the end.

"You don't have to take the chaise. You're like a foot taller than me," I say, standing in front of the couch and refusing to lay down yet.

He didn't set out any pillows or blankets for me, and it's not like I know where to get more after watching him empty the closet.

"I actually like this spot the best, but thanks," he says, pulling out his phone and engaging with it instead of me.

I'm slightly irritated by his rude behavior, but I suppose I asked for it. He's giving me what I want. Walking over to the linen closet, I double-check for more blankets. Except, the cupboard only has some sheets and towels. I take my time, hoping Chance notices I need help, but he ignores me.

"Do you know where more blankets are?" I ask.

He fights to hide a smirk while keeping his eyes on his phone. I roll my eyes. He's clearly playing games. I don't have time for this. Not with the molly making my skin buzz with a need for something warm and cozy.

"No idea. Are there not any in there?" He feigns confusion.

"You know there aren't any in here," I snap.

He looks up at me with an arched brow, as if daring me to continue my tongue-lashing. I'm sexually frustrated, horny as all hell to be touched because of these drugs, and now equally irritated that my denial is rewarded with a dickhead attitude. I stride over to him and snatch one of the pillows under his head. I rip it out from under him, tossing it to the other side of the couch as I go for a blanket next.

"Hey!" he yelps, his head falling back against the second pillow.

He barely catches hold of the escaping blanket and tugs it away from me forcefully. My blood is boiling. I double-fist one end of the blanket. We tug-o-war with teeth bared, yelling profanities at each other.

"You fucker. Give me the blanket!" I pull on my corner, using my entire body.

"No. Fuck you," he yells back, tugging it harder and making me lose my balance.

I barely catch myself from falling on top of him, stumbling to stay upright as I roughly yank the blanket. "You teasing asshole prick!" I yell as he lets go of the blanket. I fall straight onto my ass. "Ugh," I seethe.

Chance stands. He towers over me, letting the other blanket fall to the floor at his feet. He looks irritated as he says, "Are you okay?"

"No. Fuck you," I repeat his words and snatch the other blanket from his feet.

I'm feeling petty as I climb to my feet, plopping down in his spot and cocooning myself in the blankets. Chance's mouth drops open in shock at my audacity.

"Are you fucking kidding me?" he spats.

"Go away. You're ruining my molly high," I say, covering my head with the blankets.

The couch cushion shifts as Chance's body weight sinks into it. Without uncovering my face, I have no idea what part of his body now touches the length of my side, but I have some theories, and they make me warmer than both of these blankets. Slowly, I peek over the edge of the blanket.

Chance's face is inches from mine, yet again. "I dare you to call me an asshole again." He licks his lips before dragging his teeth across his bottom lip. "Your mother would be ashamed if she knew you were talking to me like that."

It's hard to focus with him so close. Thank God the blanket keeps his skin from touching mine. The entire length of him presses into my side. His leg bends, sliding over mine as he lays an arm across my stomach.

"Are we still pretending there's no attraction between us, Tessa?" he asks.

The way my name rolls off his tongue is like a snake charmer's song. I'm caught in the allure of this man, and the only thing keeping us separated are two blankets.

My Brother's Best Friend

3

"Um..." My brain tries to come up with a witty remark to escape his question, but the fire that fueled our little tussle quickly moves from my brain to my sex, making me incapable of forming sentences altogether.

"You want me just as bad as I want you. Don't you?" His voice is like a beating drum, methodical yet taunting, in a way that makes my heart rate spike.

I shake my head in denial, but my body is screaming yes. I pinch my thighs together as firmly as possible to deny the growing heat pooling there.

"Can I kiss you? One kiss. I swear. I just want to taste your lips one time." His eyes move back and forth between my lips and eyes, questioning and yearning.

I know it's the molly, but I want to feel it, too.

It's stifling under the covers, and I need air. To think. To breathe.

I shimmy the blankets down my shoulders slightly as Chance watches me with curiosity. He presses closer and moves the hand draped across my stomach to the top edge of the blanket. I nod. He pulls them down, freeing my upper body, and the air douses my desire like a bucket of cold water.

I inhale a massive, chilling breath that makes my breasts heave toward my chin, revealing more cleavage under my shirt. Chance's eyes widen and his mouth parts when he catches sight of them. Before I can cover myself, his hand latches onto my wrist again. His bare skin touching mine makes my body warm all over.

Our eyes meet, and I hold my breath. He's so close I can smell him. Sweat glistens along his hairline. I imagine it's on mine, too. Either the molly, the nerves, or a combination are making us both hot.

There's no denying my attraction to him and no denying what I truly want. I want him to fuck me harder than I've ever been fucked before. This has been years of yearning in the making.

"Fuck it," I say quietly, gasping for air to cool the inferno inside me, but nothing can calm the flames of desire. Nothing but Chance.

His lips slam onto mine. He is forbidden fruit, and I've never tasted anything so sweet. He will be my undoing in so many ways, but I'm ready to fuck it all to hell because his lips are consuming me.

Chance's hands frantically rip the covers off the rest of me while his lips and mouth explore my own. I wiggle, trying to align my body with his while he holds my face between his hands so we don't lose our connection. My body is tingling like I'm connected to an electrical plug feeding energy into my very core.

Chance climbs on top of me, holding himself up by his elbows and knees. He moves his lips from my mouth and peppers a trail of desperate kisses down my chest before stretching the top of my shirt down and letting my breasts pop free.

He hungrily devours my nipples—moving from one to the other while kneading my breast tissue. If I wasn't hot and bothered before, I am now. I can feel the wetness pooling in my panties.

Chance keeps his mouth around my nipple as his fingers trail lower, tugging at the hemline of my skirt. I lean up to stop him, insisting on removing his shirt first. I can't be the only naked one. Plus, I've been dying to see what's under his clothes. I have a feeling he feels the same insistent need to be skin-to-skin as I do.

He assists me with pulling off his shirt, kneeling to his full height, and stretching it over his torso. *Good god, those abs.* I need to run my tongue over his rippling muscles.

I pounce on him, rocking him onto his back at the end of the chaise lounge.

"Woah, Tessa," Chance laughs, holding onto the sofa's edge to avoid falling off.

My tongue is already running over the rolling waves on his abdomen and moving lower. Chance's hand finds the back of my head, balling my hair into his fist to keep it out of my face. I kiss down his stomach and run my hands along the edge of his pants. His eyes are hooded with lust, and it's the sexiest sight I've seen in a long time. The way he looks at me makes me feel wanted, needed and appreciated.

A flower blooms in my chest. It's the only way I know how to explain the feeling, but it's as if my entire soul is laid bare for him.

I kneel by the edge of the couch and remove his jeans, pulling his underwear down. Chance's heavy breaths are the only sound filling the eerily silent room as he lifts his hips so I can get them fully off.

His cock bounces out, and in the dim light of the living room, I see a subtle curve to the left. *That is something new*. New and intriguing. I can't wait to feel it inside me.

"Tessa?" Chance asks.

I look up at him, barely able to take my eyes away from his memorizing cock. "Yes?" I ask.

"Take off your clothes, babe. I want to see you," he says, sitting up and sliding his hands down my body to the bottom of my shirt.

I stand and do as he asks. When I'm naked, Chance just stares at me, and neither of us moves. This is the point of no return. If our skin makes contact, there is no going back.

"Do you want this?" he asks.

"I think so," I reply honestly.

"I'm not going to force you."

"You aren't forcing me," I say with a laugh.

"I know I came onto you strongly, but I'll only do this if you're sure. I've waited a long time, and now that you're here, I have plenty of time to keep convincing you." His cocky attitude returns.

I take a deep breath and look down at his entrancing cock again. That curve is everything—long and hooked in a way that I know at the right angle, it'll have me screaming.

"I'm sure," I whisper, dropping to my knees and sucking him into my mouth before he can object.

Chance sucks in a breath and falls backward on the chaise, placing his hands on the sides of my head and helping me go down on his manhood. "Yes, baby. You're so good at that," he says breathily.

I suck in my cheeks and take him as far into my mouth as possible, letting him hit the back of my throat as I fight a gag.

I pull away, panting and slobbering when I can't take him any further.

Looking up, I see Chance watching me with his mouth half-open. I don't think he expected me to be good at this, and I relish knowing I'm an all-powerful, dick-sucking woman.

Feeling the confidence radiating from me, I stand and straddle his lap. I center my sex over the curved tip of his cock and impale myself onto him.

My body is ridiculously turned on, to the point that my wetness is seeping down my thighs and pooling at the base of Chance's cock. When our pelvises hit one another, we both let out a guttural moan of pleasure.

I let myself sit there momentarily, soaking in the feeling of him filling me completely. As I tilt my hips and lift myself off of him, I feel that curved tip run alongside my inner wall in the most fascinating and delicious way. Needing to feel more of him, I rotate my hips up and down, lifting and dropping on him and becoming more frenzied in my movements as my head starts to spin.

Chance's hands grab my waist, helping me move faster on top of him. As my walls tighten and my eyesight blurs, I shut them and let the molly take over. I'm tossed into euphoria.

My body clenches. I can't move as an uncontrollable sensation forces me to spasm. Chance takes the lead, thrusting wildly into me as my body ignites. The sensual touches and angsty build-up of yearning all night finally reach its peak.

A long-overdue release of pleasure explodes from me like a storm of fireworks, and as Chance keeps moving, I implode, falling onto his chest. After several more thrusts, Chance stills inside me, and I feel the hot spurt of his cum release inside me.

I nearly black out during the climax. There is no coming back from that. Chance fucked me like I've never been fucked before, and I need it again.

"Round two?" he whispers in my ear.

"Yes, please," I reply.

After Dark

"You shouldn't be out here miss." A burly man in an over-sized trench coat stalks out of the shadows and circles me.

"I could say the same to you," I counter, picking at my nails and pretending not to notice him draw closer.

He walks under the last streetlight, slinking into the darkness as he approaches me. I don't move. I hold my ground, seemingly unaware of the threat he poses. The sly grin on his face tells me all I need to know. As I turn my shoulder away from him, he lunges for me, wrapping a thick arm around my waist and a scratchy hand around my throat. The callouses on his palms scrape against my sensitive skin.

"Nowhere to go. No one to help," he says.

His tobacco-scented breath creeps across my neck and tortures my nostrils. The man's erection is pressing into my backside. Only the worn fabric of his jeans and my sheer silk dress separate us.

"I wouldn't do that if I were you," I warn him, relaxing into his hold.

His hand releases my arm to adjust himself. Either he trusts me not to fight back, or he doesn't see me as a threat by only holding me by the throat. Regardless, if *he* remembers me, the man behind me is in serious trouble.

Part of me fears *he* hasn't thought twice about me, and I may very well be on my own tonight. I might very well be signing myself up to be raped. I take the risk, though. Because *he* has been on my mind for weeks, and this is my last desperate attempt to get *his* attention.

Three weeks ago, he saved me from a mugger in a situation much like tonight. I was so banged up from the attack that the strange hero helped me back to my apartment, cleaned, and bandaged my wounds. His face remained masked as he assisted me, which only made matters worse. I look into the eyes of every man I cross, hoping to see those dark brown irises again.

At the time of my rescue, I was too exhausted to ask his name, and the soft caress of his fingers as he tended to me left me speechless. The feeling of his fingers on my skin still has not faded, though. If anything, it's motivated my pursuit to find him.

I had to find him. If only to thank him.

"Step away from the girl," my mysterious savior says.

A breath of relief rushes out of me as the man behind me tightens his hold on my neck, turning our bodies to face *him.*

"Fuck off, and nobody gets hurt," my abductor yells, backing us away from the approaching masked man.

My savior follows, undeterred by my captor. The hold on my neck is tightening to frightening levels, making me silently question the decisions that led to my coordinating this event. However, some intrinsic part of me trusts the man following us will save me, even if I black out from being choked so hard.

"Stop right there or I'll slit her fucking throat," the man behind me threatens.

I tense.

"You don't have a knife. Let her go and I won't break all your bones." My savior takes long, undeterred strides forward.

We stop abruptly, my feet stumbling as my body presses against the fat man who no longer retreats. A tremble works its way through him and into me. I can practically sense his fear. I crane my neck against his hold and catch sight of a brick wall behind us. A strangled laugh chokes out of me, and the captor squeezes harder, cutting off my mockery.

My savior continues toward us. He's an arm's length away as he says, "Leave now and I won't follow. This is your last warning. I'm feeling generous tonight."

The man behind me doesn't hesitate. He releases me, shoving me into the arms of my savior as he flees the alley.

"What are you doing?" *he* asks as he helps me stand upright.

I stare into his glossy brown eyes. They're sharp and narrow, curved up toward high arching brows. His gaze pierces me like the tip of a blade.

"I don't know what you're talking about," I lie.

"You do know."

His hands leave my arms and fold into themselves, forcing his biceps to bulge. Even in the dark, I can see the thick cords of veins under his skin, like even his blood is trying to escape. I imagine most people run away from him. But not me. I ran to him.

My mouth waters as I take in the sight—from the dark fabric straining across his shoulders to the mud splattered across his military boots. If what's under the mask matches the parts of his body I can see, he is dangerously intriguing.

"Do you purposely wander down dark alleys in search of trouble or does trouble just happen to find you often?" he asks, squaring his shoulders and making no move to leave the alleyway or me behind without receiving answers to his questions.

Not just a vigilante but a detective, too. Hot.

"I guess trouble just finds me," I say, hoping our conversation never ends.

He scoffs at my response. "I think you're searching for trouble. However, I can't quite figure out what type of trouble it is. Did you want that man to rape you?"

"No! Of course not," I protest quickly.

I don't have *that* kind of forced sex fantasy. I'd rather my savior not think I'm some type of sadistic whore. Granted, if *he* wants to role-play the fantasy, I might consider it.

"Then why am I finding you hanging out in a dark alley, dressed like some club slut, on the wrong side of town? Did the first time not teach you a lesson?"

His words sting, but I forgive them. I've been searching for him to thank him. I didn't expect him to judge me for being in the wrong place at the wrong time. Plus, I think I look cute—not like some club slut.

"Thanks for saving me again. I'll be sure to take note of where to go and how to dress next time I go out," I say sarcastically, shouldering past him.

A firm grip latches onto my wrist and tugs me around. My chest slams into his, knocking the breath out of my lungs with an *oomph.*

"Ow," I say as my savior pins my arms behind my back.

"Tell me your true motivations for making such poor decisions, Essy."

I gasp.

He knows my name. How does he know my name? It makes my stomach knot excitedly.

"I didn't know how else to find you," I admit.

"Did it ever occur to you that I might not want to be found?"

"No. Well, yes. It did, but I thought you might—" I stutter, searching for the words, but all I can think about and stare at are his entrancing brown eyes.

"Why are you looking for me, Essy?" he asks.

I love the way he says my name. It rolls off his tongue like a snake hissing. The sound is as dangerous as he is mysterious.

"To thank you," I explain.

"To thank me," he says incredulously.

His grip loosens on my wrist but holds me in place as if he doesn't quite believe my agenda. But it doesn't explain why he holds me so closely. Even as we speak, he makes no attempt to put space between our bodies. I'm not a threat. Surely, he knows that. Maybe he keeps me close for another reason.

"Yes. That's all," I say softly.

The flush alignment of our bodies becomes abundantly apparent as I wait for his response. He seems happy to soak in the silence, and I swear I feel his fingers caress the back of my arms. It forces a shudder up my spine.

"Pity."

He releases me, and my knees go weak from losing his touch. But he's back on me, raising me by the elbow to help me stand straight. I'd blame it on the heels, but even I know that's a lie.

"Thank you. Again," I say shyly.

"Thanking me is unnecessary. I'd do it again in a heartbeat," he says casually.

My heart races excitedly, knowing he would rescue me without a second thought. But he lets go of me again. This time, I stand on my own as he briskly walks toward the alleyway entrance.

I rush after him, heels clicking on the concrete, cheeks flushing from the effort and his promise. Would he really look out for *me*?

"Wait! You'd do it again?"

He stops to face me. "Of course. That's what I do, but you should avoid dark alleys in the future. It's dangerous. Especially in this part of the city."

I flush, feeling like an idiot. That's what he does. He would rescue me out of duty, not out of kindness of his heart or some other type of want—like wanting to see me again. He probably thinks I'm a stupid little girl oblivious to signs of trouble. Obviously, I know this part of the city is dangerous. It's riddled with drug lords, gangs, and the type of people who have nothing better to do than harass or hurt someone else.

"Right," I say.

The masked man cocks his head curiously.

"What?" I ask.

He closes the distance between us, stopping with his face an inch from mine. "You don't step away or tense when I'm near you. Why?"

"Because I trust you." Honesty comes far too quickly. I don't know this man, but I know he won't hurt me.

"You don't even know my name."

"I know, but I believe you're trustworthy," I say confidently.

He laughs. "If you knew me, you'd be very afraid. Regardless, I like your brashness. And this little stunt you pulled to get my attention was cute."

I hold my breath. If he knew I was looking for him, why did he wait until now to see me? What game is he playing? Was he trying to see how far I would go, or did he have no interest in ever seeing me again? I realize I forced his hand tonight, but part of me wishes he wanted it forced.

Before I can think of a clever excuse, he continues, "What draws you to dark alleys, Essy?"

He says *dark alleys* like it's code for something.

"I can't stop thinking about you," I admit.

His masked face leans in, the rough cloth brushing against my cheek as he whispers in my ear, "What about me?"

My lip trembles excitedly, overwhelmed by the nearness of his mouth. It's an entirely new sensation—knowing he's so close yet remains untouchable with the mask covering his face. I'll never know what he looks like under the hood. I'll never see the expressions crossing his face, only the amusement and judgement that come and go in his gaze.

"I think about how you helped me that night. You were surprisingly gentle. Your touch...I still feel it." I gulp.

The memories come back to me, still as fresh as if they just occurred. The way his fingers gently slid the strap of my top down and wiped the blood from my wound away. The scar on my shoulder will forever remind me of that fated rescue.

"What else?" he prods, still not moving away.

I swallow again before saying, "And I think about what you did to that man."

"He hurt you. His actions were atrocious, and you'll be scarred forever because of them. I did what I had to," he says, looking away.

He defends his actions as if needing an excuse for leaving the mugger in ruins. I slide my arms out of his grasp to take his hands in mine. He lets me.

"I'm glad you did," I say.

"You're not scared of me after that?"

"No. I know I can trust you. You took care of me." I smile reassuringly.

"I should go," he says, but he doesn't move or pull away like a man who wants to be left alone.

"I don't want you to go."

"Why not?" he asks.

"Because I—because I want to feel your hands on my body again." The words rush out of me, desperate to be announced.

The fabric on the mask lifts around the masked man's mouth. A smile. He slowly reaches his free hand up and slips the shoulder of my dress to the side—much like he did that night—exposing my fresh pink scar. His thumb grazes the sensitive mound of flesh, forcing a shiver down my spine.

"Tell me where you want to be touched, Essy."

He says my name so familiarly that I nearly melt in a puddle of desire.

"Anywhere," I say as a breath I hadn't realized I was holding rushes out.

His fingers slip out of mine and find my other shoulder, sliding the thin dress strap over it. The dress falls but catches on the peaks of my breasts. They are the only thing holding it up.

The masked man slides his fingers down the back of my arms, leaving goosebumps in his wake. They trail the hemline of my dress, calloused fingertips brushing along my upper thighs.

"Anywhere. As in here?" he asks, planting a hand along my side and digging his fingers into me.

"Anywhere," I say, nodding.

My rescuer takes little time to question my response. His hands cup my backside and lift me. My legs naturally straddle his waist, pushing the dress up my hips and exposing my dainty lace panties.

He carries me back to the end of the dark alleyway and presses my back into the brick wall. His hips grind into me, and I feel his erection. His fingers dig into my butt cheeks, like blunt daggers. It's going to leave a bruise, but I don't care because feeling his bare skin on mine is like a healing tonic.

This is more than I imagined happening tonight.

I feel, more than see, a hand tug the mask from his face. In the darkness of the alley, I can barely make out his features. Yet, seeing him doesn't matter. All I want is to feel him.

His hands move quickly and shamelessly, running along the mounds of my hips and breasts. He tugs my dress down, letting the remainder cinch at my waist to expose my breasts. They fall heavily against my ribcage. The chill air nips at them.

The masked man's mouth finds my peaked breast, warming and taunting it. He flicks his tongue across one before finding and pleasuring the other. My center is aligned with his, and when I feel that stirring desire bubble in my core, I grind my hips against him.

He moans into my chest and thrusts his hips hard against mine.

"Is that what you want?" he asks.

"Yes," I pant, twining my hands into his hair and feeling it for the first time. It's short, curly, and matted. I scrape my nails along the back of his head, scratching an invisible itch as if it will scratch my own.

"Fuck." He leans back, keeping a hand under my backside to hold me up while he slides down his pants.

His cock flops out, slapping against my lace panties. It's too dark to see it fully, but the velvety skin against my thighs is all it takes to make my panties a sopping mess.

My sex tingles and aches in anticipation.

"Is this what you want, Essy? You want a strange man to take you in an alley?" He slaps his cock against my center.

He has no idea just how badly I want that and what I'm willing to do to get it.

"Yes, please," I beg, pulling my panties aside and lifting my hips so he can no longer tease me. I need him inside me.

The tip of his penis dips into my arousal. My head falls back in hazy relaxation. *Finally*. The unmasked man slowly pushes and pulls himself in and out of me, lubricating the shaft of his cock inch by inch. With his dick fully moistened, he shoves into me, penetrating me completely.

We both let out a moan of relief.

"Oh my god," I say, but his mouth captures mine.

The smooth skin of his lips dances against mine as his hips slowly, methodically move. His cock massages along my swollen walls. The sound of swapping spit and fucking is the only one in this dark, desolate alleyway—it turns me on more.

I tilt my pelvis, giving him a deeper range to impale me. He takes the queue to pull back and thoroughly fuck me. He thrusts faster, his hips pounding against me. My bare back scrapes against the wall, causing pain to erupt on one side of my body and pleasure on the other.

The opposing sensations warm my core, igniting a new desire within me that relishes this type of carnal fuckery. I wrap my arms around his shoulders while he holds me suspended in the air and fucks me. He drops me onto his cock as he thrusts upward. The force of his penetration shakes me to the core. I can feel him punishing my cervix like he's serving up a life sentence for my earlier stupidity. He's so deep, too deep.

"It—It's too much." I spasm, clenching around his cock.

My rescuer doesn't care about my feelings now, though. He takes his liberties with me and drives his hips into me harder. Once again, pain and pleasure swirl, stemming from the entry he abuses.

I dig my fingernails into his shoulder, warning him not to push me further. I can't take it. The feeling is overwhelming. But the pain only makes him moan in pleasure alongside me. His nose nudges my jaw upward, and his mouth finds the crook in my neck.

A hot, wet tongue tastes me as his teeth drag across my throat. A spine-tingling sensation causes my body to clench around him again.

"That's it. Come for me, Essy," he says as he bites down.

My legs tighten, and my cunt attempts to trap him. All of the strength in my body funnels itself into the heat of my desire, succumbing to the man biting my neck and owning my pussy. My release spurts onto his cock as he continues to rail me.

"Fuck that feels good," he says, slowing down and pushing himself into me with one final thrust.

I feel his cum shoot into me, seeming never to end as my head swirls excitedly. Now I've got him.

Eat Me

I moan and roll over. Saturdays are for sleeping in, not being woken up by a restless partner.

"Babe, go back to sleep," I mumble, shifting my hips.

His hand slides down my waist, basking in the feeling of my silky skin—like always. He could probably identify me based on my skin and scent alone.

"I'm hungry, baby," he whines.

"Go eat something then. I'm not ready to wake up," I protest as I scoot my backside into the crook of his warm body.

I love his warmth in the morning as much as he loves the feel and smell of me. His nose nuzzles into my hair.

"It's not that kind of hunger," he whispers.

Of course not. I can't be too angry with his constant arousal, though. Most other women's husbands struggle to get it up at this age. Mine struggles to get it down.

A rush of breath brushes my ear as his hand skims down my abdomen. My skin flushes as his nail circles my belly button. He takes his time softly caressing and scratching my skin, working his way around each nipple and down the sides of my hips as his lips gently press against my neck.

"Just go back to sleep," he says as his body shifts, sliding down mine and under the sheets.

His rough beard tickles my sides as he peppers kisses down my body. "Babe—," I say, fighting a giggle, but am cut off when his arms encircle my waist and squeeze playfully.

He likes to pretend he's being sneaky and taking advantage of me while I'm asleep. Technically, I should be. It's still dark in our bedroom. The blinds are open, but the sun hasn't fully risen.

My husband's long body crawls over my legs, shoving them apart. Still groggy from sleep, I don't have the energy to protest. Instead, I drift in and out of consciousness while my man spreads my thighs, stretching them so far apart that it aches.

The warmth of his hands glides across my skin as they memorize the curves of my thighs and hips for the thousandth time. He takes his time, letting me sleep as his soft touch lulls me into a deep state of relaxation while he massages my legs. The position isn't entirely uncomfortable as I relax into it.

"Mmm." He lets out a deep sound of primal appreciation that rumbles in his chest.

I feel the sound in my bones but don't move. I don't give him the satisfaction. After all, he wants me to be asleep.

"Baby," I say sleepily, reaching for him below the covers.

"Sh. Back to bed, baby," he responds, kissing my inner thigh.

His lips press against the sensitive skin near the edge of my underwear. He trails up the edge of my panties, pressing soft, subtle, tender kisses onto my body. He takes his time teasing me, happy to do this for hours.

I have yet to process today's to-do list and allow myself to instead focus on the sensation of his lips on my body. I zone in on the tingling energy that transfers directly from his lips.

Everywhere they touch, my body simmers with a growing need. And they seem to touch everywhere. Everywhere but the one part of my body I know he's really focused on.

"Baby," I whine, wanting him to get this over with already as I begin to wake up.

He torments me, making me wiggle and whimper as his kisses work their way around my panty line.

"Yes, baby," he says again, clearly enjoying himself. "I told you to sleep."

He says it as if that would have made him get to the good part faster, but I know it wouldn't have. "I thought you were hungry," I say smartly, feeling the sleepiness evaporate as my desire increases.

He chuckles against my thighs. The heat of his breath cools the puddle of arousal forming under the thin strip of fabric that separates his mouth from my sex.

"I'm starved. I just needed to warm my breakfast up," he says as his teeth graze the fabric over my clitoris, making me cry out.

I reach under the blanket and thrust my hips to meet his mouth. His mouth surrounds me, and his tongue darts out. He sweeps it across the wet panties. His saliva and my arousal soak them.

"Baby, please." I swivel my hips, rubbing myself against his mouth and chin.

"As my baby wishes," he says, forcing my hips down roughly and yanking my underwear off.

His movements toss me around, but the show of his strength only arouses me more. His tongue slips into my folds, flicking over my flesh as I grab fistfuls of his hair and grind my hips into him.

His fingers dig into my sides, warning me to let him have his way with me while bracing my hips against the bed. I eagerly follow his command. I love it when my man takes control. He knows how to pleasure me. After all, what else were all these years of practice for?

He tosses the covers over his shoulder so I can watch him at work. With the skill of a veteran pussy eater, my husband dips his tongue into me, licks up my center, and flicks his tongue across my clit again.

Our eyes connect. A silent conversation passes between us.

I smile. He smiles.

Then he opens his mouth and feasts on me. His nose pokes the top of my pussy, and he expertly uses it to stimulate one part of my body while he indulges in another. He shakes his head like a wild animal full of blood lust.

I feel the budding charge of release urging for more. He's made eating me out into a sport. A sport he's perfected and honed to the level of a professional.

"Inside me, baby, inside me," I beg.

He answers my request, sinking his digits into me and curling them. The movement forces a sinful groan to escape my throat. It motivates him, and he pumps his fingers into me, letting his knuckles pound against my flesh as his tongue flicks across my clit.

"Yes," I urge him on, grinding my teeth together as the feeling of my man devouring me overwhelms my senses.

He feels my orgasm building and looks up as he increases the pace of his attack. As he smiles, I see my arousal glistening on his chin and tongue. It drips from his nose while he smiles wickedly as if I'm the most decadent dessert he's ever tasted.

It undoes me.

"Fuck." I tighten, feeling the ecstasy on the brink of exploding within me.

A growl rumbles against my clit as he possessively eats me out, slurping down as much of my cum as possible. The crudeness throws me over the edge, electrifying my nerves, and sending a multitude of ecstasy-filled endorphins through my body.

The euphoric feeling slowly fades, leaving me dazed and satisfied. He continues licking my center, claiming his prize.

As he rises to his elbows, he says, "Yum."

Occupational Hazards

Airport Security
1

"**P**lease step to the side, ma'am," the burly security guard with muscles bulging under his blue buttoned-up shirt ordered me after the alarm on the metal detector beeped for a third time.

I was assured this would work, and yet, it was clear now that nothing could escape these detection systems; when the man waved his metal detector over my center, and it began to beep, I felt the heat rush up my cheeks.

"Ma'am, do you have any metal piercings that may be hidden under your clothing?" he asked, holding back his smile.

I gulped. "Yes, I do."

Several piercings were hidden under my clothing, but that wasn't all. I prayed to God I wouldn't have to offer proof.

"Please come with me," he instructed, taking my upper arm and steering me through the security area.

"My bags," I protested, looking back to see my bags being collected by another intimidating-looking guard.

What have I gotten myself into? If I admit what I am carrying, will they write it off as a misunderstanding and let me through?

The guard opened a door to a small, sterile-looking room and guided me inside. The other guard, who collected my bags, brought them in and set them on a metal table at the far end of the room.

"Take a seat," said the burly man, whose name tag read *Curt*.

I followed his orders and took a seat, while the two guards discussed something quietly by the door. Shortly after, the guard who collected my bags left the room.

Curt and I were alone, and when he locked the door and turned back to me, I got a sinking feeling in the pit of my stomach.

Not only was his physical presence incredibly intimidating and notably attractive, but the look on his face was borderline evil. Something about his eyes screamed *danger*.

When he discovers what is inside me, will he charge me with something? He will most definitely reprimand and embarrass me. But what else will he do to me?

Curt didn't look like the kind of man who messed around or found humor in much.

"I'll need proof of those piercings, miss…?" he asked, standing before me with his arms crossed.

"Miss Griffin. Lani Griffin," I said uneasily, squirming in my seat as I realized he wouldn't be leaving the room while I removed the piercings—he would be watching me while I removed them.

"Well, Miss Lani Griffin, let's see them then. I'll rescan you once they're removed," he stated matter-of-factly before leaning against the wall and looking down at me with threatening eyes.

"Um…Sir…They're under my clothes," I pleaded, embarrassed and hoping he would turn his back momentarily.

"I won't be taking my eyes off you for one minute, Miss Griffin, so don't even try to convince me otherwise. Now, the piercings." He motioned to my clothes as if he ordered women to undress every day.

I slowly stood and, with shaky hands, lifted the hem of my T-shirt and slid it over my head. When I looked up, he was still watching me.

His gaze slid across my exposed stomach and over the fleshy mounds of my breasts. I was only covered with a thin cotton bra, and the two matching metal bars underneath poked into the fabric, making two round bulges on each side of my hard nipples.

"Good," he said, straightening and stepping toward me.

There was already little space in this small room. His towering form now stood within touching distance, and I swear the air got hotter in here. Sweat beaded on my lower back as I watched Curt's gaze darken as they zoned in upon my nipples again.

"I don't have all day." His eyes darted to mine and narrowed menacingly.

Quickly, I slipped the cotton bralette over my head and felt my breast fall out of it, bouncing a little. Curt had my breasts in each hand before my bra even reached the floor. I staggered back, but his grip stopped me.

"I have to investigate these properly. Make sure they aren't something more nefarious," he said, rolling and tugging at the metal rods.

God damn, the tiny little piercings and the pleasurable feeling they elicit when touched!

As he moved them, my body could not resist the overwhelming desire. Each tug and twist had my inner walls clenching around the item stashed away there; I would die from the embarrassment if I had to reveal that secret to the security guard.

As Curt examined the piercings, my eyes rolled back in pleasure. *God, it felt good to have this rough man's hand playing with me.* A stranger who overpowered and controlled me—it was my ultimate fantasy.

But as soon as I let my fantasies run wild, his hands were gone, and so were the metal rods.

"There. Next one," he ordered, turning his back on me and setting the jewelry down on the metal table.

I cursed myself for being a lustful whore and blamed the item buried deep in my pussy for turning me on in a situation not meant for fuckery.

Rocket, the emo gamer I'd met online four weeks ago, had shipped the toy to my house and told me to wear it through the airport.

He controlled it at home, but I had not felt any vibrations. It was bound to happen any time now. If he knew I was held up in a security room, surely he wouldn't trigger it, but how would he know? He probably thought I was close to boarding and couldn't wait to get me off when I was sitting on the plane, flying to him.

With the guard's back turned, I thought this would be a good opportunity to slip the item out. I unbuttoned and dropped my pants. As I tugged my panties down, Curt spun around.

"Um…" I started to explain, but a vibration rocked through my body, and I clenched, bending forward and cupping my pussy to shield it from Curt. "Arrgh." I moaned, smashing my legs together.

"Miss Griffin, spread your legs now," Curt said, taking a defensive stance.

The vibrator pulsed more intensely, and I shook my head. I couldn't open my legs. My body was too tight, too tense, too electrified.

"Now!" His voice rose, and his hand moved toward his weapon.

"Shit!" I said, immediately spreading my legs and removing my hand despite the tingling vibration shooting through my core.

With my legs spread, I could feel the evidence of my arousal dripping down my inner thighs, and when the sound of a droplet hit the cold tile floor, I went molten.

"Fucking hell, woman!" Curt hissed as the vibrator beat harder.

My walls clenched around the toy, spasming after each tremor.

Curt dropped to his knees in front of me and leaned in, assessing the situation. His fingers slid over my pussy, flicking my third piercing menacingly before finding the end of the vibrator and tugging on it gently.

The movement sent pulsations shooting through new parts of my body, but still, he didn't remove it.

"Oh god," I moaned, shaking and reaching for Curt's shoulders to steady myself.

His hands found my waist to steady me. "Miss Griffin, are you aware that this shouldn't be worn through airport security? This is the type of thing you pack in your suitcase." He sounded amused.

"I know," I breathed, closing my eyes as the vibrator pounded against my inner walls. Curt's fingers returned to my pussy, and continued to rummage through my wet lips as if he was searching for more piercings to remove.

Why is he touching me like this? Why isn't he just removing it?

His actions turned me on even more.

"I'll have to remove this and this," he said, flicking the piercing on my clit and tugging on the vibrator.

I swore he thrust the vibrator in and out of me several times, but I couldn't be sure as another tremor rocked me.

"Oh my god," I moaned, pressing my nails into the firm muscles in his shoulders.

"I hate to remove it when you're enjoying it so much," Curt said, his hot breath fanning my moist pussy lips.

His face was so close, his eyes examining every part of my naughty core as if searching for additional threats. He'd found them all.

"Please," I begged again, unsure what else I begged for though.

The growing tension between my legs was overwhelming, and yet, I fought it from increasing with my entire will.

There was no way I would come in this security room with a strange man kneeling before me. However, fighting the release only made me more excited.

"Fuck this," Curt hissed, and his mouth engulfed my clit.

"Ah!" Surprised, I screamed, but his hands rounded my backside and pressed me firmly to his mouth. He lifted my right leg over his shoulder and went to town on my pussy.

The new angle gave his tongue more access to my spread sex, and his tongue laved up my dripping juice around the vibrator.

I'm not sure what type of security examination this was, but I was ready to fuck it all to hell and ride his tongue. Surely, they'd arrest me after this.

The vibrator was going crazy inside me now, and Curt's tongue matched the pace on the outside. One massive hand firmly held my backside, while his other pinched and rolled my nipple.

I felt my cunt squeezing the vibrator, intensifying the feeling as my skin heated. I arched my back and tilted my pussy upward, shifting my hips as I watched my wetness slide across Curt's face, leaving behind a glistening trail of pussy juice.

"Oh, you're a bad girl!" Curt moaned, pinching my nipple harder as he ate me out.

I stifled a groan and rode his face harder. His rewarding chuckle encouraged me to go faster.

"Ride me," he breathlessly mumbled as my hips took on a crazed rhythm.

Frantically, I shifted back and forth, rubbing my pussy across his chin, lips, tongue, and nose. Every groove of his face massaged my body while the vibrator thrummed inside me, that coiling feeling stretched tautly inside me with each swipe of his tongue.

And when the vibrator stopped, Curt yanked it out of me and plunged his fingers inside me. They filled me even more, and when they pounded in and out of me, curling at the tip of his fingers, that coiling inside me exploded into a million pieces.

My cum squirted out in juicy waves, spraying onto Curt's fingers and face as I convulsed against him. He drank me in like a delectable drink.

When he pulled his fingers out of me and set down my leg, I collapsed onto a nearby chair.

Shockwaves trickled through me so frequently that I didn't even care that I was still naked and soiled.

"My turn," Curt said, spreading my knees and dropping his pants.

"Wh…What?" I looked up in a haze right before he grabbed my neck and shoved his fat cock down my throat.

Airport Security

2

Curt didn't allow me air to breathe and didn't care that I was gagging every time he drove into me. I was in such a haze from the orgasm he'd just given me that I let him fuck my face.

He was so aggressive and dominant with the way he slammed his cock down my throat, holding the back of my head with one hand and squeezing my throat with the other.

"Tell me, is this what you imagined Rocket would do to you?"

My eyes widen in surprise. *How does he know Rocket?* He didn't allow me to respond, though, as he thrust his thick cock into my mouth so hard that saliva dripped down my chin.

"I know Rocket. And trust me when I say that little bitch wouldn't be able to please a dirty little slut like you. He called me asking for a favor. He described you perfectly. He asked that I let you through security without any trouble. When I brought you in here, I texted him and said you made it through. Bet that's why the vibrator went off."

He knew Rocket, and he knew I would be coming through with Rocket's toy inside me. And yet, he pulled me in here and used me after promising to let me through. I was so confused and so turned on.

Curt pulled out of me and picked me up. He dropped my ass on the metal table and shoved me down onto my back.

He was so domineering, and my body loved every bit of it. I was still dripping wet from my release, so I spread my legs wide to let Curt see how wet my pussy was for him.

"How do you know Rocket?" I asked, running a finger over my clit as he positioned his cock at my entrance.

"We knew each other in high school. I fucked every little nerdy girl he liked."

Curt rubbed himself over my pussy, making me moan in anticipation. I didn't even know this man, and yet, here I was, letting him rub himself raw on me. Something was deeply disturbing about this situation, but my ears were still ringing from the orgasm he gifted me. And well, you don't look a gift horse in the mouth.

"Why?" I asked, needing to know why this man would be so brutal to another. It was disgustingly evil, and my body relished it.

"Because I can," he said as he pushed the tip of his cock into my hole.

My head fell backward, savoring how my body stretched with the invasion of his massive cock. It was deliciously painful.

"Yes, more," I begged, pivoting my hips and taking more of him into me.

"I'm going to fuck your needy cunt so good that you'll limp out of this airport and never think of Rocket again. Do you understand me, Miss Lani Griffin?"

"Yes! Oh god, yes… Fuck me like that, please," I stuttered, losing myself completely to his dirty words.

It had been ages since I was fucked by anything other than a dildo, and this man's cock was thick and long and sinking deeper and deeper into me.

His cock struggled to break through my walls, but with one final push, he was sheathed to the hilt. Finally. And then he retreated and slammed back into me.

Curt pulled my hips to the edge of the table and lifted my legs, bringing my knees down to the sides of my waist and fully exposing my body while keeping me pinned.

"Flexible. I might need to have you again." He praised how my body stretched into a position that allowed the both of us to watch his dick entering and exiting me.

He pulled out fully and suddenly, making my pussy lips pop as he left me empty and begging. His massive hand slapped my cunt, making me cry out before he plunged himself back into me, only to repeat the action repeatedly.

His cock glistened with my juices, coaxing more and more of my arousal out of me as he took his time torturing my thirsty cunt. My pussy was red and raw from the stinging slaps he delivered every time his cock pulled fully out of me. It was a punishment before he rewarded me with penetration.

"Please, fuck me faster," I begged as he left me empty again. My walls clenched harder and harder around empty air as he edged me.

"Dirty girl doesn't like games?" Curt taunted, sinking into me again before pulling out with a wet pop.

"Ah!" I screamed and squirmed, but he held my pinned legs down.

"Bad girl." He delivered three fast and firm slaps to my pussy, and my body ignited.

He wasn't inside me, but the edging had taken its toll. Cum squirted out of me, straight across the space between Curt's cock and my pussy. The erotic sight of it made my orgasm keep rolling.

Curt's fingers rubbed my clit, spraying the liquid everywhere and making a mess of me, but the liquid kept coming.

My eyes rolled in the back of my head as the orgasm overtook me. Curt shoved himself into me, finally properly fucking me as his fingers continued playing with my clit. He refused to let my orgasm fade.

Curt stilled inside me, attracting my attention. "Wait!" I said, but it was too late.

A wicked smile spread on his face as his fingers dug into the back of my thighs, pinning me so hard I couldn't move as he spilled himself into me. The wrongness of this event reached its highest point, and my orgasm flared to life again. Curt smiled knowingly.

He pulled out of me and coaxed more cum from my body, slapping my pussy and rubbing my clit, helping me ride the wave of my orgasm while his cum leaked from my pussy, and we both watched.

"Oh my god," I said as he let go of my legs, and they dropped over the edge of the metal table. The last bits of cum bubbled out of me onto the tile floor.

"Clean yourself up and don't come through security wearing that shit again"—he pulled his trousers up then leaned over me—"unless you want me to feed your hungry pussy again. Then, by all means, stuff as many toys up your cunt as you can. I'll get them out and replace them with something far better."

I was speechless. Curt walked out the door, leaving it open with me lying wet and naked on the table. At that moment, the second security guard walked in and locked the door. Panic consumed me.

"Um..." I said, sitting up to gather my clothes.

"You're not done here, Ms. Griffin,' the second security guard said.

"We're not?" I asked.

"Not even close," he replied as he unbuckled his belt.

Fire erupted between my legs. "What do I have to do, Officer?" I asked, loving every minute of where this was going.

"I was told that a hungry slut needed assistance." He unbuttoned his pants and walked toward me.

I dropped to my knees before him, feeling the wetness of my release all over the floor, as I readied myself for another strange man to fuck my face.

The idea of being railed by two security officers was so disgustingly right. If only Curt would come back, and the two men would take me together.

"I'm a very hungry slut," I said, batting my eyelashes cutely.

"Then allow me the pleasure of serving you your main course." He tugged down his briefs and let his even larger than Curt's cock pop out.

"Oh my god." I admired his size, not sure how I would fit it. "Wait a second. Main course?" I asked.

"Curt will be back to help me serve dessert," he said before pulling my hair back and parting my lips with the tip of his cock.

Airport Security

3

The second security guard, whose name tag read *Dante*, was larger than any man I had ever seen—in person or on screen.

It was so thick and long that only the head of his cock could fit in my mouth. I tried to take more of him into me, but it felt like my lips would split up the sides of my cheeks.

Dante laughed at my feeble attempts. "Let me give it to you where you can handle it, honey."

I stood and turned around, showing my willingness to take him somewhere more malleable. Plus, I needed to feel his monster cock. It was larger than any dildo in my collection—even the green demon cock.

"That's a good girl," Dante said as he spanked me.

I jumped as a sharp sting spread across my backside, but his quick hands pulled me back.

He pushed himself against my center, lubing the tip of his cock with my arousal and the cum left behind by Curt. Dante had no qualms about using another man's seed to fuck a woman. It was so hot.

He rubbed his cock across my lower lips. His gigantic penis touched every part of my lower body. "Fuck me," I pleaded, spreading my legs and encouraging him to take me already.

"In due time, honey. You need to be nice and wet for me."

"I'm plenty wet," I argued.

"If you insist," he said.

He pushed the tip of his cock against my center, nudging apart my lips and sinking in inch by inch. He stretched me more than the green monster cock I loved. He worked his way in eventually, though. With shallow thrusts, he used my arousal to smooth his entrance. My core muscles shifted, adapting to his size, and I angled my entrance to take him as deep as possible.

"Come here, honey," Dante said, pulling my back into his chest.

He worked his cock into me, filling me but never fully. His cock was too large to fit all the way inside me. His hands slid up my abdomen lazily, taking his time to feel me up until they palmed my breasts. Dante pinched my nipples and tugged down.

My body fought to follow him, but he said, "Stay upright, honey. This might hurt a little."

The pinched pain in my nipple was a welcome one. I wasn't sure what he was referring to until he pinched harder and shoved himself further into me. The stretched sensation I'd felt before was nothing compared to how I felt now.

Dante didn't stop there, though. He continued to explore my pussy, thrusting further into me while pinching my nipples harder. I began to see stars, my vision blurring. My head fell back onto Dante's shoulder, and he took note. Abandoning one breast, Dante's fingers laced around my neck. He tightened his hold, bringing a whole new frightening excitement to my body as the breath escaped me.

His cock prodded at me. Except it was more than prodding, it was goddamn corrupting. His other hand abandoned my nipple and found my clit. It was equally as tormenting. He pinched my clit aggressively, sending my nerve endings into overdrive. My clit swelled under the pressure, throbbing against his thumb and forefinger.

Dante skimmed a nail across the top of my clit as he pinched it, and I nearly buckled over. If not for his hand choking me and his cock drilling into me, nearly lifting me off my toes, I would have collapsed under the pleasure. His nail scraped my clit again, right in time with his cock entering me. I screamed. Or at least, I tried to. The tight hold around my neck took the sound of my voice.

Tears streamed down my cheeks, and saliva pooled around the edges of my mouth. Dante's quick breaths heated the skin on the back of my neck.

"I saw the mess you made in here, honey. You better come on my cock like that, too," he warned.

I couldn't reply, not while he choked me. But I didn't need to. I was seconds from coming so hard on his cock that I might pass out. He took my silence as his answer, quickening the pace of his thrusts to the point that he lifted me clear off the floor. Every time his pelvis met mine, my feet left the ground, suspending me in the air on his monster cock.

God, this was unbearably hot.

My body shook with excitement.

Dante rammed into me faster.

My feet didn't touch the ground again. He leaned back, holding me against him by my neck, while his cock did all the supporting. My body bounced on him like a limp doll—a fuck toy, the security guards' fuck toy.

The moment the door opened, and Curt stepped back into the room twirling a baton, my world shattered. Dante's hands moved to my hips, holding me up as he pounded into me. Once again, my cum sprayed across the room, soaking his cock and the floor below us. My eyes rolled back into my head. My body went numb as I slumped against Dante, and he continued to drill into me as if he had no intention of stopping. Gurgling sounds came out of my mouth as I tried and failed to form words.

"Damn, Dante. You fucked her dumb," Curt said, walking over to us.

Dante continued to lazily fuck me as I slumped against him, my pussy wet, stretched, and used. "She'll come back to in a minute," he said.

Curt knelt before us, and Dante slowed his thrusts. "You've got a giant cock, man. Looks like I'll be taking the back."

"No argument there," Dante replied.

Curt flicked the piercing on my clit, and I shuddered. The feeling had begun to return to my body.

"Hold her still. Let me suck her delicious little clit," Curt said.

Dante stilled, keeping his cock buried in me while Curt's mouth engulfed the front of me. My body exploded with pleasure as Curt's tongue swirled over the most sensitive part of my body. Dante's cock twitched inside me as if he, too, could feel it.

Suddenly, my body went rigid in his arms, and a new impending orgasm bloomed.

The Flight Attendant

"Would you like another drink, sir?" the flight attendant with a blonde bob asks.

I swear the woman is trying to get me drunk. The flight is thirteen hours long, yet at only three hours in, I'm already four beers deep. I'll be sleeping well tonight.

"I'm good. Thank you...Victoria," I respond, glancing at her name tag.

"Of course. Let me know if you change your mind or need anything else," she says. Her eyes flick down to the hand clutching the remainder of my fourth beer. I can't help but wonder if she's searching for a ring.

She won't find one.

"Really," she continues, "if you need anything, just call for me." The cute blonde points to the call button above my head. Her politeness is suffocating.

"Will do," I say curtly.

Victoria walks away, swaying her hips ostentatiously. The woman is practically begging to get laid. That need is something I can relate to, but right now, my only vise is at the bottle of a bottle—or, in this case, a glass.

I've been abstinent since my wife died two and a half years ago. The tan line on my ring finger only recently filled in; no longer seeing a silver band or a pale band of skin has been difficult to deal with. As a result, I drown myself in work. That's why I'm on this flight, heading halfway across the world: to work myself to death—because life has no purpose without my wife.

The global supply chain company I work for is a lucrative business. It allows me to fly first class and indulge in the best of what life offers. It would be a coveted position for most people, but I'm not most people, and I don't really enjoy much of anything anymore.

I drink the last of my beer and place the empty glass in the cup holder. Victoria will retrieve it soon enough, and I'll do my best to ignore those swaying hips and perfect manners.

Beautiful women have no place in my life. Especially not temporary ones who work as flight attendants and flirt with the customers riding in their aircraft. The lack of professionalism grates on my nerves. If the need to distract myself from my own lackluster life weren't so characteristically fond of her own form of silent protest, I might report her for coming onto me. We all deal with life in our own ways. Who am I to betray the woman for living on the more provocative side?

I recline my chair and select a movie as I settle in for the evening. The cabin lights are already dim, and most people in first class have closed the doors to their sleeping accommodations. The doors are more like paperboard, but they offer some privacy amidst the noise of the aircraft and other awake passengers.

A quiet knock and soft voice address me on the other side of my door, "Sir, did you call for me?" Victoria asks.

"No," I respond gruffly.

The door to my pod—or room—cracks open, and Victoria dips her head in, smiling sweetly.

"Can I help you?" I ask.

"May I come in for a moment?" she says shyly.

I stifle a groan as I look around at the small amount of floor space for her to stand. The pod is designed so I can change, although not easily with my height, and lie fully flat in the chair to sleep. This particular seat is insanely expensive, but it helps me fight jet lag and be ready to work as soon as I leave the airplane.

Victoria steps in, pressing down the pleated lines in her skirt.

"What can I do for you, Victoria?" I incline the chair, swiveling to face her. The tight space causes our knees to touch.

"This is entirely inappropriate, but I must say it," she begins.

I have an inkling of what she's about to say. She's going to proposition me, which I will politely decline, no matter how unprofessional, and I won't even report her. She's lucky I'm feeling generous.

Victoria stutters as she explains. "Do you remember me at all? I've served you on this same flight for the past six months, and today is the first time you said my name...And you had to look at my name tag before you said it."

"And?" I ask, feeling slightly guilty for not noticing her on my prior flights. I must have taken at least ten.

"I just want to know, am I that unnoticeable?" Her eyes are pinned to the floor.

"Oh." I don't know how to respond. I feel like a dick for not only assuming she was hitting on me but also failing to notice the same person has been serving me for six months.

I'm an asshole.

"I'm sorry. It's not that I haven't noticed you; I zone out on these flights." Shame washes over me.

"Really? Because I serve you a lot of drinks. It's not like we crossed paths once on this flight. We've talked a lot!"

The words spill out of her like she's been holding them in for a while, but her voice remains hushed, aware that the thin paperboard door only stifles so much sound.

"Look, I'm sorry." I have no other explanation.

"It's okay," Victoria says, looking around sheepishly.

I want to make her feel better if only to make myself feel better. "I honestly thought you were coming in here to proposition me, but I'm glad you called me out. I've been a dick."

Her eyebrows shoot up, and she says, "Proposition you?"

If I was trying to improve this situation and look less like an asshole, revealing my internal thoughts was not the way to do it. "That was the wrong thing to say." It's been a long time since I've been in a position to ease an offended woman's mind, especially after *I* offended her.

"Yeah, it was. I mean, you're hot and all, but I've mainly been more offended by the fact that you haven't even noticed that I serve you on every flight. Most people would at least remember my name." Victoria's lips press into a thin, determined line as she crosses her arms.

"It won't happen again," I promise, placing a hand over my heart.

"Good. Thank you," she says, turning on her heel to exit the pod.

Right as Victoria pushes on the door, turbulence hits, and she stumbles backward. Her ass plops right into my lap. The plane shakes violently, and I'm forced to hold on to the only thing within reach—the flight attendant.

When the shock of the plane's abrupt jerking stops, Victoria's neck cranes to the side. Her cheeks are cherry blossom red. I can't be sure if it's from falling on my lap or the intensity of the turbulence.

"Sorry," I say, releasing my grip around her stomach.

The hemline of her skirt has slid up her thighs, revealing muscular legs and the point at which they meet. My eyes are glued to the spot between her legs, with only pantyhose to block my view of what lies beneath.

I find myself fully entranced by her. It's been so long since I saw another woman. I haven't even looked at porn since my wife's passing. I haven't been this close to touching a woman in years, and right now my arms are around one very sexy woman.

"Sir," Victoria asks, but my hold around her waist tightens as my balls contract.

I swallow the dry, bulging lump in my throat. "Victoria," I say, unsure what to do next. My shame is displaced by undeserved raw desire and the embarrassment to match. Victoria has every right to slap me. Part of me hopes she will. I need something, someone, to get me in line.

"Oh my gosh," she whispers, no doubt feeling my erection against her backside.

"I'm sorry." I lean my forehead against her back and inhale her sweet floral scent.

I forgot how amazing women smell. The richness of their scent, the smoothness of their skin. I've withheld my desire for too long. Work and booze have sated me, but with Victoria this close, I need something else.

"Sorry," I say, sighing as I release her.

She stands abruptly, spinning around to face me. I'm certain she's about to berate me, but she's silent. My pants are straining, and Victoria can't take her eyes off me. I don't know why she doesn't leave, but I need to take care of this. I *need* privacy.

"Sir," she whispers again.

"What?" I ask gravely as I adjust myself. It's not as if she can't see all of it anyway.

"You're... "

She can't finish her sentence, so I finish for her. "I'm hard."

Victoria's mouth hangs open. Her eyes locked on my crotch. I believe my earlier assessment was correct—she needs to get laid—so I toss all professionalism and self-loathing aside.

"Victoria, unless you need something, I really need to take care of some business," I say, alluding to the business in my pants.

She nods her head in understanding and turns to leave. Suddenly, she halts. "Is it the type of business I might be able to assist you with, sir?" she asks.

Her boldness surprises and delights me. It would be nice to feel a woman again. Even as I'm contemplating, unsure if the reward is worth the risk, I say, "Maybe."

Victoria drops to her knees, surprising me again as she licks her lips. Her hands are on my waistband within moments, sliding my cotton pants and briefs down to my knees. My cock bounces out, but she catches it in her hand before it can slap against my thigh. She's so eager. The ferocity of her actions leaves no room for me to question this decision.

It's all happening so fast.

"Victoria." I try to slow her, but her mouth is on me.

She licks up my shaft, from the base to the tip, and twirls her tongue around the top. I shudder at the sensation of the warm moisture she trails across me.

This is so much better than lotion and my hand.

She slaps a hand over my mouth, and I realize my satisfaction is giving away what she's doing to me: sucking me off on an airplane. This isn't even a fantasy I've had, but damn, it makes me horny.

Victoria keeps her hand pressed firmly against my mouth as she bobs her head up and down on my cock. Her slurping is quiet and skilled like she's done this before. But honestly, I don't give a fuck if she's sucked off every other damn passenger as long as she doesn't stop.

Her head pops up, and she smiles, spit dripping down her chin erotically.

"Don't stop," I tell her.

"I don't plan to." She stands and places a leg on the arm of my chair, lifting her skirt.

The pesky pantyhose cover her bare pussy. Using her nails, Victoria tears a hole in the center of the tights, exposing herself to me. Her glistening arousal is all I can see before I drag her against my mouth, and taste her.

God. It's been too long since I tasted a woman.

She's delectable, and the feel of her soft lower lips on my tongue is a sensation that can't be replicated.

I slide my tongue through her center as her hands wind around my hair. Victoria confidently bucks her hips against my face, covering my entire mouth in her juices.

"I need you inside me," she whispers as she pushes me back.

I fall against the back of the chair as Victoria expertly lifts the armrests and straddles me.

"Wait," I say, remembering we should use a condom, but Victoria sinks down on my shaft before the words leave my mouth.

My cock delves into her wetness, and the world around me disappears.

It's been too long since I felt this, and I'm not sure I'll recover. Booze and work can't even touch the type of distraction this elicits. Her warmth is all-consuming, and when she begins to ride me, I let go of all control. Fuck everyone else on this plane.

I take hold of her hips, lifting her to thrust myself into her. With wild abandon, I slam my cock into her as quickly and viciously as possible.

When a tiny squeak slips through her lips, I cover her mouth and growl into her ear, "Quiet." This is my moment.

Victoria nods, seeing the need for control in my eyes. She melts into my touch, moving where I direct her, absorbing every thrust like her hole is made for me. I punish her pussy with my cock as thoroughly as this tiny seat allows. She shakes against me, her orgasm looming. I rub her clit, urging her to come. Arousal covers my hand as it leaks out of her.

"Are you going to come?" I ask quietly.

She nods.

"Good, because I'm going to come in you."

I grab her hips, turning us so Victoria's ass rests on the edge of the chair as I kneel in front of her. I pin her legs above her head, giving myself the optimal angle to take her. I dive back into her, hard and thorough. Her eyes roll into the back of her head as her hands squeeze the sides of the chair. White, sticky cum coats my cock as I continue thrusting into her.

Victoria's body clenches around me as she finds her release, which brings me to mine. I thrust into her bare pussy, watching as her cum mixes with mine, coating my cock as I push it deeper inside of her.

"Yes, baby," I growl between gritted teeth as the last of my seed spills into her.

When I pull out, a long string of cum drips from her pussy to her asshole. I keep her legs pinned above her head, swipe my fingers across the cum, and stuff it back inside of her.

"You look so beautiful with my cum inside you, Victoria."

Her answering smile is all I need to recharge and take her again.

Record Daddy

"One of the bartenders said a famous music producer from New York is sitting in the back booth! You've better turn it on tonight girl!" said Shane, my very gay-licious drummer.

Pre-performance jitters worked their way up my spine, tightening at the base of my neck. I rolled my head, shaking my shoulders, willing the tension to release. I was used to performing, so nerves weren't a common occurrence. Every night, it was the same thing—the same set, the same stage, the same vibe. Nerves were a thing of the past. Until someone like this mysterious "famous music producer" showed up and got my head swirling with possibilities.

My performance was solid, but past failures constantly reminded me of the repercussions and missed opportunities of one bad show. These were make-or-break situations. Or at least, that's what I told myself. In the past, I'd get so worked up about one misstep or off-key note that I spiraled into a tornado of mistakes, leading to an epic fuck-up.

Tonight was not the night for a fuck-up.

Whoever this music producer was, I didn't care. I had a consistent gig here. I didn't need to worry about making it big anymore. While the monotony of performing here dulled the performance high, it paid the bills, and for the most part, me and my band had fun doing it.

"It doesn't matter," I told Shane as our bass guitarist, Buzz, walked up.

"What doesn't matter?" Buzz asked.

"Shane said a music producer is in one of the bottle service tables, but it doesn't matter. Let's go out there and do our thing like we always do! Nashville wants a show, and a show is what we'll give them!" I said confidently, shaking my long red hair out of my face as I pulled my guitar strap over my shoulder.

Shane and Buzz put their hands in the middle of our little group. Kinsley, the keyboard player, ran up to us with smeared red lipstick across her mouth. She was likely just fucking a groupie on the side stage. That girl was as free-spirited as they come.

"You good Kins?" Shane asked.

"Better than good! Let's do this shit!" Kinsley said excitedly, slapping her hand on the stack of ours.

I yelled our mantra, and the band chanted with me, "To the people who came before, to the people who came tonight, to the people who will come tomorrow! Let's get fucked!"

Shane and Kinsley came up with the chant one night when they both hooked up with someone on the side stage between sets—those nasty whores. But regardless, I loved the chant! It reminded me of our younger, wilder days when we thought fame was two seconds away.

We walked onto the stage. I completely forgot about the music producer, and we played one hell of a show. Once we finished, the band and I headed to the bar for an after-show celebratory drink.

Mickey, my favorite bartender, had beers and a whiskey shot waiting for us when we bellied up to the bar.

"You're the best, Mick!" I held up the shot in thanks before knocking it back.

It burned in the best way.

"Oh shit," Kinsley said, ducking behind me.

I searched for her latest conquest-gone-wrong. "Who's the unlucky guy?"

She laughed and pulled Buzz into my side so she could hide behind us. "Well…Technically, he was the lucky guy before the show, but he seems like the type to get attached. Plus, I spotted this super-hot guy giving me fuck-me eyes during the show. I need to find him." Kins grabbed her beer and Shane's hand. "Come with me. I need you as a buffer!"

"Only if guy number one swings both ways. Otherwise, I'm leaving your ass to find some tail, honey," Shane said.

"Deal. Let's go!" They headed off, leaving Buzz and me to enjoy our drinks and watch the shenanigans unfold.

"What's your plan tonight?" I asked Buzz.

He shrugged and said, "I'll probably head home. I've got an early shift at the club tomorrow."

On top of our gigs, Buzz worked as a bouncer for a strip club downtown. While it wasn't the most fun job, especially for someone as sweet as Buzz—I couldn't imagine him dragging anyone out of a strip club, but I could see him berating a man for touching a woman wrong—he said it paid well.

"What about you?" he asked.

"I'll probably go home too. There's not much to do around here other than watch Kins and Shane make out with strangers, and I don't have much space left in my brain for another one of those memories."

"Ha! Me either. That's why I'm going home. Tina's waiting for me anyway." Buzz chugged the last of his beer. "Want me to walk you to your car?"

I looked down at my half-full beer, feeling no urge to finish it. However, something made me want to stick around a little longer. Maybe it was to avoid being utterly alone for the rest of the night, or maybe it had something to do with the music producer. I told myself it didn't, but that part of me who always hoped for a big break still wanted to give it a chance.

"Nah. I'll stick around for a bit. Thanks, though. See you tomorrow, Buzz."

Buzz nodded goodbye and made a quick exit. Our relationship was simple like that. A *yes* or *no* did the trick. There was no pushing. No trying to tell the other person what was best for them. We had an understanding and a deep level of respect for each other. The band wouldn't have been able to stick together this long if the dynamic was anything else.

As I scanned the crowd, I caught Shane and Kinsley dirty dancing between two guys. I admired their ability to let loose, like tonight was their last on Earth. Once, I had been as wild as they were, but as soon as I hit twenty-six, the reckless decisions of my teenage years and early twenties didn't seem as fun or smart.

Unfortunately, the right kind of guys weren't usually attracted to women entering their late twenties and still trying to get famous. One day, I'd be that washed-up forty-year-old still singing top country hits in Nashville bars.

Not that anything was wrong with that lifestyle. I loved the idea of it. I chose this. But I didn't want to date another struggling singer, and lately, those were the other people who "got" me.

I wanted a man. A man with his shit together. A man I could rely on and go home to, like Buzz went home to Tina. I envied what he had: a faithful woman with a desk job, who, despite the crazy schedule, made their hours together work because they respected each other's dreams and admired each other for it. She was amazing. Maybe I needed to switch teams and find a Tina.

"Hey," a deep voice said behind me.

I turned around and faced the man of my dreams—literally. I had to blink a few times to make sure I was seeing reality and not a figment of my imagination. *Was God listening extra hard and delivering extra fast tonight?* Because he just delivered my male Tina.

The man was tall with salt-and-pepper hair. A faint five o'clock shadow lined his jaw. His lips were pursed in a serious, thin line that made him look unapproachable, especially with those hard, narrow eyes. And those hard, narrow eyes were directed at me. While I wanted to curl up in a ball and run away from this stern-looking man, I also wanted to disappear into those dangerously hazel eyes.

I wanted to run my fingers over his stubble, down his neck, and around those broad shoulders…Because those broad shoulders looked super fucking sexy in his sport coat. He was not the typical customer for a tourist bar in the middle of Nashville. He looked like he would fit in better at some ritzy rooftop cocktail bar specializing in thirty-dollar martinis.

"Hi," I replied, taking in my fill of him.

"I'm Grey," he said, putting his elbow on the bar top and leaning into it.

He didn't even care about how dirty and sticky the bar was. Why would he? Grey looked like the kind of man who owned twenty jackets and got them dry-cleaned after every wear.

"Hi, Grey. I'm Abby." I mimicked his stance and curtness. I wasn't sure who this man was or his agenda, but I was certainly willing to find out.

"Nice show," Grey said, waving at the bartender. "Let me buy you a drink."

I lifted a brow. *Let me buy you a drink.* Not a question. A command.

"And if I don't want a drink?"

He paused and cocked his head predatorially. "Then let me take you out for a bite to eat. You must be hungry after putting on a show like that."

"And if I'm not hungry?" I played along, secretly loving his persistence and wanting to see how much he'd push my rejections. Never mind the fact that he complimented my performance. That didn't hit home nearly as much as this banter.

"Then I guess I should ask what you need right now, Abby. Because whatever it is, I'll get it for you."

Mick walked over, slinging a towel over his shoulder, and asked, "What'll it be?"

Grey looked at me expectantly.

"A whiskey. Thanks, Mick," I said.

"Make it two. The best you've got," Grey said, pulling out his wallet and smiling at me.

His face transformed when he smiled, and I found myself mesmerized by him in an entirely new way. The man was probably in his late forties, maybe older. He was totally different from the men I usually went after. Yet, I found my knees weak and my stomach full of butterflies just from his presence.

"So, Abby, how long have you been performing?" he asked, his face turning serious again.

"I've been on stage professionally since I was fifteen. What are you in town for?"

I needed to know if he was just another tourist. Not that I was above chatting it up with a tourist—especially one this hot—but this man had serious potential. The go-home-to-after-work kind of potential, so I sincerely hoped he was a local and that this would be more than a one-night conversation.

"I'm here on business. I often am, but for some reason, I've never seen you play. I don't know how I could've missed you. You're beautiful up there. It's intoxicating."

My cheeks flushed at his compliment. He said it so matter-of-factly, leaving no room for argument. The way he expressed it was like everyone could see it, and everyone agreed. Intoxicating? Like I was a drug. No one had ever described my performance like that. I liked it.

Was I a good singer? Yes. Was I a good performer? Most nights. Was I beautiful? More like sexy.

Being called beautiful felt like a flower blooming in my chest. It was like he saw through all the bullshit and recognized the craft for what it was—art. Although I felt it when I played and sang, I could never tell if the audience felt it too. But this strange older man felt it and expressed it in such simple words. My chest swelled in appreciation.

"Thank you," I said, removing all sass from my tone. Grey just made my night.

Mick set down the whiskeys, and Grey handed over a black card, telling him to close it.

I guess he only planned on buying me one drink tonight.

My stomach sank in disappointment. Either I'd just totally ruined it with Grey somehow, or he was just being a gentleman and buying the performer a drink for a job well done. It was basically a tip and not the kind of tip I wanted. I pondered how to make him change his plans.

"Do you have any plans tonight?" Grey asked, signing the bill and tucking his wallet into his coat.

"No," I replied.

"I have a proposition for you, Abby," he said, leaning back against the bar and drinking his whiskey. His voice held power. There was no hint of insecurity or doubt. Just the simple confidence he exuded to the point that it was nearly arrogant. Yet somehow, it wasn't.

"What's your proposition?"

"Spend the night with me."

I nearly spit out my whiskey.

Does he think I'm some kind of prostitute? I'm not that desperate!

"No, thanks." I slammed my glass down and turned away.

A firm hand gripped my wrist, twisting me back around. "The only thing you'll regret tonight is walking away from me. Maybe I should have told you that you *will* spend the night with me, instead of asking if you would."

He tugged me toward his chest. My hands flew up to stop the collision of our bodies, planting themselves on his chest. For a man of his age, he was fit. Extremely fit. And firm.

His whiskey breath fanned my face as he looked down at me, still clutching my wrist between our bodies. The pressure squeezed to the point of bruising.

"I'm telling you now… You're mine tonight, pretty little singer. I'm going to make you sing like you've never sung before."

Oh my god. That sensual promise… And using my talent as an innuendo for all the ways he'll make me feel.

My stomach knotted with the aching desire to know what he would do and how he would do it. But this man was dangerous. Those eyes might have been light in color, but they held dark promises. I wanted to flee, but I also wanted him to hold me tighter.

"I don't think that's a good idea," I said, using my brain rather than my overly excited, underappreciated lady parts that were screaming for some attention. In my wilder days, I'd tell this guy to fuck me backstage. Right. Fucking. Now.

Grey leaned in and whispered into my ear, "You're a performer, Abby, but you could use some improvement. Let a man with experience show you how to achieve what you truly desire."

What was he talking about? How was my performing on stage anything like performing during sex?

I attempted to cross my arms and challenge the infuriatingly sexy man holding my wrists, but he held me firm and nipped my neck when I fought. The sting of his bite sent a shiver down my spine, making my knees weak. I nearly crumbled. A heated passion stirred deep within my core. I should have been running for the hills, away from this man, but I found myself relaxing against him, waiting for another bite.

"You like that. Let me show you what else you'll like," Grey whispered, his voice husky and hot against my skin.

I failed to voice anything and instead groaned—literally groaned. I was officially at this powerful man's mercy.

"What's that?" Grey laughed, sliding my hands up his shoulders.

Those shoulders. They felt as good as they looked. He was so stiff, so firm, so immovable. It was like touching a sleeping dragon. It excited me. Adrenaline pumped through me like it hadn't in years, flexing muscles and awakening the side of me that threw all caution to the wind.

"The back," I managed to get out, suggesting we get backstage as fast as possible because I wasn't a total idiot. I wasn't going anywhere unfamiliar with this man.

But even though he seemed like a bad idea, I was totally fucking him. I was too far gone.

Grey grabbed my hand and pushed through the crowd to the side of the stage. He ducked under the black curtain I had emerged from earlier. Apparently, he had been paying attention.

His head moved back and forth, searching for a private space. His urgency turned me on even more.

"Follow me," I rushed past him, nearly jogging to the dressing room.

We got to the room, and two women were inside, touching up their makeup.

"Out," Grey barked.

They looked at the man and instantly went pale.

"Please," I added sweetly.

It wasn't necessary. They grabbed their makeup and ran out the door. Grey locked it and turned around. I was facing him, but the look on his face had me backing up.

Is this a bad idea? Is he going to skin me alive and wear my skin around until it got all dried up and crusty?

The thought made me sick as I backed away. My legs bumped into the couch behind me, and I dropped onto it, plopping down with an *oomph*. Grey chuckled and stalked closer. He ran a hand through his salt and pepper hair, the only thing that physically revealed his age.

"Take your dress off," he demanded, shrugging off his jacket and casually tossing it onto a chair.

This is happening. This is really happening.

I struggled out of my dress, and by the time I dropped it to the floor, Grey was unzipping his pants. His shirt was already off, revealing the toned body I'd felt underneath.

Wow. He's hot. Mouthwateringly hot.

Grey—the man of my dreams—stepped out of his pants and slid his boxers off with them. He was so to the point, wasting no time.

As for me, I didn't even know what to do. This was not how I usually started sex. But after seeing his length and the hand that stroked his cock to life, I was on board with however he approached getting it on.

"Um…" I started to ask the question, but his hand slung out and pinched my cheeks, pushing my lips into a pout.

"Don't talk, little singer. Save that voice for when I'm making you scream."

Is it possible for a body to feel like it's melted into a puddle on the floor more than once in a night? Because I just full-body melted. I was totally liquified.

I nodded and waited for his next command. Grey dropped to his knees and slid his hands over my legs. His tongue followed the line of his thumb, sweeping up my inner thighs.

When his lips landed on the outside of my panties, I groaned again.

"That's it. That's the sound I want to hear more of," he murmured against my center.

I wiggled underneath him, begging him to make me make more of those sounds, and he took the hint, no longer wasting time. He pulled my panties down to my knees, then lifted my legs onto his shoulders, placing his head between my legs.

I had him trapped. We both knew he, ultimately, had me trapped, but I liked having an older man on his knees, surrounded by all things me, worshipping me. His mouth engulfed me, and I threw back my head, letting another moan fill the silent room. With as much seriousness as the man himself exuded, his tongue worked me. He ran his long, flat tongue over my moistened lips, stopping to flick my little bundle of nerves that had a penchant for this type of foreplay.

"Say my name," Grey demanded, lifting his head and giving me a view of just how aroused I was. His entire chin was covered in my juices, and instead of wiping it away, he licked his lips.

I melted again, and just as I did, I felt more arousal slicking my thighs.

Grey looked down at my pussy and growled. Literally growled.

Oh yeah, I'm in trouble.

With a fervor unlike before, he attacked my vagina. His tongue, lips, and entire mouth devoured me raw while his fingers dug into my sides to hold me still. I bucked, grinding my hips into his face as my hands pushed his face harder into me. My moans and his hungry appreciation were like music to my ears.

Where has this man been my whole life?

He ate me like I was his breakfast, lunch, and dinner. Like he was coming out of a week-long fast, and I was exactly what he'd been craving all those days of starvation.

As I felt an orgasm swelling, I pressed his face firmly into me, not even caring if I suffocated him because I needed him. I needed him to keep doing that thing with his tongue where it felt like he was touching my entrance, my walls, and my clit all at the same time. He was everywhere.

"Grey," I moaned.

My hips lifted from the couch, and my thighs squeezed his head as my orgasm threatened to hit, but he kept going. My entire body clenched, tingled, and erupted. A wave of pleasure spilled out of me, awakening a dark desire in my soul and shaking me to the core.

Grey didn't give my racing heart a chance to calm down. He stood, grabbed a condom from his pants pocket, and slid it on. I was in an orgasmic daze as he pulled my hips to the edge of the couch, got on his knees, and shoved himself inside my sensitive walls.

My head fell back as a moan of pleasure escaped us both.

His fingers found my clit again, stimulating it once more. I was swollen and loosening for him, stretching to accommodate his size perfectly, so that we both had maximum pleasure.

"Grey," I said again, looking him square in the eyes.

A wicked gleam lit up his face as we challenged each other. "Time to sing again," he said, pulling out and slamming back into me.

His cock pounded into the back of my cervix, making me cry out. Grey did it again, then harder, then faster. I was breathless and pliant. I was at this man's mercy while he vigorously buried himself inside me.

"Yes. Yes. Yes!" I cried out as he owned my body.

"Say my name," Grey demanded, pulling my bra down to expose my breasts.

He leaned down and sucked one of the nipples into his mouth, flicking his tongue over the tip in time with the thrusts of his pelvis. My body rocked and writhed as I moaned. The heated pace, the violent rhythm—Grey had me climaxing before I even knew what was happening.

"Grey," I screamed, closing my eyes and clenching around his cock as I came.

"Fuck yeah! Come on me, baby. Soak me," Grey growled, tightening his hold on my breasts.

The pain intensified my release. Liquid rushed out of me, lubricating Grey's dick and making it easier for him to fuck me. He moved, deepening his thrusts, and drawing out my ear-deafening climax.

When my orgasm subsided, I was still shaking. My lower body was overstimulated and sensitive to touch. I reached underneath my legs to find his testicles. I massaged his tight balls and watched his eyes close as he tensed. His thrusts were less controlled, and his face contorted.

I relished the moment. After making me feel so good, I wanted to make him unravel. I pulled his face toward mine, and the moment our lips locked, I saw the wild beast inside him emerge. I kissed him provocatively, slipping my tongue between his lips and tasting myself on him. It was nasty in the best kind of way. This time, Grey moaned.

His member stiffened inside me, becoming unbearably hard. With two slow and deep upward thrusts, Grey stilled inside me and came. His body convulsed. Our lips pulled apart, and one vigorous shudder ran from his shoulders to his cock.

"Abby," he said hoarsely as he came inside me.

When the orgasm ended, he rested his forehead against mine. I felt like I had just mated with a wild animal. It made me want to do it again.

"Grey," I said softly as he pulled out of me and stood.

"I'll be in touch." With those final words, Grey, the mysterious older man, dressed and left the room.

Be in touch?

For more sex?

God, I hoped so.

Soccer Mom

"Get in the car! We're going to be late." I rush Dylan to the door, grabbing his cleats on the way out.

If it weren't for my unreliable ex-husband, we wouldn't be in this situation, yet again. As usual, he dropped Dylan off late, exhausted, and hungry.

The coach has never said anything about his star player consistently arriving late to practice, but the intensity in his gaze every time tells me more than words ever will. He thinks I am a horrible mother, always showing up to practice and games late with a half-starved son. I know how it looks. But I can't exactly blame everything on my ex-husband without looking like a bitter woman. So, I glare right back at the sour man.

Let the coach and everyone else judge. Without my son on the team, they wouldn't be on track to winning the state finals.

"Buckle up," I tell Dylan, who is only half paying attention to me as he shoves a turkey sandwich in his mouth while texting on his phone.

He's a growing boy, turning fifteen years old just last month, so he needs the calories, especially since he's about to run around for two hours. I honestly don't know how he does it and keeps a smile on his face. Between his schedule, mine, and his dad's, Dylan is constantly on the go with the go bag to prove it. He's adapted well to the new life this divorce forced on him.

My heart aches for the pain and inconvenience this has caused him. He doesn't show resentment or irritation, though. He deals with it and moves forward. He's so strong.

The field is ten minutes away, but I reach the gate in eight. Dylan jumps out of the car.

"Thanks, mom," he says before sprinting toward the field.

"Good luck," I call after him.

Despite being across the field, his coach instantly targets me with those blazing eyes. I'm a hundred yards away, yet he still finds me. It makes my spine tingle dangerously. That look. It haunts me in my dreams, serving as a constant reminder of how I continually fail as a mother.

"Fuck that guy," I say under my breath, pulling away to look for a parking spot.

By the time I take my stadium seat, the game is well under-way. Dylan is doing his thing, running circles around the other team.

Gerald, his coach, thankfully, has his full attention on the game, as he rightfully should. I no longer feel his judgment, even though my own judgment always lingers, tainting the very cold, hard stadium bench below me and making me feel even more like life itself is a never-ending battle.

As expected, we beat the other team. Dylan texts me after the game, asking if he can go to a friend's house to celebrate.

Of course, I told him it was okay. I'll do anything to keep his spirits high. And leaning on friends during a tough time at home is so much better than him caving in on himself like so many other children do.

The parents are all participating in after-game gossip, but I'm not in the mood to make small talk. I return to my car on the far side of the field house—the only parking lot with open spaces since I arrived late. Most of the cars back here belong to players, but since I was waiting around for Dylan, most of them have already left for the party, leaving only a few cars in the back lot.

And it seems my luck keeps getting worse because Gerald is also walking to his car, which is not too far away from my own. I should have known he parks out back—it's the quickest way into the field house. If I'd thought this through, I would have waited longer to leave the field, but a large glass of wine and a romance movie are calling my name.

It's impossible to ignore Gerald as we near the cars. Not that he would allow me to ignore him—he's already coming toward me. The beeline to me, instead of his car, is obvious.

"Good game, coach," I say.

"Dylan was outstanding, as usual," he remarks curtly.

Regardless of his judgment of me, I know his admiration for my son is real. "Yes, he was," I say.

"Have you thought about the leagues I mentioned? If he wants to play in college or professionally, he needs to start competing with more advanced players and playing year round."

Gerald is walking beside me now, avoiding his car altogether. It appears I will not be getting out of this conversation quickly.

"Yes. The only problem is getting him to the games when Max has him. He's not exactly reliable when it comes to being on time or even present." Sourness tinges my words.

Gerald looks at me sternly. "Max, your husband?"

"Ex-husband," I correct him, even though technically, the divorce is still being finalized.

He makes a sound. It's something like an approving grunt, but I can't be sure with the British accent.

"Does he not support his son's future as a soccer player, or is it something else?"

Gerald has never been one to pry, but I know he's only concerned about helping Dylan.

"Max is being spiteful. He loves his son, but anything that inconveniences my life takes priority. We'll work it out, though. Thank you, Gerald," I say sincerely. I don't need this man to tell me how to manage my son or ex, no matter how right he might be.

We reach my car. I unlock the door and open it, hopping into the driver's seat. Gerald plants a hand on the side of my car, stepping into the space between my open door, and halting my attempt to close it. I look at him, confused.

"I find it hard to believe a man could treat you so poorly, messy divorce or not," he says lowly.

I don't understand what he means. He doesn't know the details of our divorce, and I know he's never been married. There's no way Gerald can empathize, and I don't want his sympathy.

Most men would be spiteful if the court ruled that they had to share custody and give up half their paycheck. But that's the price you pay for cheating. Max should have thought of that before he stuck his penis in his secretary. Frankly, I think it serves him right.

"Max has his reasons," I say.

"Kate, you're a wonderful mother—even I can see how hard you work. What type of man wouldn't respect the mother of their child, especially when she's raising such a fine young man? You deserve praise, not to be treated poorly by a man who never deserved you in the first place. He should be thanking you for the favor you're doing him—hiding his transgressions and lack of honor."

My blood turns as cold as the stadium bench I sat on earlier. Then, it goes hot. For a soccer coach, he sure knows a lot more about my divorce than I expect. The gossiping moms know everything. It's hard to hide much in this town, but Gerald doesn't seem the type to invest his energy in local drama.

His intense gaze returns, zeroing in on me as if I am the goal and he's the soccer ball aiming for the back of the net. I'm not sure what's gotten into him today. I always thought he hated me. I thought he pegged me as a lackadaisical mother.

"Thank you," I finally mutter.

Gerald smirks. The expression transforms his face. He's so handsome. Young, but handsome. Suddenly, I feel like the space between Gerald and my seat is shrinking.

I try to excuse myself. "Well, I better get going."

"Where are you going? I heard the boys gossiping about a party tonight, and Dylan obviously isn't with you." He peers around the car, amused.

Unable to help myself, I laugh. The coach and I have never had a lighthearted conversation like this, but I'm beginning to relax. His stern looks don't feel so judgmental anymore.

"He's with friends tonight. I'm just going home. I'll probably have a glass of wine and take a bath."

Gerald's eyes skim down my body when I mention a bath. My lower lip drops open as the realization hits me.

He's into me!

"Care for some company?" he asks brazenly.

My mouth is hanging agape. Gerald reaches up and lifts my chin, a chuckle slipping through his lips.

"Did I say something surprising, Kate?"

I swallow. "Um…Company drinking wine?"

"Sure. And other things, if you'd like."

I find myself nodding. Except, I don't know what I'm agreeing to. His rewarding smile is answer enough. Before I can fully process whatever is happening, Gerald leans in. At his height, he towers over my car, but he bends down easily, his head ducking under the roof.

My heart stammers, preparing for something to occur that hasn't occurred in a very long time, but he simply reaches a hand around my steering wheel and presses the ignition button. The car roars to life, blocking out the sound of my pounding heart as Gerald gets close to me.

"Let's not waste time then. I'll follow you."

"Okay." I breathe heavily.

My breath fans his face as he moves away. He must feel the same tension growing in the air because he pauses his retreat. Our eyes lock. No words are exchanged.

Suddenly, something carnal takes over my body, and I lunge for him. My fingers dive into his curly hair, tugging him forward as I crush my lips against his.

Gerald falls into me with hasty movements. I'm not sure when it happens—between my tongue plunging into his mouth or his thumb scraping along my jaw—but he's turning off the car and pulling me out.

My back hits the back of my car door as Gerald aligns his body with mine. He presses into me, the hard planes of his body ridged and enticing. His hands snake up the sides of my thighs. Then he lifts me.

The movement catches me off guard, and our lips disconnect. I'm panting. Gerald's lips glisten with my saliva, proof of our savage kiss. He wraps my legs around his waist, pinning me to the car with his pelvis.

"Jesus, Kate…I don't think I can wait," he says.

I feel a new hardness pressing into my hips. The spot between my thighs heats and aches.

This is wrong. So wrong. I haven't been with a man since my ex-husband and I separated a year ago. And this man—my son's soccer coach—has to be ten years younger than me, maybe more!

"Gerald. I don't know if we should do this," I say.

My body says otherwise, though, because when he dismisses my words by kissing my neck, I let go of all rational thought. With his lips and tongue working my neck, he replies, "Why not? I want you, Kate. You want me. We've been eye fucking each other for months. It's been long enough."

Is that what we've been doing?
I recall the battle of our stares.

Maybe we were eye-fucking each other. By the way my body, and, if I'm being honest, my mind is reacting to Gerald, I want this.

"Uh-huh," I say, tilting my hips forward.

His cock presses achingly hard against my core, driving me wild. The thin fabric of my leggings is a hindrance, but not for Gerald. He wraps an arm around my waist while the other supports my backside as he opens the door to the back of my SUV and lays me on the backseat.

"This is not how I normally treat a woman, and you deserve much more than to be fucked in the backseat of a car, but I don't plan on stopping here. I'm going to fuck you senseless tonight. First, we both need to get off, though."

I couldn't agree more.

"Get these off me," I order, scrambling further into the car as I slide my leggings down.

Gerald tugs my tennis shoes off, then takes my leggings fully off as he climbs into the backseat and closes the door. He slides his athletic shorts down with ease. I don't have time to appreciate his cock because I'm pulling him forward. He leans over me as my nails dig into his firm backside. His cock is achingly close to my center. I grab it, rubbing his shaft through my folds, and wetting him with my arousal.

"Oh my god." My head falls back in a sinful moan. No vibrator will ever feel as good as the rounded tip of a cock.

Gerald pulls back, taking his delightful penis away from me.

"I don't have a condom, but I swear I'm clean. Is that okay?" he asks.

"Yes. Just put it inside me already!" I say impatiently. It's careless, but something tells me I can trust the man. I know where to find him; he'd be an idiot to lie.

Gerald leans over me and aligns his cock with my center. Wasting no time, he thrusts into my pussy. The sudden intrusion makes me cry out, but his lips capture my cries as his hips move greedily. Sweat slickens my brow as the sensation of finally being fucked overwhelms me. My hands roam Gerald's perfectly cut body, pulling up his shirt to skim my fingers over the groves in his abdomen.

Jesus. This man is ripped.
He tears off his shirt so I can have my fill of him.

With his impeccable strength, Gerald supports himself with one hand, then reaches the other between my thighs. He sits up so I can watch him. "You feel fucking amazing, Kate," he says, circling his thumb over my clit.

I bite my lip to avoid crying out. The pace of his thrusts slows to match the timing of his thumb. My pleasure heightens.

I tremble. "Oh my god."

"Come for me." Gerald grits his teeth. He presses his thumb harder, grabbing my waist with his other hand to drill into me.

My body tenses and lifts off the seat. Gerald holds on and fucks me harder. I cry out as my orgasm flares to life. The shock-wave of ecstasy starts at the base of my neck and slices straight down to my core. My nails dig into Gerald's arms, encouraging him to fuck harder.

He groans, grinding his teeth as his orgasm overwhelms him. He slows his thrusts, shoving as deep into me as possible. The hot ropes of his cum spurt inside me as I come down from my own release.

"Wow," Gerald pulls out, our combined cum covering his cock.

"Yeah," I agree.

My breathing is shallow as I struggle to recover, but Gerald isn't done. His fingers explore my sex. I'm still swollen and numb from release, but I like the intimacy and familiarity of this moment. He touches me gently, appreciating my body as he takes the cum dripping from me and stuffs it back into me.

A shiver rolls down my spine. I've never had a breeding kink, but having Gerald save every last drop of his seed and ensuring it stays inside me might be the hottest thing ever.

"I'm going to take you home now," Gerald says, dipping his fingers back into me and slowing moving them in and out.

Cum covers his hand, but he keeps putting it back into me. He pins my legs beside my head, putting my pussy on full display as he stuffs me full. My body reignites, wanting more.

"Fuck me again," I say boldly.

Gerald smiles and says, "You should tell Dylan to stay at a friend's tonight. I'm going to put fresh cum in you every hour, until you're so full there's no way I can keep stuffing it back into you."

The Rockstar and The Actress

Zane

"**B**angin' show, man." A dark-skinned man with too many piercings slaps my back as I walk by.

Security is supposed to keep people away from the gate, but the crowd tonight was restless, and the venue was over capacity. The people are still pumped up, even after I played a third encore. I'd be flattered if this didn't happen every three to four days at a different venue in a different city. I'd smile at the emo-punk fool yelling *bangin' show, man* if he wasn't one in a thousand who said it before.

My booking agent is running me ragged with this schedule. He tells me: *Hold on a bit longer. You'll get a reprieve, and the payout will be worth it when you're done. Put on a good show, every night, and the fans will reward me for years.*

This lifestyle can't last forever, so I do what he advises—I leave my soul on the stage every time I step off it. The fans feed on my energy like a succubus. The merch sales have boomed ever since I started cutting the sleeves off my band tees and wearing them on stage. I toss the T-shirt to a lucky fan at the end of every show, giving my fans a good tease before I leave them.

At the end of this tour, I'll have a fat ticket to thank my marketer for that idea. I'm not above selling my body to make a penny. I sold a lot more than that to get to where I am. Punk-rock wasn't exactly popular when I stepped onto the scene. Pair a pretty boy face with a bad boy look, date the right people, tip the right gossip mags, and it wasn't long until I started bringing punk back.

I step around the final barrier, cutting off the crowd's view. Security escorts me through the hallways of the stadium toward the exit. I like to get out of the area as fast as possible. The quickest escape is to the waiting SUV that will take me to my hotel. The tour bus will circle the venue, drawing everyone's attention to it, in hopes they will spot me inside, while I'm actually long gone.

My head of security, John, opens the passenger door, and I slide in the backseat. The driver never makes eye contact with me. He drives away when John hops in the front and tells him to *drive* in his brutal, raspy voice.

It's nearly midnight. I can't wait to shower, put on a fresh pair of sweats, and sink into the overly plush bed in my hotel room.

When we arrive at our destination, I enter the hotel with John at my side. In silence, as usual, he walks me to my room, makes sure it is secure before I enter, and then returns to his own accommodations next door. The protocol is a bit much for my liking, but a crazy fan at the beginning of the tour freaked the record label out, so they stuck me with a bodyguard. Unfortunately for John, every bone in my body is naturally defiant, so I like to test the limits of my security when given the chance.

As soon as he is safely out of earshot, and I am cleaned up, I take a trip to the hotel lobby. There's a secret speakeasy behind the front desk. The access point is a hidden door pressed into the wood veneer that lines the walls.

It's brilliant.

A little jazz and whiskey is the perfect combo to put me to sleep. I might sing punk, but I'm an artist, and all music is connected by instruments, no matter how they're used.

After providing the password, the receptionist opens the door, and I enter the dimly lit passage. A steep stone stairwell leads down. As far as I can tell, there's only one path in and out of here. I'd be nervous about what lurks below if the sound of moody jazz music didn't pull me forward.

When I reach the bottom, I'm not prepared for how busy this place is or how large. I expected a tiny room, but it's a massive underground venue, supported by large, ageless stone pillars running down the middle. A hundred people are laughing, drinking, and dancing to the music. Sconces lining the walls cast a red hue over the people. It gives a sensual, yet mysterious energy to the room. Lush fabrics and antique decorations give the place an avant-garde-esque look.

It's perfect.

"What can I get you?" the bartender asks as I approach.

"Whiskey sour," I say, as I continue to scan the room. I love that no one recognizes me here. I can take it all in. I can relax.

"Make that two," a sultry voice says.

I feel her presence as she slides onto the barstool next to me. I'm forced to acknowledge her. *Her.* A woman around her late twenties, with hair as black as night and eyes as dark as the ocean's deepest water. She would visually embody the woman of my dreams if it weren't for the cut-off T-shirt she's sporting.

"Where the fuck did you get that?" I ask, recognizing it immediately. I fucked up cutting the sleeves off earlier today when my drummer distracted me. There's a slit that cuts into the chest, exposing her collarbone.

"Get what?" She places her hands on her hips, smiling.

She knows.

"Whatever." I dismiss her as I pay the bartender.

"It's on me." The woman pushes my card back across the counter and throws down two twenties.

By the look on her face, I can tell she's leaving no room for argument about paying for my drink, so I force manners as I grit my teeth and say, "Thanks."

"Anytime. I'm Shea," she says, extending a hand.

Her sweet smile doesn't match the black paint on her taloned fingernails. Frankly, her entire look is too dark for that innocent face. With my T-shirt on, she looks like the female version of me, minus the genuine positivity she displays and the complete lack of tattoos.

I shake her hand a bit too aggressively, unsure what's fueling this disconcertment other than the fact that someone recognized me when I was convinced no one would know me here. "I'm Zane," I say.

"I know—obviously." She points at her shirt, previously my shirt, jokingly.

I don't find her attempt to be funny or cute. I find it annoying. "Yeah...How'd you like the show?" I say dismissively.

"I don't know. I wasn't there."

I roll my eyes, but my interest has officially peaked. *Does she think I like the sweet little liar act? I don't.*

"You weren't there?" I say incredulously.

"That's what I said," she says.

"Why are you wearing my shirt then?"

"It's a long story. Essentially my top broke. My girlfriend said she found this on the ground, and I thought it was pretty badass looking, plus I didn't want my tits hanging out, so I put it on."

Shea smiles again. It unnerves me. It's so at odds with her dark look.

"She found it on the ground?" I ask, playing along.

Shea didn't deny knowing it was my shirt, which meant she was at the concert. She saw me wearing the shirt, and she knowingly put it on. I let it slide because I mostly want to know what type of top she was wearing that could break and result in her tits hanging out—which I don't see much of under my oversized shirt. She's nearly as flat-chested as I am.

"Yeah, sorry to burst your bubble. I'm not the girl who caught your shirt, but I'm also not the one who discarded the smelly thing on the ground, so you should be happy about that."

I can't decide what to think of this woman. Her cheery behavior and moody look make my brain spin. It's like staring into one of those optical illusion mirrors.

"I guess so," I say.

"Anyway, cheers!" Shea says bubbly.

"For a scene chick, you're kind of a lot."

Shea pauses. Her smile falters. "Excuse me?"

"Your look—it doesn't match your personality."

"And yours does?" she counters sassily.

I stumble on her quick retort but answer honestly. "Duh. It's kind of my thing."

The bubbly mood is gone in an instant. Shea runs her tongue over her teeth as if smiling too long has made them dry. She tilts her head, letting a ribbon of midnight hair streak across her face. Her lips part as she leans into me. I can smell my sweat on her—still lingering on the shirt—mixing with the sweet scent of her floral perfume. It's a heady concoction—my sweat and her perfume. I begin to doubt the story about my shirt being discarded on the ground. Something about this woman tells me she has a plan, and putting on my shirt was only just the start of it.

"Would you prefer I act all dark and mysterious? Should I say cryptic things that make you question my sanity? What would please you most, Zane?"

She mocks me, but her words are like a spark to my flame. And her quick transition from bubbly to bitchy checks all my boner boxes. I question the level of both of our sanity, but I'm too tired to care much.

"What are you doing here?" I lean back against the bar, taking a sip of my drink. The bartender has a heavy hand. The liquid is potent and burns as I swallow.

On cue, Shea reaches beside me, retrieving her drink and mimicking my sips. She's a chameleon—adapting to her environment, blending in to give a sense that she belongs. I begin to like the little actress. Her audacity is intriguing.

"So?" I say, prodding for an answer.

"I like this bar. I come here often—ask the bartender."

I glance at the bartender. He's busy assisting other patrons. I don't need to ask him for confirmation, though, because I don't care if Shea is telling the truth. We're all liars in this world—saying and doing whatever it takes to get through the day. We may lie to each other, or we may lie to ourselves. In my and Shea's case, I think it's a little bit of both.

"Who are you with?" I ask. Shea smiles, but this time, it doesn't reach her eyes. It's more seductive and mysterious—like the scene girl she pretends to be. "That's better," I whisper.

"What's better?"

Fuck it.

Something stirs inside me. Maybe it's boredom, maybe it's intrigue. Regardless, I've reached my limit on this tour and need an outlet.

"Nothing. You going to tell me who you're with or not?" I say impatiently.

"You're being kind of pushy with these questions. What do you care, Rockstar?"

There it is. My calling. My name. My category.

She's unintentionally drawn a line in the sand that tells me exactly who she is and exactly who I am. I know her goals, and I know how to get us both what we want. Although, I'll still be left hanging, knowing there is no real connection. There is no real attraction to anything other than the man I am on stage.

"I don't," I say.

"Liar." Shea's tongue flicks between her teeth as she calls me out.

I don't care. But I also do. It's late. She's hot. I'm hot for her.

This is a pretty simple equation to figure out, and all the banter in the world isn't going to make it clearer. The only difference tonight is that she's wearing my shirt—she's a fan, trying to act like an actual emo girl that I'd be into. It'd be hilarious if she weren't so sexy.

Since I've been in this scenario a million different times, I start with the usual proposition. "This can go two ways," I say.

Shea smirks.

I continue, "We can keep talking, drinking, get wasted, and then eventually stumble up to my room. When we wake up tomorrow, we'll hardly remember how good last night was. Or we can go up to my room right now and take our time with each other. I will thoroughly exhaust myself on your hot ass, and tomorrow you can tell all your friends about it in detail."

"Two options?" she asks, barely able to contain her excitement.

I down the rest of my drink, ready to take things upstairs. "Yeah, sweetheart. Two options. Pick one."

"Since there aren't any other better options, I'll have to pick the second." Shea finishes her drink and sets it down on the counter beside mine.

"Good choice. Let's go."

I take her hand and lead her up the stairs, leaving the sound of jazz behind. *So much for relaxing.* Although, I can't say the alternative is worse. When we enter my hotel room, she doesn't look around as I expect. She slides out of the black jean shorts that are hiding under my oversized t-shirt.

"You're quick about it," I chuckle but pull off my shirt and toss it beside her shorts on the floor.

"Why waste time? You should be thoroughly exhausting yourself on me already."

"Point taken," I say, stripping my pants next.

Shea doesn't remove the shirt, though.

"Off," I tell her.

"No. This stays on," Shea says with a smug smile.

"That's kind of fucked. I'm not self-absorbed enough to be into that."

"Then don't look."

"I want to see you, sweetheart. Not myself or a reminder of it. I'll put my mark on you in a different way. Now take it off," I say.

Shea rolls her eyes but takes off the shirt. She's naked underneath. Not that she needs a bra anyway; her tits are A-cups. The size fits perfectly on her petite little body, though.

"Happy?" she pouts.

"Ecstatic. Those too." I point to her black satin thong—fitting for a wannabe emo chick. The whole outfit is on point. It'll be interesting to see how it translates into sex.

"Take them off me yourself, Rockstar." Shea spins on her heel and saunters to the bed.

Her hips sway seductively, captivating my gaze on her ass.

"You know I'm not a fan of that either. I'm beginning to think I may need to be fucked up to enjoy this," I say honestly.

"Seriously?" She drops onto the bed with a careless plop.

This woman's attitude is all over the place. I hate that I continue to find it hot even though it feels like we're arguing.

"Yes, seriously. I don't want to hook up with a fan. It's not as cool as it sounds. So please, try not to remind me of what you are by calling me something I don't want to be in the bedroom."

Shea laughs. "Oh, trust me, I'm not a fan of yours. You're just hot, and technically, that is your profession. But I get it, fucking a fan is so not what it's chalked up to be. They can turn stalkerish."

As if she can relate. "Yeah…So can we continue?"

"Let's just not talk," she suggests.

I draw a line across my lips, pretending to zip them together. Shea does the same. As soon as the playfulness is finished, our gazes intensify.

Shea crooks a finger at me, commanding me forward. I stalk toward her. The closer we get, the hotter my skin feels. Her face goes slack, and her eyes narrow, taking on all the seriousness of a woman who found her prey and is ready to attack.

Forgetting all about her fan status and focusing on the outrageously sexy woman in front of me instead, I lean in and capture her lips with mine. Shea falls back onto the bed, taking me with her. Our lips remain connected as we slide up the bed. I can taste the whiskey on her tongue. She's clearly had a few more than me tonight.

Breathless pants slip between her lips as I settle between her legs, pushing my groin into hers as we kiss. Our underwear is the only barrier between us. Something about knowing nothing about this woman but being so insanely attracted to her makes my mind whirl excitedly, and my balls tighten.

I break our kiss so I can focus on her neck. I want to hear her panting and begging underneath me before I am inside her. A sadistic part of me wants to make her pay for being so combative.

Her neck is salty and dry. She was probably head-banging and dancing to my songs all night. I lick the sweat off her neck, removing proof of her fandom. Her pelvis flexes against my cock as she rolls her hips, shoving herself against my erection.

"Yes, Zane," she says, breaking the oath not to speak.

Shea's fingers knit in my hair and hold me against her neck. I keep working her erogenous zone as she grinds her hips against me. For such a petite woman, she's got a firm grip and strong hips. And those nails—they prick my scalp deliciously. I suck in a chunk of her neck, rolling her skin in my mouth, knowing I'll leave a mark, while I grind my hips into her, pinning her to the bed. She pulls me in tighter, encouraging me to leave a mark—proof for the story she'll share with her friends later.

I release her neck with a pop and push-up, admiring the red, swelling skin. Shea's eyes are narrowed in on the space between us. They scan over the length of my erection pressing against the thin fabric of my boxers.

"You like that?" I say, grinding myself against her. My cock is as hard as it's ever been or will be.

"I love it." Shea licks her lips. "Let me see."

Using one hand, I pull my underwear down enough to let my cock fall out. It stands straight, ready to penetrate.

"This what you want?" I take my penis and slap it against her pussy. The satin on her black underwear darkens. "Yeah, you want it," I say.

Shea pulls her underwear to the side in invitation. "Get it wet," she says.

A voice in my head tells me to find a condom, but her wet pussy is so inviting. And a hell of a lot closer than a condom—if I even have one.

I can't resist. Her pussy glistens beautifully. Her labia is swollen, and I swear I can see it quiver. I shove my cock between her folds, running through them, passing by her entrance to coat myself in her arousal. I roll my hips, mimicking how I'll fuck her as I cover my shaft in her juice.

We both watch in silence, intoxicated by the sensual way our bodies move together. Teasing. Taunting. I pinch her nipple as I continue to glide myself against her. Shea's eyes close, and her head falls back into the plush pillows.

"Yes," she moans. Her nails dig into my thighs, urging me forward, asking for more.

"Careful." I bite my lip through the pain of her piercing nails, focusing on the pleasure of her warmth coating the underside of my cock. My balls begin to drip with her juice. She's so fucking wet. Plenty wet enough for me to enter her, but I wait.

"Fuck me already," she says.

That's what I need. I reach into the bedside drawer, shuffling around the free shit I threw into it two nights ago as I make a silent prayer that there's a condom in there. My fingers find a foil package.

"Got it," I say, kneeling back to slide it on.

"Is that latex-free?" she asks.

"Huh?" I look at the condom. "Um…No."

"I'm allergic to latex. We can't use that." She sits up, investigating the packaging.

"This is all I've got," I say.

"I'm clean and on birth control. Are you?"

"I'm clean, but not on birth control," I joke, weighing the potential risk of this while continuing to rub myself against her. I can't stop touching her. My cock desperately wants to feel more.

"If you're lying to me. I'll fuck your life up," Shea threatens. Her thighs squeeze mine, attempting to stop my movements.

I stop moving and take a second to deliberate.

"Yeah. I'm not lying. That's fucked. I wouldn't do that. But just in case, I'm taking a picture of your license after this, and I'll have plan B delivered here in the morning."

She nods. It's agreed.

Great.

Even though it's a risk, I don't care. My balls ache with the need for release. This wouldn't be the first time I've been irresponsible. At least, this chick questioned it, and I'll take care of it in the morning. My cock nudges her entrance.

"You good?" I ask for consent again.

"Just fuck me already, Zane." She bends her knees, planting her feet beside me and lifting her hips to push herself against me.

The tip of my cock enters her one snug inch at a time. Shea pushes into me, taking more of my cock like a good girl. The inside of her pussy is so soft, so warm, and so tight.

"You feel so fucking good," I groan as my shaft is fully engulfed in her.

"You do, too," she moans.

I let her walls contract and relax before I begin my retreat. Slowly, I work myself in and out of her with shallow thrusts, letting her adjust to my size as her juices fully lubricate my cock and her entrance. Soon, I find a rhythm, playing her body like my electric guitar.

There's nothing intimate or animalistic about the way we fuck, but there is a deep need growing between us. It's something I don't understand and can't fully explain, and yet, I'm ready for whatever it is.

I flip Shea onto her stomach, needing to see, to feel her ass as I fuck her. The way it bounces every time my cock disappears inside her is an erotic symphony. I grip her hips, watching them jiggle against my hold as I fuck her harder.

"More," she begs.

I give her more. I pound into her, spreading her ass cheeks so I can watch the show. The veins on my cock bulge, ready to explode at any minute, but I need more of this woman. Grabbing a leg, I turn her onto her side. I pin her leg over my shoulder and lean into her, stretching her body until she's trapped in the splits. We both let out a sigh of satisfaction that turns me on more.

My cock protrudes from her flat stomach, going deeper than the other position allows. Shea howls her delight as I increase the depth of my thrusts. Her mouth hangs open as she pants for breath, leaking little *yes's* and *more's* and *please* each time I slam into the back of her pussy. I planned to exhaust myself on her, so that's what I'll do.

I pull her face to mine and suck on her lower lip. I kiss her so aggressively that our teeth scrape. But neither of us pulls away. Instead, I stretch her legs with my body while my cock finds the deepest part of her. It's not enough. I need more of her. My free hand fists her hair, bending her neck backward as I roughly kiss and fuck her.

Shea bites my lip, forcing me to cry out, but it doesn't stop me. I pull her hair tighter. I fuck her harder. Shea bites harder.

When the taste of iron touches my tongue, I'm not sure if it's Shea or me that cries out this time because my orgasm crashes into me so hard that I swear my cum must burst through her. It takes a solid minute for my orgasm to end, for my cum to stop squirting out of me, and for my hips to stop moving. Shea feels too good for it to end.

Eventually, my hips do stop moving, though.

Shea slumps, a sign that she, too, just had her release. I loosen her leg, which she lets gratefully drop onto the bed. Her lips are ruby red, covered in my…blood. My cock is still inside her, and it begins to harden from the sight of it.

When she smiles, and I see more of my blood in her teeth, I go rock hard.

"Are you not done?" Shea asks.

I look down, but there's nothing to see. I'm still buried inside her as I feel her walls tightening around me.

"Apparently not," I say.

The Rockstar and The Actress
Shea

I t can't be him. There's no way he would show his face here. I bend over the bar top, taking another long look from my seat across the dimly lit bar. My suspicions are, unfortunately, confirmed.

It's him.

As if this night could get any worse. My agent conned me into attending his show, placing me in the VIP section directly in front of the stage. The asshole tossed me his sweaty T-shirt like I was a thirsty groupie who wanted to hump it all night.

Although, I ended up being forced to put on the shirt when some *other* asshole spilled a bright red drink on my brand-new white top. I will never again be conned into attending a punk rock show. The people were out of control.

Tack on the fact that *Zane* walked directly past me as he exited the stage and said nothing—absolutely nothing. Trish, my agent, promised it would be a quick meet and greet. She forgot to mention *that quick* meant *not happening at all*. The exposure from this publicity stunt is supposed to help my upcoming movie—where I play a moody teen who falls for a bad boy—when it hits the box office.

Apparently, being seen with Zane in public will make my character in the movie more believable. He is the epitome of a bad boy. Tattoos cover every inch of his body, piercings line his ears, and the disheveled, forever-bashful-but-still-a-bad-boy haircut perfects his image. The fans went crazy when he tore his shirt off and tossed it into the crowd. No matter how much of an asshole he is, I have to admit he has a nice body underneath all that black ink.

Zane perches against the bar like he owns the place. He has an arrogant vibe about him that makes me want to cut him down a level. It doesn't matter that I hardly know the man. He disrespected me, and that is not going to fly.

I strut across the bar slowly, swaying my hips casually, as if I have nowhere important to be and would love some company. Zane has a reputation that makes me positive he'll notice.

But he doesn't.

He's busy ordering a drink, forcing *me* to make a move. The three drinks prior to this moment are certainly not doing anything to damper my plan. If anything, they're encouraging me to throw all caution to the wind. Making a scene in public is highly discouraged by my publicist, but putting the man who ditched me this evening in his place would be progress for my therapy.

"Make that two," I say seductively.

Finally, he notices me. Zane's head cocks to the side as he regards me, working his way up and halfway down my body. His brows narrow on my chest.

"Where the fuck did you get that?" he asks.

"Get what?" I play dumb, putting my hands on my hips and pushing my chest out. *Sue me*. I'm an actress. Plus, he should recognize me in a matter of moments. I can't wait for my apology.

"Whatever." He ignores me, tossing a black card at the bartender.

My plan to annoy him quickly evaporates. Zane is acting like I actually *am* some wannabe groupie wasting his time. I might be the one with a perversion for pissing off men who wronged me, but this guy's an actual asshole. There's officially no doubt in my plan to make him pay.

"It's on me." I slide the card back to him and throw out two twenties. The bartenders prefer cash here, which is something Zane wouldn't know since *he's* never been here. I come often, which is why people aren't bothering me. Locals don't bother the locals. Zane's hardly famous enough to be bothered anywhere—even in a small town where, by some odd chance, someone might be impressed with his music.

"Thanks," he says.

I feign geniality and extend my hand. "Anytime. I'm Shea."

He stares at my nails for far too long before he accepts my hand and shakes it like it might be poison. My nails are an aggressive shade of black with pointed tips—it saves the costume department time when I have them ready to go—but they aren't toxic.

"I'm Zane."

"I know—obviously," I say. Sarcasm leaks through my voice. I can't help it. People don't act like I'm some grotesque waste of space—ever. Zane, apparently, doesn't have the time of day for anyone, no matter how much they might skyrocket his own career.

"Yeah…How'd you like the show?" He asks. The tension in his shoulders loosens with a sag as if he's giving up on something.

"I don't know. I wasn't there," I lie.

"You weren't there?"

"That's what I said."

"Why are you wearing my shirt then?" He leans forward, engaging in the conversation.

"It's a long story. Essentially my top broke, my girlfriend said she found this on the ground, and I thought it was pretty badass looking, plus I didn't want my tits hanging out, so I put it on." I easily lie. There's no way I'm admitting someone spilled a red drink on me or that I wore a white top to a punk concert—it became a clear mistake as soon as I arrived and saw everyone in shades of black. I stuck out like a sore thumb.

"She found it on the ground?" he asks.

"Yeah, sorry to burst your bubble. I'm not the girl who caught your shirt, but I'm also not the one who discarded the smelly thing on the ground so you should be happy about that," I say.

Take that for a reality check, Zane. I'm not just some fan girl.

"I guess so," he says, shifting in his seat.

"Anyway, cheers," I say.

Zane lets the silence between us grow into a nearly pregnant pause before saying, "For a scene chick, you're kind of a lot."

A lot?

"Excuse me?" I've been playing a *scene* chick for months. If he wants to see *scene*, I will give him scene.

"Your look—it doesn't match your personality."

"And yours does?" I say quickly.

He points at his body. "Duh. It's kind of my thing."

Instead of playing all sweet and flirty, I flip the script on this *bad boy*. "Would you prefer I act all dark and mysterious? Should I say cryptic things that make you question my sanity? What would please you most, Zane?"

His eyes narrow into a dark gaze, and his left lip quirks into a smirk. *It seems bad boy has a type.*

"What are you doing here?" He casually leans against the bar, sipping his drink.

My inner actress takes the cue and mimics Zane—mirroring movements is a sign of attraction and trust. And after a second sip, Zane mimics me. My new personality hooks him, intriguing him past the level of friendly flirtation.

"So?" he says leadingly.

"I like this bar. I come here often—ask the bartender."

He looks around the bar as if for a sign of proof, but shrugs when there's no one within talking distance to confirm.

"Who are you with?" he asks.

This time, it's an effort not to roll my eyes. *Is he really trying to pick me up and still doesn't recognize me?*

"That's better," he says, sliding his hand across the bar top in my direction as if he's about to touch me.

"What's better?" I ask.

He smirks and leans back. "Nothing. You going to tell me who you're with?"

"You're being kind of pushy with these questions. What do you care, Rockstar?" I say, mocking him.

I'm beginning to question my agent for setting up a publicity stunt with him at all. This is a train wreck, and Zane only thinks with his dick. We're more likely to end up choking each other out in a battle of who's right than pretend we're friends.

"I don't," he says.

"Liar." I smooth a hand down my side, straightening his wrinkly shirt against me as I decide which route to go next. This conversation isn't exactly going according to plan.

Zane's eyes scan my body as he says, "This can go two ways. We can keep talking, drinking, get wasted, and then eventually stumble up to my room. When we wake up tomorrow, we'll hardly remember how good last night was. Or we can go up to my room right now and take our time with each other. I will thoroughly exhaust myself on your hot ass, and tomorrow you can tell all your friends about it in detail."

I choke on my drink, then manage to get out, "Two options?"

Zane guzzles the rest of his drink and sets it down on the bar with a thud. "Yeah, sweetheart. Two options. Pick one."

This turned into a sexual advance really quickly. Part of me questions whether he's fucking with me. Does he finally recognize me, and this is his way of pissing me off more so I forget about his other transgression? This man has my head spinning. But if there's a possibility that he *is* fucking with me, then I have to fuck him back harder.

"Since there aren't any other better options, I'll have to pick the second." I finish my drink and set it down beside his, taking the bate.

"Good choice. Let's go."

He grabs my hand and roughly tugs me after him while I deliberate how to handle what happens next. I was set on acting my way through our conversation, hoping to disturb his perfect façade and go from there. Zane wasn't disturbed in the way I hoped, though. And while hooking up with him under the guise of a fan is definitely not how I thought our meeting would go—it's also kind of awesome to think that when he eventually realizes who I am and what he did with me, he'll also realize I knew who he was all along.

I'm beginning to think this emo character with a penchant for revenge is a total badass, and I need to lean into her more.

When we enter the room, I immerse myself in the dark side of my character. Her transformation from good girl to bad is sensual in nature, and I need to harness that energy now if I'm going to make Zane sick when he realizes the best sex of his life was with *me*.

I slide out of my black jean shorts, keeping my eyes on Zane as I do so.

"You're quick about it," he says, following my lead and tossing his shirt on the ground.

Touché, Rockstar.

"Why waste time? You should be thoroughly exhausting yourself on me already."

"Point taken. Off," Zane says, pointing at my shirt.

"No. This stays on."

"That's kind of fucked. I'm not self-absorbed enough to be into that."

The dominance in his tone surprises me but doesn't deter me. I like a power struggle.

"Then don't look," I say, taunting him.

"I want to see you, sweetheart, not myself or a reminder of it. I'll put my mark on you in a different way. Now take it off." Zane's tone softens but holds no less dominance.

I roll my eyes as I pull the shirt over my head. I don't have a bra on because I never wear a bra. My boobs aren't big enough to need support, and by the smile on his face, Zane seems perfectly delighted by it.

"Happy?" I ask, dropping his shirt.

"Ecstatic. Those too," Zane says, biting his lower lip and pointing to my black thong.

"Take them off me yourself, Rockstar," I say, spinning around and swinging my hips in an alluring walk toward the bed.

"You know I'm not a fan of that either. I'm beginning to think I may need to be fucked up to enjoy this," Zane says, stalking after me.

"Seriously?"

"Yes, seriously. I don't want to hook up with a fan. It's not as cool as it sounds. So please, try not to remind me of what you are by calling me something I don't want to be in the bedroom."

This man is such an ass. I momentarily question my revenge plan to sleep with him. "Oh, trust me, I'm not a fan of yours. You're just hot, and technically, that is your profession. But I get it, fucking a fan is so not what it's chalked up to be. They can turn stalkerish," I say, feigning an excuse to appeal to him.

His brow furrows as if he's beginning to recognize me, but he doesn't. "Yeah…So can we continue?" he asks.

"Yes. Let's just not talk," I suggest.

Zane takes the cue and seals his lips. The sensual energy in the room intensifies as Zane's focus narrows on my lips. He's pressing against me so quickly that I fall back onto the bed, dragging him with me. His arms are already pushing me further up the bed. He crawls over me, keeping our lips locked and our bodies skimming each other. I'm not prepared for how well he kisses. Nor am I prepared for his tongue ring—I hadn't noticed it before. But the smooth edges of it massage across my lips and tongue as our mouths explore each other.

I turn away from his invasive kiss, trying to catch my breath, but Zane is moving on. He nuzzles my neck, finding the spot that makes my breath hitch, and then he devours me.

"Yes, Zane," I say, driving my fingers into his hair. It's surprisingly soft and so at odds with his rough-around-the-edges look and personality.

The more my nails press against his scalp, the faster his tongue works on my neck. He's covering me in his saliva, but I relish it. His hips grind against my pelvis, mimicking a thrust and teasing my lower body as his mouth teases my upper body. He harshly sucks in my skin, making my back arch as I cry out from the pain. There's going to be a mark there. My character would fucking love the fact that he marked me, so I love it too.

"You like that?" he asks.

"I love it. Let me see." I motion to his underwear. I wonder if his cock is tattooed like the rest of him. Doubtful, but I've never been with a guy like Zane. All the tattoos and mystery piercings—it's exciting. It's pleasurable.

Using one hand, he tugs his briefs down, letting his cock fall out. "This what you want?" He slaps his bare penis against my pussy. "Yeah, you want it," he says.

I'm pretty sure the floodgates to my vagina burst open. His cock isn't tattooed or pierced, but good lord, it is perfect. And the curve in it—I love a good curve.

"Get it wet," I say, arching my hips toward him and pulling my underwear aside to expose myself.

Zane lowers himself to me, taking his sweet time. I'm shaking with anticipation as the smooth underside of his shaft slides against me effortlessly, soaking with my arousal. Zane pinches my nipple as he moves like he's fucking me. I cry out when his nail bites into the tip of my breast. I'm not prepared for the heat that transpires between us as his cock presses against my clit and his fingers dig into my chest. That feeling builds.

"Yes," I moan, digging my nails into the back of his thighs to urge him on.

"Careful," he says through gritted teeth.

"Fuck me already," I say.

He pulls away from me, leaving me cold and wanting as he collects a condom from the bedside drawer. I wonder how many women he's brought up here, how many *fans* he's fucked. My perversion to his impending discovery of my identity soars, heightening the excitement.

He's ripping open the condom when I remember to ask, "Is that latex-free?"

"Huh?" He looks at the condom wrapper. "Um…No."

"I'm allergic to latex. We can't use that."

I grab the wrapper to confirm, and sure enough, it's latex. Fucking idiot…He probably hasn't been with the same woman long enough to realize most of our bodies disagree with latex. Even without my allergy, it wouldn't be comfortable. Condoms dry out. Frankly, I don't sleep around often enough to need them. I keep a man around, we get tested, and we don't use condoms.

"This is all I've got," he says.

"I'm clean and on birth control. Are you?" I say quickly.

He's still grinding against me as if we shouldn't be having this conversation. The more he moves, the more I hate him, and the wetter I get. He's so stupidly disgusting, but that cock of his is perfect, with a face and body to match.

"I'm clean, but not on birth control," he says.

I already decided to take the risk. This sweet revenge will be so good when he figures it out. Regardless, I feel the need to plant a seed. A little warning to make sure this *Rockstar* knows what will happen to him if he's lied to me.

"If you're lying to me. I'll fuck your life up," I say seriously.

"Yeah. I'm not lying. That's fucked. I wouldn't do that. But just in case. I'm taking a picture of your license after this, and I'll have plan B delivered here in the morning," he says.

I said I was on birth control, but whatever. Double precaution is smart on his part. If I actually was a fan, I might try to get pregnant with his baby and trap him. He's smart not to trust me.

"You good?" he asks.

"Just fuck me already, Zane."

He enters me slowly as if he is still debating doing this, so I grab his ass and pull him against me. He lets out a groan when he's fully sheathed.

"You feel so fucking good," he says.

"You do, too."

I urge him to move, but he takes his time. Zane rolls his hips, clearly having done this a thousand times. But I don't care about that tonight. I care about getting off. I care about getting him off. And I definitely care about how shocked he's going to be in the morning when he discovers he's not fucking some fan.

I close my eyes, and hold onto his hips, pulling him forward when he tries to pull out of me. Zane answers my plea, increasing his pace. He leans into me, kissing me softly, too softly. The way this man fucks is more like lovemaking. He's soft and gentle in the ways that count, and domineering in the other ways that count. I dig my fingers into his ass, and he rips my hands away, pinning them above my head. He flips me onto my stomach with unexpected force, and the fire inside me is ignited as he twists my upper body into a pretzel.

"More," I say.

He gives me more.

My belly flutters excitedly as he plunges back into me, holding my hands down with one hand and digging his other into my backside. His nails bite into my ass, and I let out a breathy squeal. He chuckles, releasing my hands to grab my butt cheeks. He pulls them apart as he squeezes, using them like handles to drive himself into me faster. Harder.

He growls wildly, spanking me so hard that the sound rings in my ears. I nearly lose it. I clench around him, forcing his thrusts to slow, but Zane flips me onto my side. He pulls my left leg over his shoulder and leans into me, forcing my body into the splits. The stretch is nearly unbearable, but I'm quickly lost to the pain when Zane sinks back into me. His cock pounds against the deepest part of my vagina, slamming into my G-spot.

I circle my clit, spurring myself on. Zane watches me intently as he fucks me with a possessive need. He pushes my leg against my chest and kisses me while his hand pushes mine out of the way, and his fingers take over. This man refuses to let me bring myself to climax. It's his for the taking, and I love it.

"Yes, Zane," I say.

His other hand fists my hair, tugging my head back and exposing my neck, but Zane doesn't stop kissing me, nor does he slow his fingers. They move faster, as do his hips. They move in tune with each other, making me feel him everywhere, all at once.

I pant, trying to catch my breath as the tightening feeling builds inside me, but Zane kisses me harder, stealing the air from my lungs. I bite him, channeling my inner bad girl. The sound that leaves his throat is so dark and sensual that it triggers me to do something completely out of character. I bite him so hard that the taste of blood fills my mouth, and I lose it completely. Everything in my body tenses. I clamp around him as the orgasm hits me. Zane groans into my mouth, his body stilling before a hot wave of pleasure unfurls inside me. I swallow his blood as my body swallows him cum.

This is easily the most erotic sex I've ever had. He rears back and gives me a sideways look, with blood still pooling on his lower lip. I lick my lips, giving him a lazy, very satisfied smile because I am satisfied. Acting like my bad-girl character or not, that was amazing. Knowing he's going to shit himself when he realizes who scarred his lip in the morning only makes it that much better.

He left his mark. I left mine.

Zane licks the wound as if he knows what I am thinking. His dick twitches inside me, still erect.

"Are you not done?" I ask.

He looks between us and shifts his hips, testing the resiliency of his cock. "Apparently not," he says.

Heady Holidays

A Very Merry Christmas

"Now that our flights are canceled, what should we do for Christmas?" Rachelle asks as she plops down on the couch beside me.

My wife isn't nearly as upset about missing her family Christmas as I expected. I'm personally relieved. Spending the holiday with her family typically results in me being constantly hungover or drunk. Her family is from Wisconsin and loves drinking me under the table. I do my best to keep up, but a skinny boy from Staten Island is better at doing drugs than drinking bottles of hard liquor.

"Should we get some whiskey and pass the bottle? It won't be a Peters' family Christmas unless we're drunk," I joke, using her surname to indicate that drinking is her family's holiday tradition, not mine.

Rachelle laughs and rests her head on my lap, looking up at me. "I'd prefer you don't puke your guts up and sleep on the bathroom floor all night."

Unconsciously, I begin tucking my wife's hair behind her ears. I want to see all of her so I can lean down and kiss her without getting a face full of hair.

"You know," she says thoughtfully. "There is one thing we never get to do during Christmas at my folks."

"Oh yeah, what's that?" I ask, slipping my gangly arms around her tiny torso and pulling her up my chest.

As she talks, I inhale her intoxicating scent. She doesn't wear perfume, but she always smells like berries and vanilla. It's a sweet and soothing combination.

"I'll show you," she says.

Rachelle pops up from the couch and speed-walks down the hallway toward our bedroom. I have no idea what she has in mind and get up to follow her. The bedroom door slams shut loudly before I make it to the hallway. I take the closed door as my cue to wait in the living room.

"What are you doing in there, babe?" I call down the hallway.

She opens the door slightly and pokes her head around the corner. "Go sit down, Steven. I'll be right back. It's a surprise!"

I know better than to push when she uses my first name. While I'm curious about the surprise, waiting a few minutes won't kill me. For the life of me, I can't remember what we don't get to do while at her parents. We celebrate nearly every holiday tradition I've ever heard of in the week we visit her family.

After what feels like an eternity, I lose my patience, so I pull out my phone and mindlessly scroll through social media.

"Surprise," Rachelle says in front of me.

My head snaps up in surprise, and my jaw practically drops to the floor. In all five years of being married to Rach, she's never donned anything sexier than a lacy nightgown during our honeymoon. It's not that she can't rock lingerie. She isn't that type of girl, and I prefer her naked. Or so I thought I preferred her naked. The strappy black thing that barely covers her most intimate parts makes my dick shoot up like a rocket.

"Rach…" I say, my voice sounds all kinds of husky and needy without even trying.

She spins around slowly so I can get a visual of the backside. Thick black straps with circular metal hooks run under and over her butt. No straps are covering her butt crack, and I immediately imagine why. It must be for easy access. My dick twitches in anticipation.

Before Rachelle can turn back around, I tug her down onto my lap. She squeals and squeaks when she feels my erection digging into her backside. I grind her hips against me and admire the view of her two butt cheeks gripping my cock through my sweatpants. I need fewer clothes on.

As quick as I got her in my lap, she's out of it. I stand, shuffling around her to get my socks and pants off. Rachelle laughs as I scramble to get fully naked and nearly trip over the coffee table.

"You're making me feel inadequate in that dominatrix outfit. Quit laughing at my clumsy ass. I've never been more turned on while feeling so emasculated," I tease, pulling my shirt off.

She bites her tongue and spanks my ass. The emasculated, turned-on feeling only heightens. I shed my briefs and let my cock bounce free. Before it stops bouncing, Rach is on her knees in front of me. The leather straps hiding her nipples and surrounding her breasts make them stand out even more than usual. I peer down at the swollen mounds of her breasts and lips. My wife is so fucking beautiful.

Rachelle leans forward and wraps her silky voluptuous lips around my cock, and I nearly collapse. Her tongue circles around the tip and drenches it in saliva. Her hot, cavernous mouth feels like home. Blood pulses and rushes to the tip of my cock as she bobs her head on my erection—taking every inch of me until she gags and is forced to pull back for a breath.

I gaze down at my wife and see her in a new light. In this outfit, on her knees, it's like a stranger is sucking my cock right now. I love the idea of role-playing with her.

"Babe, get up here," I say, reaching under her shoulders and pulling her off me before I come in her mouth and not in her tight cunt.

She giggles as I pull her onto my lap. Her thick thighs straddle me, and the tip of my cock searches for her center. She's already soaked, and it gives me the same reaction every time I feel it. That hot, soaking center is a baby-making oven built just for me, and I need to spill my load inside it.

Rach holds herself over me, sliding her warm pussy along the length of my cock and lubricating me for entry. I lay my head on the back of the couch and close my eyes, fighting the tight feeling in my balls that threatens to make me explode before I'm even inside her.

Before I combust, my wife plops down onto me, and the tight warmth that encompasses me is like coming home after a long vacation. "Oh, baby," I moan, gripping her hips tightly as she starts to ride me.

I lose all semblance of control and open my eyes. I drag her forward and capture her nipple in my mouth, sucking it harshly and reveling in the feeling of her walls clenching around me as I pleasure her body.

"Yes, harder," she says, bucking harder and faster on top of me.

My balls are nearly sucked into my stomach, I'm so close, but I need her to find her release before me. I lift her plump ass, plant my feet firmly on the floor, and drill into her from below. The cold air hits my cock as I pull fully from her and then slam back into her tight cunt. Her arousal drips down the base of my cock to my balls, and the slapping, sloshing sound of our fucking makes my entire body tense.

Yet, I fight the release and pound into her harder. I grab her breasts, kneading them between my hand. Rach moans above me, and her back arches. Her vagina grips me like a vise. She stills.

I lean back to watch her face. That pleasurable O-face contorts her features as she squeezes unbearably hard around my cock. It's all I need. I thrust harder. As she moans my name, my balls tighten and explode, squirting my cum into her warm oven.

Slowly, I lower Rach onto me and let my cum sink further inside her. I don't want to lose a drop of it. This is the best holiday tradition I've participated in for a very long time.

"Merry Christmas, babe," Rach whispers, slumping against my shoulder.

"Merry Christmas, love. Hope you can handle round two because this is about to be a marathon night," I say, flipping her back onto the couch and climbing over her.

Let the sex marathon begin. Happy Holidays!

New Years Resolution

"**I** swear, Char, I'm not hooking up with another random dude this year. Not even for a New Year's kiss. I'd rather kiss you," I shout to my best friend, Char, over the booming club music.

"Well, Dusty is coming tonight, so don't count on my lips being free for you. Unless you want to have a threesome, I'm sure he'd be down for that," Char jokes.

We're at a nightclub in downtown Portland. Despite the freezing cold temperature outside, I'm in a long-sleeve, deep V-neck velvet mini dress with black stockings and knee-high boots. Char is in a similar outfit, but her dress is covered in gold sequins. She looks hot and flashy, while I look more obscurely hot.

That was my goal, though. I didn't want to be tempted by some hot man again. It's not like I've never had a boyfriend. I did. I just never had a boyfriend during the New Year holiday, so I developed a history of New Year's Eve one-night stands—a tradition I'm trying to break this year.

I got so drunk last year that I took home a total of four men. The sex was great, but most sex seems great when you're half falling over and nearly blacking out. Plus, four…That was one for the books.

"Dusty would bust his load by the mere mention of a three-some," I say, rolling my eyes.

"Look, there he is!" Char points to the other side of the bar and takes off through the crowd, not bothering to wait for me.

I follow her as best I can, but lose sight of her. Heading in the same general direction, I weave through the numerous bodies packing the club. A girl stumbles into my side, and I turn just in time to catch her forearms before she face-plants onto the disgusting floor.

"Oh my god, I'm so sorry. This guy seriously just hip-checked the shit out of me," she says, straightening her jacket and smoothing her hair.

Her short dark bob and black cat eyeliner catch my attention. She has that Portland hipster chic look that I've always admired but have never been able to pull off myself.

"It's okay," I say, giving her an understanding smile. There are so many tall guys in here. It's hard for us short girls to get around in a crowd like this. She's nearly my exact same height. I'm five foot two and a half, which is slightly below average. My boots add a couple of inches.

"I love your dress! Oh, and your boots, those are really cute," she says, complimenting my outfit.

"Thanks! I love your hair. I wish I could pull off a bob," I gush, feeling an instant connection.

"My name is Gabby." She extends her hand.

I shake it. "Betty. Nice to meet you," I say.

"Are you here with anyone?" Gabby asks.

"Yeah, my girlfriend and her guy. We know some other people who are supposed to show up tonight, but I haven't seen them yet. What about you?"

"A few friends, they're supposed to be at the bar. I just got here, so I was trying to find them," she explains, blushing.

She looks cute when flustered. "Well, I'm headed to that side of the bar if you want to join us until you find your friends," I offer, knowing what a pain it is to search for people when you're a short girl.

"You're a lifesaver, thank you," Gabby says, squeezing my upper arm.

"Come on," I say, wrapping my hand in hers and leading her through the crowd to where Char and Dusty should be.

We find them ordering drinks. Char stands beside Dusty to make room for us at the bar. I let Gabby slide in next to it so she doesn't get knocked into again as I take up the space next to her.

"What do you want? It's my treat for letting me hang out with you while I search for my friends," Gabby says, having to yell in my ear so we can hear each other. Her arm rests on mine as we speak.

"Whatever you're having," I shout back.

After we get our drinks, Gabby and I follow Char and Dusty to the dance floor. The couple immediately starts grinding. They just started dating, so they're still super horny for each other. Plus, the three or four drinks Char and I had earlier are starting to make us both feel buzzed and carefree.

Gabby grabs my free hand and spins me around playfully before doing a sexy swivel with her hips.

"You've got moves, girl," I say, looking her up and down to encourage her to dance more.

As she dances, I mimic the sway of her hips—wanting to appear as chic and sexy as she does. Soon, she's twirling me around and dancing behind me. She intertwines our fingers before placing them on my hips. Following her lead, I shake my hips back and forth with the rhythm of hers. We are totally grinding now, but I don't care. It feels good to be carefree and not worry about breaking my rule of hooking up with a random guy this New Year's Eve.

Gabby spins me around just as I'm finishing my drink. Char motions toward the bar, giving the universal signal for another round, so Gabby and I follow. We set our empty cups down as we wait for a refill. With our hands now free, Gabby wraps her arms around my waist, and I slide mine over her shoulders. We move together to the beat of the music. Our legs lock around each other when we dip and rock our hips. The music coaxes us closer, and soon, our pelvises are bumping and grinding each other.

My chest heaves heavily, sweat beginning to slick my lower back. The bass pounds against my feet, vibrating my whole body as I rub against Gabby. This is what I love about dancing in the club—the tempo beating through one body and flowing directly into the next. It's like a tribal dance, connecting you to each other through a shared appreciation of the act.

"Guys, it's one minute until midnight!" Char yells as she pushes people away to get closer to us.

She's holding two champagne flutes. Dusty is behind her with two more. Gabby and I break apart slowly to accept the drinks. I'm still in a daze from the dancing, and I'm sure she is still, too. The DJ begins to count down from twenty seconds.

"Sorry you didn't find your friends." I say to Gabby.

"Oh, I saw them, but I was having fun with you." She gives me a sweet smile that makes my chest feel warm.

"Me too. I'm glad you stayed to hang out," I agree.

When the countdown reaches ten, we shout the last remaining numbers out loud—"Three! Two! One!"

Confetti rains down on the crowd, drinks are thrust into the air, Char and Dusty kiss—with tongue—and I turn to hug Gabby, but she goes the same way. Mine and her lips collide. I try to pull back and apologize, but her hand cups my cheeks, and before I know it, she's kissing me.

And I'm kissing her back.

This isn't like when you kiss or make out with your friends for fun or on a dare. This is the type of kiss I'd normally receive from a man every New Year's Eve—sloppy, passionate, leading. Except, this time around, it's with a woman.

My stomach turns excitedly when I realized she isn't going anywhere. She's into this. So instead of breaking our kiss, I wrap my arm around her small waist, dig my fingers into the back of her hair, and kiss her back. The softness of a woman's mouth is something I've never taken the time to appreciate before fully, but damn have I been missing out. Kissing her is like sucking on a juicy orange slice. I find our mouths meld and mush together so easily that it makes kissing her more enjoyable.

Before long, I've completely lost myself in Gabby, much like I lost myself in our dancing. I don't know where, when, or how it happened, but eventually, we're climbing into a cab and heading back to my apartment. Our hands and mouths haven't left one another long enough to make a plan. Few words are spoken, but they don't need to be in the heat of the moment. Bodies can say a lot more than words.

I've never felt skin so soft and hands so gentle. It's as intoxicating as the liquor buzzing through my veins.

We stumble into my apartment, breaking apart only so I can unlock the door. Gabby walks into the living room, absorbing the bits of my personality littered throughout the apartment's aesthetic. She turns toward me, smiling like she likes what she sees. I've never been looked at like this by another woman.

I'm frozen in place by nerves. Normally, I'm confident in the next steps. Normally, I know how the man will approach me and what to do to turn him on. But with Gabby…I'm uncertain and don't want to screw this up. I want to touch her and taste her.

"Where's your bedroom?" she asks.

"That way," I glance to the hallway on the other side of my kitchen.

Gabby struts up to me, takes my hand, and leads me to the bedroom. I'm thankful for her confidence.

She walks me to the side of my bed and turns me around. Silently, her nimble fingers slide down the zipper of my dress. She glides the dress from my shoulders, letting her fingertips skim my arms as she lets it fall to the floor.

"Damn. Why were you covering all this up? You're so sexy," she says, running her hands around my waist and pulling my back into her chest.

Her warm body presses into me. I've never been called sexy by a woman, and it means more than an observational compliment. The way she speaks is like an erotic language. She kisses the back of my neck, and it feels like electricity skates down my back.

Gabby turns me around to watch her remove her own clothes, giving me a wink and bending over, twisting and turning so I can see all of her. She's so effortlessly confident. And rightfully so. Her body is perfect, not a dimple or scar in sight on her flawless skin.

My eyes roam further south, taking in the dips and swells of her womanly body. Her curves are firm yet luscious.

"You're so fucking hot," I say, meaning it as more than an observation. This is the first time I'll touch a woman's body as intimately as my own. I want to know what it feels like to ravage such beautiful, smooth skin. I need to know what it's like to watch someone else come undone by doing to them what I like done to me.

"Come here," Gabby says as she crawls onto my bed.

Her mouth moves seductively, and the words are coated in heady desire. I follow her like a lost puppy, admiring her graceful movements that are so unlike the masculine brutality of a man. Unable to resist touching her any longer, I glide a hand up her leg. The skin turns to silk when I reach her inner thigh, and her breath hitches.

"Is this okay?" I ask, pausing.

"More than okay."

I bite my lip and let my other hand wander, rubbing up the outside, then the inside of her toned legs. Her panties are the neutral, seamless kind, and I can already see a dark spot forming in the middle of them. She's wet for me, and the confirmation of her lust has my own underwear soaking.

I like touching her and turning her on. The more she wants me, the more confident I am in my approach.

"I've never done this before," I say, keeping my eyes on her center as I deliberate exactly what I want to try next.

"Just do what feels right," she responds, lifting my chin with her hand. "Or just let me make you feel good," she offers.

Shaking my head, I say, "No. I want to taste you."

I slide her sticky panties down, exposing her womanly body parts, and my stomach twists with desire. I've never seen it from this angle, but it's beautiful. Before I can second guess my ability to perform, I lick up the center of her vagina. Gabby's back arches off the bed as she moans.

"I've been waiting for that all night," she breathes heavily.

Tasting her feels so good. She's soft and malleable. I want to feel and taste more of her. I lave my tongue over her, flicking it across her clit before I open my mouth and cover her pussy. Gabby writhes above me, grinding her hips into my mouth and pushing my head down onto her. My tongue works in overdrive while I consume her entire pussy.

"Fuck. You're so good at that."

Gabby's hips buck against me, but I reach up to hold her down. I brace her arm across her stomach as I sink two fingers into her pussy. At this angle, I can reach all the way up to my knuckles. Using my thumb in the way I normally like, I curl my fingers inside her and rub my thumb in tiny circles right below her clit.

Gabby clenches around my fingers and grabs my wrist. Her knees shake on either side of my head as I feel her pussy tremble against my fingers. It's so quick. A smile graces my face as Gabby finds her release. I don't stop. I work her through the orgasm, sucking her clit at the peak of her climax.

"Wow," I say, looking down at my fingers as I slowly pull them out of her. They're soaking wet. Gabby is still panting below me. I kiss her throbbing vagina and crawl up her body, feeling like a powerful bad bitch.

While still recovering, Gabby rallies and starts peeling my underwear off. She straddles me, pushing my back to the bed.

"What are you doing?" I ask.

"I want to feel your pussy on mine," Gabby says, tugging my hips forward.

Our vaginas are inches apart. I've seen scissoring done before, but the intricacies of the position are foreign to me, so I let Gabby line herself up with me. The minute her sopping folds touch mine, my mouth drops open. She massages herself against me, coating me in her juices and mixing with my arousal. The pressure, the friction, the god-damn erotic sight of this entire thing has my pussy aching.

"Oh my god, that's so good," I say, forcing my eyes shut before I totally lose it. This feels too good. I want it to last forever.

"I want you to come on me," Gabby requests.

"Come with me," I say.

"Okay, yeah," Gabby replies. "Harder then. I need it harder."

I plant a hand on her waist and use it to grind my pussy harder against her hers. Our moans of pleasure fill the room, and that familiar taut coil of an orgasm building embraces me. Just as I am about to climax, Gabby pinches and twists my nipples. It sends me overboard. The floodgates release.

My cum spurts out in small bursts, and Gabby rubs her pussy harder against mine.

"Fuck," she moans, her body shaking as her hips move in jerky motions.

Our clits scrape together, and another orgasm hits me, making me squirt onto Gabby's pussy again. We pump and grind ourselves raw against each other, fully soaked and slippery from our release. When the orgasms end, I fall back onto the bed again, and Gabby climbs on top of me.

"Next, I want you to do that into my mouth," she says lewdly while kissing me.

I have to admit, this New Year's resolution panned out to be more unexpected and satisfying than any year yet.

Valentine

“Mi Amor! You shouldn't have. He is too delicious," Angelio says, stalking around the handsome man.

The Anglo-Saxon-looking male I brought home to share our bed tonight is kneeling on the floor between us. He looks up at us with pleading eyes. I forced him to kneel for the last hour while we waited for Angelio to arrive. Meanwhile, I played with myself on the bed, letting him watch me circle my clit and ready myself for tonight's activities. His boner has to be aching. It's been straining against his pants so tight I thought the fabric would eventually give out and tear.

"I'm so glad you like him," I purr, leaning against the red silk pillows on our bed and continuing to play with myself. I'm soaking wet from the hour of rubbing myself as I thought about having two male cocks inside me and my fangs deep in them.

"Stand, pet," Angelio orders the young human man, who promptly complies. "Have you enjoyed watching my wife play with her delectable lady bits?"

"Yes," the pet answers, cupping the outline of his cock in his pants and rubbing himself.

"Well, be a good pet and pleasure my wife already. After all, it is Valentine's Day. She'll get everything she wants today. And I can tell the first thing she wants is for you to suck her tight little cunt."

While we aren't ones to play into the commercialized holidays—having seen these things die out and be renamed over the centuries—there are always hungry men and women looking to satisfy their empty desires on days like today, and we'd be fools not to take advantage. Plus, the man I brought home to enjoy was practically dripping with insatiable need when I found him. He was such an easy target. I couldn't wait to have him between my legs, showing me what a good pet he could be.

Our pet for the night does as Angelio tells him and crawls across the bed to kneel between my legs. As his tongue swipes across my center before mouthing my clit, our audible groans release in union.

"Our pet is hungry, my love," I tell Angelio.

The pet's tongue flicks across my tiny bundle of nerves, and the familiar ache of desire starts throbbing more intensely between my legs. It is like a heartbeat, which is a feeling I miss occasionally. This pulse between my legs is nostalgic and fulfilling in a way a human will never understand. My pet has no idea how much I relish each quick whisk of his tongue that makes the throbbing beat harder.

"Do you like watching another man make me feel this way, Angelio?" I ask my husband, who is climbing onto the bed beside our pet.

"I love it," Angelio answers, placing his hand on the top of our pet's head and pushing him firmly onto my vagina. "Eat her like it's your last meal, pet."

Our pet opens his mouth wider, spitting on my cunt, then licking the entirety of it.

"Yes," I buck my hips against his face as I lace my fingers in Angelio's. "Taste me through him," I say.

My husband smiles. His fangs elongate, and quick as an asp, he strikes. The pet jerks in his hold, but Angelio and I's laced hands hold his head down. When the numbing toxin in Angelio's bite takes effect, the tension in our pet dissipates, and he continues languidly sucking on me while Angelio sucks the blood from his body.

"You taste so good in him, mi amor," Angelio says, lapping up the blood that drips from the pet's fresh bite. "But I want to taste you for myself."

My husband spreads my legs as he lays bed beside our pet.

"She's so delicious," the pet says, moving his lips to one side of my dripping cunt.

"Yes, she is," Angelio agrees, sucking on the other side of me.

The two males work in tandem, licking the inner groves of my lower lips. One sucks the top of my clit while the other plunges his tongue into my entry. And when I feel that familiar coiling tension growing unbearable, ready to send me soaring, the male's tongues tangle together as they eat me out simultaneously. Their mouths glisten with my juices, their spit, and our pet's blood on Angelio's lips.

"I'm going to come," I moan, holding both males' heads down as Angelio's tongue darts in and out of me.

My pussy moistens, leaking its approval and reading itself for more. I attempt to tighten around his tongue, but my husband is too quick. He brings me to the edge without letting me fully get off because he knows the teasing will make me come harder later.

"Pet," Angelio says, tugging the pet's head off me.

"No, Angelio," I protest.

"Pull your dick out and fuck my wife's mouth. I want her choking on your cock."

The pet nods happily, moving into a kneeling position at the top of the bed and sliding his pants down to his thighs. His thick cock flops out and smacks me in the face. His veiny cock looks delicious. I open my mouth, and the pet shoves into me. He thrusts without restraint. His patience and control from waiting an hour are broken. The tip of his dick jabs into the back of my throat. Saliva slides down my chin, but I don't fight for breath. I don't need to breathe. I slurp him down, and his eyes go wide. My body hums with delight, knowing I'm giving him the best head of his life.

Angelio slams his equally as large penis into my pussy, and when a moan escapes my lips, the pet captures the sounds by shoving his penis all the way down my throat. His balls slap my cheek. The two males pump in and out of my holes, rocking my body back and forth as I suck each of them into me.

"Good, wife. You're so good at that. Fuck her mouth faster, pet," Angelio says, lifting my hips and using the angle to drive himself deeper into me.

Our pet follows his order, grabbing the sides of my face as he thrusts into my mouth. My teeth scrape against his ridiculously wide girth, causing my canines to tingle and extend in the promise of fresh, pulsating blood below his thin layer of skin. I moan when my tooth knicks the base of his penis, and he cries out. His cock strokes by my teeth once more as he settles into me, not moving as my fangs shoot out. They anchor themselves in the base of his cock.

The pet cries out as blood fills my mouth. It floods my throat, and I gulp on his tangy, abundant elixir.

"That's what I've been waiting for," Angelio says, slowing his thrusts but continuing the tantalizing movement in shallow thrusts that massage my pussy.

I gaze up at the pet whose eyes are closed, and whose head is thrown back as he soaks in the ecstasy of my bite. His cock pulses in my mouth like a second heartbeat as I suck on his juice. Warm liquid seeps down my tongue and into my throat. His cock swells, and salty cum accompanies the rich iron taste of his blood. It heats my body, giving me life.

When my fangs retract, the pet withdraws his cock from my mouth. The tiny puncture wounds slowly clot, a result of the toxins in my bite allowing our pet to heal faster for later use.

Angelio leans over my body, keeping his cock buried deep in my pussy, and licks the last droplets of blood from our pet's penis. He comes to my mouth next, cleaning my face of our pet's precious offering.

"Put your delicious thick cock inside my wife's cunt," Angelio says.

The pet pumps his cock back to life. He only went to half-mast after coming. It won't take him long.

Angelio places me on my knees. The pet is ready now, his dick full and pumping with blood again. He nudges my entry. I'm sopping wet and already stretched from Angelio, so the pet slips in easily. My husband straddles the pet's legs, sitting behind me. He prods my asshole with his cock.

"No. It's too much, Angelio," I beg him to stop, remembering how overwhelming this was the last time he entered my backside. I might not be fully alive, but there are no toxins to nullify the bite of him fucking my ass. The feeling of being stretched and filled so fully is an indescribable pain and pleasure that I hate and love. But I know by the end of tonight, I'll be begging Angelio for more.

"You can do it, mi amor. Focus on our pet so I can enter you." Angelio encourages me as the head of his penis pushes past the first barrier of my tight hole.

"Argh," I groan and moan my pain as he continues pushing into my backside, and our pet slowly thrusts into my cunt.

My husband pushes past the final part of my backside's resistance and enters me fully. He waits for my walls to stretch. The pain scorches my insides, heating my body to unbearable levels. My body shifts and tightens around the two male's cocks. It's too much. Too deliciously filling, and I become lightheaded as my body simmers from being possessed by these two massive cocks.

I surrender to their desires as they relentlessly drill me, one moving in as the other pulls out. They take turns pounding into my holes and ravishing my body with their rough hands. Our pet gropes my butt cheeks hungrily while my husband wraps his long fingers around my neck. A hazed, drug feeling starts to fog my brain as I give myself over to them completely. The pain is gone, and only pleasure exists.

As the incendiary pleasure builds in my core, Angelio pulls me up and sinks his fang into me, sucking the fresh blood from our pet from my veins. His bite is like an electric fire. It doesn't nullify the pain as it does for humans. It feels like wildfire rushing through my body. I rear my head back and scream. Angelio releases me, moving faster than the blink of an eye to reposition us.

He's underneath me now, fucking my ass. The pet stands in front, plunging back into my cunt. I wrap my arms around his shoulders and strike again as the males penetrate me.

Angelio bites me again.

More fire. More searing pain and pleasure.

Energy and euphoria pass between our bodies at the sharing of blood. Then, a climactic shockwave pulses through each of us in a feverish, spellbinding euphoria, causing me to writhe between the two males. Our pet grunts and spills his seed inside my achy cunt. When he's done, Angelio moves again—too fast to be seen by the human eye. He throws me on the bed and spears into my pussy.

"I love this cunt. It will be mine forever, Valentine," he purrs in my ear.

"Yours forever," I agree, leaning my head against the plush pillows as my husband thrust into my dripping hole and pushes our pet's cum further into my cervix.

"Mine," he groans, stilling inside me, and filling me with his hot ancient seed.

My husband pulls out of me to watch as their cum slips out of my empty hole. "Come clean up my wife, pet," he says.

Our pet crawls between my legs and feasts on the intermingled cum. My body hums in approval as our pet readies me for a never-ending night of pleasure.

Pride Ride

"That looks like a big cut, Wess. Are you sure you shouldn't get it looked at?" Darren asks.

"It's not that big. I've been dealt worse," Wess says, shrugging off Darren's soft hands.

He's halfway to reaching for Wess again when the other man stands, straightening the lapels of his jacket. It's a cold winter day, and layers won't keep him warm. Only work. Only movement will bring heat to icy fingers and toes.

"They're serving tomato soup and grilled cheese at the diner today. You should at least warm up. Let that cut clot a bit before returning to work," Darren suggests. He helps with the milk cows—too young and inexperienced to work the heavier machinery, but he was finishing his master's degree in agriculture and wanted part-time work in the field. Despite his doe-eyes and meager smile, he's a hard worker. Caring. Attentive. Firm when necessary—with the cows.

Wess gives him a stern look, but Darren's pleading eyes soften his response. "Fine. I'll see about some food first." Darren's answering smile makes him happy to have agreed to the suggestion and prompts Wess to continue, "And I suppose I could wrap my hand up so the wound doesn't get dirty."

Darren jumps up from the stool. Some of the cows frighten by the abrupt movement, shuffling in their pens. "I'll get the first aid kit," he says, briskly walking toward the cabinet at the barn's far end.

Wess could swear his hips move more vivaciously in those overalls, but it could also be an effect of the countless layers they're all forced to wear. He briefly wonders exactly how many layers Darren has on under that faded khaki fabric. He turns on his heel, returning to Wess as fast as possible. Darren makes quick work of Wess's cut, cleaning it with antiseptic, adding ointment, and wrapping gauze tightly around his hand so there's no chance of it splitting under his gloves or dirt slipping through the opening.

"Thanks, Darren," Wess says curtly.

He bats his eyelashes, sparing a quick glance at Wess to say—"Of course. I'm always happy to help you"—while pulling Wess's glove over his fingers. His nails brush against Wess's palm, leaving a sharp tingling in their wake.

A sudden urge to return niceties consumes Wess. Darren is always helping him. Anytime he needs an extra hand. Whenever he's working through a problem or simply wants to take a break and chat with someone. The younger man is always available for him. He's never understood why or appreciated him enough for it.

"Why don't you go home early today? I can have Judd finish up here," Wess offers.

Darren's cheeks redden, and it's not from the bitter cold. "That's not necessary. I like it here. I don't have anything to do at home anyways," Darren says.

"Nothing? No boyfriend to go home to or friends to go out with?" Wess doesn't know why he's asking. It's none of his business as Darren's employer, but they have become something kindred to friends over the past few months.

Darren plays with his fingers. They're ghostly pale. Wess reaches for them, bundling Darren's icy cold hands in his own. Their knees bump as he pulls them toward him. He breathes into the space between his thumbs, warming Darren's fingers.

"Oh, Wess. You're so sweet," Darren says shyly.

His giggle delights Wess. "Well, you're too cold to stay in this barn any longer. I'm not taking no for an answer," Wess decides, pulling Darren up and steering him toward the exit.

Darren puts on the gloves and winter coat hanging by the door. His movements are stiff and efficient. "Is something wrong?" Wess asks, waiting for Darren to zip his jacket before opening the barn door.

"I told you I don't have anything to do today. I don't mind working…" Darren's words trail off as if he isn't talking about milking the cows.

Wess takes a different approach. "Yes, I know. You're a great worker, so I'm giving you the day. You should take a hot bath. Warm up and relax. There's plenty to do tomorrow." He offers Darren a warm smile and a gentle pat on the back.

Darren cranes his neck, giving Wess a sour look. "If I have to take off the rest of the day because it's too cold to work, then you do too!" Wess snorts, but Darren stops him. "Don't give me that attitude. Come on, whiskey and a fire should do nicely." Darren grasps Wess's hand, tugging open the barn door in one swift pull.

A harsh, unrelenting wind slams into them as Darren pulls Wess along with newfound confidence. They head for Wess's work truck, climbing in without saying a word. Wess is breathless and speechless by the time he closes the truck door. Darren's rosy cheeks and watery eyes gleam with amusement.

"What?" Wess asks.

"You should see your face right now! Come on. I'm forcing you. You're taking the day off. Drive!" He points down the dirt road in the only other direction from the barn.

"To where?" Wess asks dubiously.

"You're house, silly," Darren says, turning the heat on full blast.

Wess starts the vehicle. "My house?" he asks, wanting to make sure he heard Darren correctly.

"Yep," Darren says, leaning against the oversized passenger seat. He feels so small in Wess's truck. He realizes he's never been in it. And he's most certainly never been in his boss's house. The only remotely secluded place he's been with Wess is the barn. But even alone, there are still animals around.

They drive down the road. It's not far from Wess's house. Darren sings along to a song on the radio, and Wess enjoys his jovial presence. When they reach the house, Wess shuts down the engine, and Darren hesitates to get out.

"All good?" Wess asks hesitantly. He's not sure why Darren suggested they come here instead of the diner or to a bar. The house is closer, but it's not like Darren even knows if he has whiskey or firewood. Obviously, Wess does, but still, how would Darren know?

Darren assesses him thoroughly, his eyes far more pressing than usual. All humor is gone. "I'm good. Are you good?" Darren says softly.

Wess's voice is scratchy as he responds, "I'm good."

They rush inside to beat the wind, shrugging off layers as the warmth of Wess's home greets them. Darren helps himself to look around, going into the kitchen to find glasses and whiskey. Wess likes how assertive and unphased he is by being in a new space. "Where's the booze?" Darren calls from the kitchen as Wess starts the fire.

"Above the fridge," he replies.

"I can't reach that!" Darren hollers, exasperated.

Wess chuckles as the fire catches. He leaves it behind to help Darren. As he enters the kitchen, he's taken aback by the image before him. Darren's overalls are unbuttoned. The front and back flaps hang loosely at his sides while a white cotton t-shirt is the only thing covering his very lean body. Wess didn't see him remove the thick sweatshirt beneath the coat, but he certainly notices everything the man is wearing now.

"A little help," Darren says on his tiptoes, still reaching for the liquor cabinet.

Wess slowly approaches, planting a hand on his lower back in dismissal. Darren backs away as Wess pulls down a decent bottle of whiskey. "This good enough for you?" he asks.

Darren nods. "More than," he smiles devilishly, watching Wess as he fills two glasses with ice and carries all three items back to the fire.

They sit in the middle of the couch, directly in front of the blazing fire, as Wess fills their glasses with whiskey. His nerves get the better of him, prompting him to fill their glasses slightly higher than might be deemed appropriate, but Darren doesn't say anything as he takes the glass and sips the amber-colored liquid.

"It feels kind of naughty drinking during work hours," Darren says.

Wess smirks. "Well, you're doing it with your boss, so I don't think you'll get into trouble."

Darren's giggle lights up the room. He drains his glass to the middle, welcoming its brazen effects as he says, "I like getting in trouble sometimes."

Wess's eyes darken with interest. "I don't recall a single time you've ever got in trouble on the farm or got remotely close to doing something wrong."

"I didn't say I like getting in trouble at work," Darren teases him, playfully poking his shoulder. He notes the way Wess's eyes skim down his chest, taking in the lack of layers as if Wess is just now seeing him.

"I'd prefer to get out of these work clothes. You good here for a minute?" Wess asks, standing.

Darren's hand latches onto his forearm, halting him. "Wait," he says, breathlessly. "What about me?"

"What about you?" Wess asks, turning toward him.

Their knees bump as Wess towers over the other man. Darren leans back against the couch, the movement far more confident than he feels. Wess can't help but think about ripping that thin white shirt off of Darren and devouring his lean frame. Wess doesn't know why the thought consumes him so deeply, making it impossible to look away, but his attraction to Darren has been a long time coming.

Wess pushes thoughts of his crush aside for the sake of being professional. But having Darren here—in his home, drinking whiskey in front of the fire—makes being professional very, very hard.

"I hate these itchy overalls." Darren crosses his arms, releasing Wess's wrist.

"Then take them off," Wess says before he can stop himself. He wouldn't mind seeing what else is under Darren's overalls.

Darren cocks his head to the side, smirking while looking at the ground. He's playing with fire. "But I don't wear anything under these."

Wess's balls tighten. "Jesus Christ, Darren." he says, grinding his teeth.

Darren looks Wess in the eye. "If you take off yours, I'll take mine off."

Darren is a little vixen, brought here to tempt him, but Wess doesn't care. He shrugs off his shirt and jerks open the fly of his jeans, kicking them off in a matter of seconds. Darren watches, biting his bottom lip as he absorbs every bare inch of Wess. Wess feels his cock strain against his briefs as Darren's eyes lock onto it. Darren sucks in a breath.

Before he gets too distracted, Wess says, "Are you comfortable now?"

Darren nods, fully encapsulated by the outline of Wess's cock.

"Then take off your overalls, Darren," Wess says, his voice gentle but demanding.

Darren lifts his hips from the couch, sliding the overalls down his legs and letting them drop to the floor. He's not wearing anything under his overalls, and he's only half-mast.

"Good boy," Wess says, receiving a shy smile from Darren.

"What about this?" Darren asks, running his fingers along the bottom hemline of his shirt.

Wess watches as the movement forces the fabric to snag on Darren's hard nipples, rubbing back and forth. "You look a little nippy, Darren," he says.

"I am. But maybe if I take it off, you could warm me up," Darren suggests.

Wess is moving before Darren can finish his sentence. Wess drops to his knees and spreads Darren's thighs. He opens his mouth and sucks Darren's half-hard cock into his mouth. Darren's body jolts, and Wess is pleased by the *harumph* Darren lets out as Wess bottoms out on his dick.

"Wess," Darren says his name like a prayer.

"I'd be happy to warm you up…here,"—Wess's knuckles brush over Darren's nipples, flicking the barb pierced there, making Darren's back arch—"And here," Wess says, cupping Darren's balls. A squeal escapes Darren.

"Yes. I'm so cold there," Darren pants as his lower lip quivers.

Wess's hands are surprisingly steady as he raises Darren's shirt over his head. He can't wait to roll those piercings in his tongue and make Darren scream. Wess tosses the scrap of fabric aside, knowing it's not going back on Darren's perfect body for a very long time. If Darren wants him, Wess will give him more than he bargained for.

He lowers his mouth to Darren's nipple, sucking it into his mouth, and twirling his tongue around the two-pronged barb. Darren moans, sinking his hands into Wess's hair. Wess pulls back, snatching Darren's hands and pinning them behind his back with one of his.

"None of that," Wess says.

"Why not?" Darren asks.

"You feel what I want you to feel," Wess says.

Darren has no idea what Wess is indicating, but he needs Wess's mouth on him, so he says, "Okay. Whatever you want, please, don't stop."

Wess obliges. Keeping Darren's hands pinned, he teases his nipples with his mouth and his teeth. His hips buck into Wess, their cocks brushing, but Wess uses his weight to keep Darren pinned. Darren's little whimpers of protest, asking for more, make Wess's cock even harder. Darren begs him to touch more of him, his cock impossibly hard as it stabs Wess in the stomach, but Wess doesn't touch him yet.

Wess pulls back, blowing against Dareren's swollen pink nipples.

Darren's body shudders. "Ah! Wess, please," Darren pleads.

"Are you going to be a good boy and keep those hands behind your back?" Wess asks.

"Yes. Of course," he says quickly.

Wess releases his hands. Darren follows his instructions, keeping them behind his back as Wess slides his hands down Darren's abdomen. His body shakes in anticipation. His hips wiggle as Wess fails to touch him where he wants it most.

"Patience," Wess says.

Darren groans in protest. "I'm trying, but I want you. I want to feel you."

"Oh, you're going to feel me, sweetheart. You're going to feel a lot of me, but not until I'm ready. I'm the boss, remember."

"I remember." Darren's eyes meet Wess's as he spreads his knees. His cock throbs and twitches, but Wess still doesn't touch him.

"You're so fucking hard," Wess says, eyeing the thick vein running up Darren's shaft.

"You make me hard all the time," Darren says.

"Is that so?"

"Yes. Oh my god, yes. I've wanted you for so long. Please, Wess." Darren's hands reach for him, but Wess is there first.

"I told you not to move these," Wess says through gritted teeth. "Is this the kind of punishment you're looking for?"

A wicked smile spreads across Darren's face. "Yes," he says darkly.

Wess knows exactly what Darren needs to be put in his place. "Wait here."

He leaves Darren in the room, knowing the other man will wait. He might be acting impatient and begging for Wess's cock, but Wess will make Darren realize how much more satisfying obedience can be. Wess grabs the items he's looking for from the bottom drawer of his dresser. He used a few of these items just last week, but they weren't nearly as satisfying as they were about to be. How long has Wess imagined it was Darren who he was fucking into oblivion and not some dirty fucking slut filling the void?

Darren is exactly where Wess left him when he returns. The smaller man's eyes widen as he notes what Wess holds, but he waits for instruction.

"Stand," Wess says.

Darren stands. Wess spins him around, running a palm up his pert, smooth backside before cuffing Darren's wrists. The other part of this particular bondage set loops around the neck. Wess brushes Darren's perfectly shaved jawline as he tightens the collar. He tightens the chain between binds so Darren's movement is limited, forcing him to push his shoulder blades together and arch his back. It makes Darren's ass stick out in a delicious taunt that encourages Wess to spank him. The sound rings in their ears as Wess delivers a hard blow to Darren's right buttcheek.

"Ow," he wails. But Darren's body only tingles for more as the sting settles into his skin.

"Be a good boy, and I won't spank you so hard," Wess says.

Darren doesn't like that promise, though. "I like it. Don't tempt me to misbehave," he says.

Wess chuckles. "Okay, sweetheart. Then I guess that'll be your reward, and this will be your punishment." He pushes Darren's upper back down until his face presses into the back of the couch. Wess kicks his feet apart just enough that his buttcheeks are spread for him. "What a pretty little hole you have, sweetheart."

Wess can't help the erotic delight that makes his throat dry, and his cock throb as Darren's reply is muffled by the couch cushion. Wess spreads Darren's ass cheeks even further apart as he squirts lube between them, watching as the cool liquid slides down the center of his body. He uses a finger to direct it, swirling his thumb around Darren's asshole. Darren's body goes slack as Wess finally touches him. His moan seeps into the cushion.

"Do you like your asshole being filled, sweetheart?" Wess asks.

Darren twerks his backside, a silent answer of agreement. "Good boy," Wess says. Somehow he knew Darren would be an amazing fuck. He picks up the anal plug he brought from his room, pressing the tip against the tight hole. Darren's hole puckers, begging for more, so Wess teases him. He circles the cool metal tip around, pushing in, then pulling out. Darren's body is tight and thirsty when he forces the plug all the way in. A low moan releases from them both.

Darren turns his head to the side so he can say, "I'm going to need a lot of punishing if you don't touch my cock already!" His breath is strained, and sweat slicks his forehead. Darren wants Wess desperately. He can't remember the last time he needed anything this desperately.

Wess taunts him, though. He lowers the band of his briefs, letting his cock bounce out. He fists himself. "You want this, sweetheart? Is this what you want in your tight little holes?"

Darren's eyes widen at the size of Wess, but he licks his lips, ready to take him. "Yes, Wess. I want that. I need that. I can't live without it," he wines.

Wess smacks Darren's ass with his cock, stroking himself until pre-cum beads at the tip. Then, he slides the head of his cock against Darren's ball sack, marking him with his cum.

"Oh my god, yes," Darren moans.

Wess spanks him, leaving a red handprint in his wake. Darren cries out again, his balls clenching, then releasing. Wess watches in satisfaction as Darren begs to be fucked.

"You're a needy boy, aren't you?"

"You have no idea," Darren says.

Wess tugs him up and whips him around. "Get on your knees, and let me give you something to suck on then."

Darren drops to his knees, opening his mouth. Wess nearly cums from seeing this beautiful man on his knees for him. Darren looks messy in the best way. Hair sticks to his face, slicked with sweat. His eyes hood with too much arousal and not enough release.

Wess pinches his cheeks and says, "Tongue out."

Darren sticks out his tongue, and Wess slaps it with his cock.

"That's a good boy," Wess says.

Darren smiles but keeps his tongue out so Wess can slide his cock along it. Again, they both release a much-needed moan as Wess sinks his cock into Darren's mouth. He grabs the back of

Darren's head and holds him against his shaft. The way Darren's lips press against his groin makes Wess want to explode into his mouth, but he's saving it. Wess still plans on fucking him.

Wess waits until he feels the back of Darren's throat constrict before pulling out. Darren gasps for breath. Before he can suck down another breath, Wess does it again, shoving himself down Darren's throat until he's gagging, and Wess is forced to pull out again. They do this for several minutes, to the point that Darren is shaking from exhaustion, and Wess is shaking from holding back his orgasm.

Darren's mouth feels so fucking good. He takes Wess so well.

"You're such a good boy, sweetheart. You deserve to be rewarded," Wess says.

Darren can only nod. His body is tense. Tired. Wess helps him stand, loosening the restraint so his arms can relax. "Thank you," Darren says.

"Lay down on your stomach, ass in the air, Darren," Wess tells him.

Darren works his way onto the couch, pushing his ass into the air. Wess kneels behind him, admiring the anal plug. Wess fists Darren's shaft. Darren's body relaxes as Wess finally touches him.

Wess fiddles with Darren's perfect little asshole, pulling the plug out as he jerks him off. He leans down and tastes Darren.

"Ah! Wess, I'm going to come if you do that," Darren says.

"Come like a good boy," Wess answers, flattening his tongue against Darren's hole before sticking his thumb in.

Darren's body jerks, but Wess holds him still as he goes to town on his ass, showing Darren how a real man eats ass before he fucks it into nothing. Darren moans and bucks, the orgasm nearly ready to explode.

"Wess," Darren says as Wess sinks two fingers into him and curls them.

Wess rears back, giving himself the leverage to thrust his fingers into Darren's ass while his hand jerks him off. Darren is shaking, and Wess wants him to get off, but he's selfish. Wess wants Darren's orgasm to be from his cock, not his fingers. He pulls out of Darren and shoves his cock into his hole. Darren screams out, but Wess doesn't slow down. He rocks his hips, slamming into Darren's prostate. Wess feels Darren's cock swelling in his hand. He focuses his hand toward the tip, squeezing from the base as he jerks him. Darren groans, his body tensing, as liquid shoots out of his cock.

Wess's balls tighten, urging him not to stop. "Where do you want my cum, sweetheart?" he asks.

"My ass," Darren says. "Fill my ass up!" Darren doesn't need to tell Wess twice.

Wess loosens his control, focusing on Darren's tight asshole. Darren's moans of pleasure have him nearing the edge.

"Uhhh. Yes," Darren moans.

Wess's hand is soaked in Darren's cum. Fucking bare has his balls tightening, but Wess wants Darren coming again. He uses Darren's cum to jerk him off again, bringing his cock to full staff. Darren's body is limp and tight, but Wess works him as his cock glides effortlessly in and out of Darren's tight hole. Wess slaps Darren's ass again, making him cry out. He spanks him again. Darren yells Wess's name. Wess slams his hips into him, and Darren's cock swells again.

"Fuck yes, Wess. I'm going to come again. Fill me up while I come," Darren begs.

Wess pulls Darren up, putting his back flush to his chest so he has easier access to fuck Darren. "I'm going to fill you up with so much cum it'll be dripping out of your ass for days," Wess says as he shoves two fingers down Darren's throat and pumps Darren's cock with his other hand.

Darren gargles on the fingers in his mouth and clenches around the cock in his ass as his balls tighten. Wess picks up the pace of his thrusts, fucking his ass like Darren has been waiting for since he met Wess. Wess controls Darren's entire body, fucking every part of him, and Darren only wants more. He chokes on the tips of Wess's fingers, trying to cry out for *more, more*, but Wess likes shutting him up.

Wess's pelvis pounds against Darren's backside with every thrust. Darren's body has never been so thoroughly used. The orgasm hits both of them suddenly. Darren comes onto Wess's hand, his ass clenching so hard that Wess's cock can't handle it, and his hot cum shoots into Darren's ass. He continues fucking Darren, more cum filling him.

They're both shaking when their release stops. Wess is careful about pulling out of Darren, taking a moment to watch as his cum drips out of his asshole and down his balls. Darren's entire lower body is soaked with their cum. It's a marvel to look at. Wess kisses his backside, over the mark his hand left.

Darren is so tired he hardly notices when Wess removes the bindings and helps him stand.

"Let's clean you up before we do more," Wess says.

"More?" Darren asks.

Wess smirks. "Sweetheart, I have so much more planned for you."

Darren gapes at him, then bites his lip. "I don't care what you do to me. Just make me come like that again."

Office Daydreams
Birthdays

"Hi!" Amanda squeals, running up to Thomas and me.

She hugs both of us, wobbling a bit. The booze has clearly been flowing heavily already.

"I'm Amanda. Nice to meet you," Amanda says with a dubious grin.

"Tom." Thomas introduces himself but puts distance between himself and Amanda.

I never felt right calling him Tom, but he seems to request other people call him that instead of his full given name. He never corrected me for using his full name though, so I assume it's because he likes me.

"Come on, we've got a table in the back." Amanda motions for us to follow as she leads us toward the back of the nightclub.

Neither Thomas nor I were in a rush at dinner, so we are arriving late to the birthday festivities. I'll need to take a few shots to catch up to everyone else's level. And after that kiss with Thomas outside the restaurant, I need a shot to steady my buzzing body.

I catch sight of Jen's head as we near the table—the birthday girl is dancing on the couch. It isn't too early in the evening to be drunk, but it's too early to be trashed.

She's attempting to twerk for the man standing below her. He's tall, a little too lean for my taste, but he's enraptured with Jen. His eyes are locked on her backside. I stifle a laugh. If they weren't drunk, I doubt either would be so ostentatiously mugging each other.

I feel a slight pang of jealousy for the birthday girl. She's definitely getting lucky tonight. Me, on the other hand—to be decided.

"Veronica! Finally, bitch, get up here," Jen waves at me as she jumps off the couch.

"Happy birthday! I see I've been missing out! You look amazing, by the way." I hug her and eye her sexy little black dress appreciatively—she really does look like a birthday queen.

"What's up, Tom?" Mr. Tall and Lanky Man throws an arm around Jen after he greets Thomas with a bro hug.

Thomas and I don't run in the same friend group, but things are changing. Courtesy of working at the same company, Jen's crush coincidentally is friends with Thomas.

"Drinks? Who needs drinks? You two look way too sober for this," Amanda chimes in, taking a head count for drinks.

"Please," Thomas says, moving past me to join Amanda at the table, who is holding bottles of liquor and mixers.

I catch up with Jen about her day and other weekend plans. She tries to quiz me about my date with Thomas, but I reverse the topic and ask about Mr. Tall and Lanky, whose name is Luke.

They've been dating or talking—as Jen puts it—off and on for several weeks. When she invited him out for her birthday, he jumped on the chance to meet her friends, which I'm taking as a good sign of an impending relationship.

Not that meeting friends has to be a prerequisite for dating someone, but having your friends validate a potential partner is helpful in finding blind spots within your own decision-making. If I'd had my friend's opinion on any of my exes, I might have avoided the disasters they turned out to be.

"Here you go," Thomas says, extending one of two glasses of clear liquid to me.

Damn. I do not want vodka right now, but my dumb ass acted as if I liked it twice before, and now this dude thinks I actually prefer it. If I drink vodka all night, I'll be an absolute mess.

I take the drink without complaint and sip it eagerly. Soon, I'll have to switch to my drink of choice—whiskey.

"Thanks," I say, scanning over the other guests at the table.

The majority of people here are just party friends. The type I only ever see while out drinking on weekends and never spend time with elsewhere. Amanda and Jen are the type of friends I can have a chill movie night with. These are the friends who know how to party and are always reliably present when you've got no one else to go out with. We'll have a good time with this group, but if I'm not careful, I will definitely overdo it.

I introduce Thomas to everyone. It surprises me that he knows a few of them. Honestly, I'm not sure how he and I hadn't ran into each other before I became obsessed with him at work.

Had I overlooked him before? Looking at him now, there's no way I would've missed him at the club. He's not the tall, dark, and handsome type. He's the boy next door type—and I'm all for it.

After introductions, Thomas and I are ready for drink number two. The night is going fairly smoothly, and I'm thanking the gods we haven't run into James yet.

As if on cue, James's boisterous, Australian-accented voice rings out over the music. "Happy Birthdee, lady! Nice to meet ya, mate. Ah Amanda, how are ya, Sheila? Thank ya for the invite."

Thomas greets James with a cursory nod as James pulls me into a rib-crushing hug before kissing my cheek. His lips hover over my skin momentarily as if he is debating on moving the placement of his lips. *God, please forgive me for sort of wanting him to.* My toes curl with the nearness of his body at my front and Thomas at my side. I doubt a threesome is Thomas's vibe, but it crosses my mind.

"Who wants a fuhkin' shot?" James asks no one in particular. "Veronica, whiskey gal, right?" He points at me while grabbing a shot and filling it with the delicious amber liquor.

I grit my teeth, hoping Thomas doesn't pick up on the blunder.

"You like whiskey?" Thomas whispers in my ear, still holding the empty glass he took to top off for me.

"Yeah, I do. Sometimes," I stutter nervously.

Thomas shrugs and sets my glass down, taking the shot from James and handing it to me. Their eyes lock for a moment too long, making my skin prickle. Before anyone else has their shot, I toss the liquid back, letting it burn down my throat pleasantly, and hand it back to Thomas for a refill.

"If I'd known you were so thirsty for whiskey, I would have gotten it for you sooner," Thomas says seductively, emphasizing *thirsty*.

Oh my, Thomas. If this man is speaking in innuendos, tonight will be very interesting. The shots are filled and being passed out, including my refill. We all wish Jen a happy birthday and drink.

Despite James showing up with all his sexy swagger after my date with Thomas, it isn't nearly as awkward as I thought it might be. James has hit on me quite a bit since I met him, but his advances aren't only directed at me. He's making moves on Amanda, and she's eating it up. There's an occasional curious glance or two thrown mine and Thomas's way, but otherwise, James is being super chill about this entire thing.

James hasn't pressed me about his offer to go on a date tomorrow either, which I think means the opportunity is off the table. I'm not entirely sure. However, if so, it's for the best. I don't want to screw up this opportunity at work over a one-night stand, especially after things with Rob, another co-worker, turned out so poorly.

Right now, I'm happy with my current path—Thomas. James is a sexy temptation, like a cold popsicle on a hot day, but that temporary relief only lasts so long. Thomas is a calm and steady presence that can act as an anchor during any storm.

Tonight's storm is a drunken mess that goes by the name of Jen and Luke.

"I think it's time to leave," I yell over the music to Jen.

Thomas is trying to corral Luke while I collect Jen, but both parties are actively ignoring us and grinding on each other instead.

"Dude, let's get you guys home where you can take this to your bedroom—where it belongs. Not here in public." Thomas tries to talk sense to his friend, who is sliding his hand up the back of Jen's top.

"Jen," I yell again, tugging her arm and receiving a deadly glare.

"Ugh. Fine. Let's fucking go," Jen groans, tugging Luke toward the exit, who follows her with the defeated look of a broken puppy dog.

Thomas and I follow them. He's already ordering a ride to take them home. None of us are sober, and since Thomas and I both took Uber's to dinner and the club, it puts us in that awkward position where one of the two parties either asks the other to go home with them or they both have to order their own ride and awkwardly wait on the curb together.

I loathe this situation.

Usually, I'm drunk enough to request the person go home with me, or I don't have to because we're already making out, and it's obvious where things are leading.

"So I got them a ride to Luke's place, but I can't figure out how to book two Uber's at once. Would you mind booking one for us? You don't live far, right?" Thomas asks.

"Book a ride to my place? For us?" I ask in surprise.

I didn't expect Thomas to be so forward about his intentions. It makes my stomach fill with butterflies. This man, whom I've only had the pleasure of tasting his lips, will be coming home with me tonight.

"Yes. Is that okay?" he asks warily.

"Yes," I interrupt, internally cursing myself for being so obviously excited.

"Great. Let's get these assholes into their Uber and get the fuck out of here," he says, grabbing my hand and walking toward Jen and Luke, who are making out against a brick wall.

Their make-out session is sloppy, not hot, but it leads my thoughts to what it'll be like to make out with the man beside me, and that thought alone is enough to heat my skin a degree.

Thomas retrieves a blunt from his jeans pocket and lights it up. The smell of marijuana draws Jen away from Luke. She meanders over to us, holding out an expectant hand for the blunt. We all know the booze come down is not going to be a good one without something to level it out.

Shortly after we finish the blunt, Jen and Luke are in an Uber and on their way to finish what they started. I hope they play Birthday Sex by Jeremih while fucking tonight.

Just as my head is clearing from the smoke sesh, Thomas and I walk around the corner toward our ride and pass Rob, Alex, and two women. Rob's arm is slung around a tall, thin, brown-haired woman. He's half stumbling, half making out with her neck.

Fuck me.

Just when I thought I was over Rob, I run into him on my way to take Thomas home. Fire erupts in my veins. My feet melt into the concrete as I halt to watch them. The icing on the cake, or should I say creme brulee, is that he walks past me like I don't even exist.

Office Daydreams
Mystery Man No More

"Veronica. Veronica?" Thomas tugs at my hand, trying to get my attention.

I'm so caught off guard by seeing Rob with another woman. My gut feels empty, yet my chest is heavy. This reaction is more than jealousy, and spite, and far more than I expected to happen when I saw him next. I know feelings developed for him, but they shouldn't be this deep.

"S—Sorry," I stutter, shaking my head and trying to clear the fog overwhelming my senses and threatening to tear through my eyes.

"Was that Rob?" he asks, moving in front of me and taking my hands.

"Yeah." I avoid eye contact and look at the dark concrete sidewalk. The last thing I want Thomas to know is how I feel about Rob, especially after having just gone on a date with him. I feel like such a bitch.

"He's a dick and an idiot, clearly." Thomas tilts my head up and forces me to look into his eyes.

His words are just like things Rob said to me before. How can one man say essentially the same thing to me, and then treat me like this? I feel used again.

"Hey. Hey. Don't do that," Thomas coos, swiping his thumb across my cheek.

His thumb glistens with the proof of my feelings. I'm an idiot, crying about some asshole at the end of the night, outside of a bar, in front of my new crush. To make matters worse, I feel like a whore for going on a date with Thomas and trying to take him home when I so clearly have strong feelings for another man.

"Sorry," I mutter the only words I can express right now—an apology.

Thomas cups my jaw with both hands, completely undeterred by my admission, and says huskily, "I'm not. Let me make you forget about him."

Then, he kisses me fiercely.

Through sobbing tears, I let this man remove my pain with his sensual, erotic lips. He sucks and nips my bottom lip before plunging his tongue deep into my mouth. His tongue licks up the backside of my teeth and swirls in a tantalizing tangle with mine. The fire and heat from my anger turn into a hot, frantic need.

I focus solely on the mutual yearning between us. The emotions inside me are overwhelming, and it fuels a desperate demand to suffocate the pain with something more primal and satisfying.

A horn honks and Thomas breaks away from me, leaving me breathless with my head spinning. I breathe deeply, trying to steady my racing heart.

"Come on. Let's find that Uber," he says, as out of breath as me.

Thomas resembles a mannequin in the car ride to my apartment. His hands stay perfectly perched on his thighs, and he keeps his eyes forward on the road. My lips still tingle from his touch, and my hands are itching for more. I desperately hope he's not regretting what just happened. If not, how he maintains his composure right now is beyond me —the man is a paradox.

Jiggling the keys in my janky lock, I nervously unlock my front door and swing it open. I step in slowly as I try to ignore the unnervingly loud steps my heels make as I walk down the hallway toward my living room. Thomas follows me in and shuts the door softly, locking it behind him. My heart skips a beat. He's still here. He still wants me.

I walk to the fridge to pour two glasses of chilled water. One for myself—to cool down this overwhelming hot desire before it gets out of control and I embarrass myself—and the other for Thomas because I'm not sure what else to do.

As I pour the pitcher of water into each glass, Thomas's silent steps approach me. He snakes his arms around my waist and snuggles me into his chest while still giving me space to pour the water and set down the pitcher.

Since Thomas isn't much taller than me, our bodies align and touch in all the most sensitive spots. My backside presses into his groin, and I silently beg it to start growing behind me. I want to feel him. I need the distraction of his touch, so I wiggle my hips against his groin.

"No. Not yet," he warns, pushing my hair to the side and nuzzling my neck.

His silky lips brush my shoulder, kissing up and down my collarbone and neck. I relax my head, letting it fall onto his shoulder to give him easier access to my erogenous zone. Thomas rewards me by sucking my neck into his mouth, rolling his tongue over the sensitive skin.

"Mmm," I moan, lulling my head to the side and feeling my shoulders sag against his chest. His lips massage my neck as well as fingers would.

Thomas holds me against him as he kisses my body, soothing my mind, body, and soul. His hands glide from my waist to the hemline of my dress with practiced ease. Grabbing the bottom of my dress, he slides it slowly over my hips, my waist, my chest, and my shoulders, lifting it up and over my head without letting me turn around to face him.

"That's better," he says, dropping the dress on the floor beside us.

I'm trapped between the kitchen counter and Thomas, wearing only a little lace thong and bra. I feel vulnerable standing with my back to this mystifying man. I have lusted after him for so long, and we're finally here—about to do it. My office daydreams are coming to fruition.

With newfound fervor, I steel my nerves and turn around. Thomas keeps his hands at my waist as I reveal myself to him. His eyes roam my body approvingly, like a man satisfied with his choice of wine.

"You're so fucking beautiful, Veronica," Thomas says, trailing his fingers along my waist. "Should we do this here or in the bedroom?"

His steely gaze shows no signs of his preference or desire. It takes all my effort not to quake under his control. Thomas has a way of unnerving me to the point that I don't know where this should go next. Should I run and hide? Would he come for me, or would he leave? Should I kiss him here and now? Does he want me to?

The tension in the air is thick with confusion, speculation, and wild excitement that makes my bones shiver. A glimmer of amusement traces the fine lines of his sly smile.

"Don't be confused, Veronica. I want to do this. What happened to that persistent woman in the elevator? The one who demanded I fuck her?" His lip quirks into a smile, recalling the heated events of our first tangle.

I gulp down the thick, suffocating lump in my throat that forces my nerves to prickle and my confidence to hide. He's right. Where is that woman? I waited long enough to get this—I might as well enjoy it.

"Here," I say, biting my bottom lip in anticipation.

"Good, because I can't fucking wait any longer," he growls, spinning me around and yanking my underwear down.

He drops to his knees. His tongue is on me, licking up the dewy folds of my sex and through the thick line of my backside. *Oh my*. His mouth is as skilled on my vulva as it was on my neck. I lean against the counter, using it to steady myself as his mouth sucks in my clit and flicks it with his tongue, sending electric spasms shooting through my body.

"Ah," I arch my back, and my knuckles turn white as I grip the counter in a death hold.

Thomas spreads my butt cheeks as my back arches, and he uses the angle to dig his tongue deeper into me as he continues his hypnotic sequence of licking, sucking, and nipping. My pulse hammers faster with each stroke of his tongue. I'm panting, nails nearly breaking against the granite counter as the coil of desire in my center winds tighter and tighter.

As my body begins to quiver, Thomas engulfs my clitoris with his mouth, flicking his tongue so quickly over the swollen bundle of nerves that my body clenches. Suddenly, he drives his fingers inside my entry and thrusts into me vigorously. My body strains and tightens around his fingers, but he forces through my tight inner walls.

A throbbing sensation pulses heavily from my body, against Thomas's mouth and hand. My skin is scorching, and I feel my orgasm growing, nearing the tipping point. My body shudders, and Thomas reacts. His free hand yanks down my bra. His fingers pinch, pull, and roll my nipple in a painful and pleasurable release.

My orgasm unleashes itself. I writhe against his mouth as the glorifying feeling of euphoria washes over my body and through my mind.

Office Daydreams
Stretches

I'm panting as I teeter against the kitchen counter. Thomas removes his fingers from my sex and kisses down my inner thigh before he stands. He runs his hands up and around my backside appreciatively.

"No wonder you can squat so much. This ass is so fucking nice, baby," he whispers in my ear, squeezing my butt cheeks.

"A little soon to be calling me baby," I say sassily.

"What would you like me to call you?" Thomas chuckles, spinning me around to face him. He presses his groin into me.

I gasp from the friction of his erection rubbing into my front. My leg naturally rises to his waist, wrapping around him as I snake my arms over his chest and around his shoulders. Thomas presses his erection into me harder. My lower back digs into the kitchen counter, but I don't care. As his lips meet mine again, I roll my hips and grind my bare sex against the rough material of his jeans. The fabric rubs my clit in enticing ways and only serves to awaken my deepest, most erotic desires.

His lips are like a siren's calls. They beguile and consume me so utterly that I lose control of my mind and body. Keeping our lips connected, Thomas bends and lifts the back of my thighs. I follow his unspoken instructions and wrap my arms tighter around his shoulders as he guides my other leg around his waist.

He holds me in mid-air as we kiss passionately, and just as I'm about to grind against him, Thomas lifts me higher. Holding me with one arm, he reaches between us to unbutton his pants.

I break our kiss to watch him, desperate to see him finally. I'm nearly drooling in anticipation of seeing Thomas's penis. While he unbuttons his pants, his arm hair tickles my sex. I swear he's doing it on purpose. And when he rubs his forearm through my wet folds, I moan.

The buttons on his pants finally open. It's as if my moaning speeds up his actions. He tugs down his pants and briefs just enough for his cock to pop out. I release another moan, one of longing and appreciation. I need him inside me.

Thomas slaps his cock against my sex. He rubs his shaft through my folds, lubricating his cock. I'm damn near salivating to feel him inside me.

"Oh my god, fuck me already," I beg, shifting my hips.

The tip of his cock prods at my entry. My clit is on fire. I'm near combusting.

"Condom. Back pocket," he says breathily, resting his forehead against mine as he holds me up.

He keeps my entry away from his cock, not letting us go any further until he has a condom on, but he keeps his rock-hard shaft pressed against my clit, and that alone is enough to get me off.

"Hurry, baby," Thomas says light-heartedly.

He knows I'm close. I hear the heat in his voice, though. He's just as desperate as me.

I reach behind him, searching for a condom. Thankfully, his pants are still around his ass. My fingers feel the rigged groves of the foil packet, pulling it out like it's the last cookie in the cookie jar. I rip it open with my teeth.

Thomas sets me on the counter and takes the condom. He rolls it over his long, skinny cock. I lick my lips, imagining what he tastes like, but that will have to wait until later. Right now, I need him inside me. Thomas gazes up at me with hooded eyes and sucks in his bottom lip. He strokes his cock as he slides the condom down his shaft, and I shudder at the provocative display of him pleasuring himself.

"Come here," he says, as he kicks off his pants and takes off his shirt.

Finally, he's naked. I thirstily follow his command. I'll do anything he tells me to right now.

"Turn around," he states.

As he demands, I face the counter once again.

"Lift your right leg onto the counter."

I peek behind me to find his gaze serious and hot. He looks at me like I am a decadent meal on a platter. It makes my skin tingle with excitement, and I quickly lift my leg onto the counter as he instructs. Thomas's hands are back on me. I sigh in relief as he repositions my leg to extend fully across the counter. My back arches with the stretch, and he pushes my chest down to the counter. The position has my pussy spread wide open.

"Damn. You're flexible," he says admirably before slapping my ass.

The sharp sting of his hand sends a hot rob of electricity straight to my aching sex.

"Ah," I yelp. My hips flex, and my backside curls upward, exposing more of my wet pussy to him.

"Such a nice ass and pretty pussy," he says.

Thomas digs his fingers into my hips as his cock nudges my center. I hold my breath, anxiously awaiting the feel of him. He breaches the tip, and without warning, he slams the rest of the way into me. An audible moan rewards me. My pussy engulfs him like his cock is made for me, and just as I thought he would, his long cock pounds into my G-spot.

"Oh god. Yes." I thank the universe for this indescribable cock. He's hitting me in all the right places.

"You like that? You think you can handle more, baby?" Thomas asks, reaching a hand around my side to palm my breast.

"Yes. Give me more," I beg.

At my plea, Thomas's thrusts pick up their fervorous pace. The base of his cock hits my ass as his cock sinks deeper with each thrust, hitting my g-spot in a rhythmic song that has my body buzzing. His balls slap against my clit, making me impossibly wetter. When I don't think our bodies can be any more attuned to each other, Thomas hooks an arm under my leg and lifts it higher, stretching my center wide open and giving him an even deeper angle to fuck me.

"Fuck," I yell, feeling on the verge of breaking.

My pussy and legs are being stretched to new levels. The strain of the painful position has me sweating, yet I want to stretch more and take him deeper.

"Oh, baby. I'm close. Come for me," Thomas says, his pace becoming erratic and strained.

I feel his cock swelling inside me, so I clench my walls around him. He pinches my nipple between his thumb and forefinger and lifts my leg even higher to the point that my knee is hooked around his shoulder. I take in the sight of our provocative position, and my mouth drops open, letting out a low, guttural moan as I come so hard around his cock bright lights blur my vision.

At this indecent angle, I can watch as my pussy clenches and pulses around him. My thick, white cum coats his cock each time he pulls out and pushes back in. I'm shaking as the orgasm bursts to life, and using his free hand, Thomas presses his thumb against my clit, rubbing it furiously.

"Fuck. No. No. No," I breathe, feeling an unfamiliar, overwhelming feeling building inside me.

He's relentless. He doesn't cease circling his thumb or thrusting his hips. My cum turns thin and clear on his cock. My lip quivers and my stomach knots as a lightness fills my head.

"Oh my god—"

My nails bite into Thomas's shoulders, fighting the oncoming release. I have no control over it. It hits me like a freight train. Clear fluid shoots from my pussy, coating Thomas's stomach and our groins, and my orgasm officially transcends all other orgasms.

"Veronica," he says.

With one final thrust, his cock swells inside me, and he comes too.

Acknowledgements

This is my second self-published book, but my first proper book release. I've been fortunate enough to have a community behind me every step of the way. Whether it be the words of encouragement or the sharing of resources, every person and conversation that has led me here has been an integral part of my growth, for which I will be forever grateful!

I would be remiss if I did not credit my Craving Darkness anthology group for giving me the knowledge and insight necessary to publish wide. This group of ladies are incredibly helpful, supportive, and insanely hard workers. I'm honored to have collaborated with them on such a fun dark romance project and have learned how to expand my career by walking in their footsteps. Thank you ladies!

I must also give credit to the people who were there for me since day one: Inkitt and Patreon subscribers. These online communities were an essential part of encouraging me to continue writing. When I thought no one would care or read it, they did. They continue to support me online and are the reason I can afford to pursue more costly endeavors related to publishing. Thank you for your continued support!

Thank you to the men and women who offered to read my stories, provide much-needed feedback, and promote my book even though I'm new to the writing scene. Your support for indie authors like myself is why we can keep doing it. Thank you, thank you, thank you! Please keep doing what you're doing.

As they say, it takes a village. My village is my friends and family. It's been a year of many changes, but the support and encouragement from my army have kept my mindset positive and my focus clear. Others in this position can relate, but it can be hard to move forward without a true North guiding your life. I've had my moments. My path has been more like a zig-zag than a straight line, but one thing has remained consistent—my people. And for that, I thank my loved ones!

Lastly, my cutie patootie, my sweet baby girl—Goldie Lu. A pup once on the cusp of death with a heart as pure as they get. Thank you for warming my feet, making me laugh, and providing endless cuddles. You aren't my first fur child, but you're no less important. You light up my life!

Author's Note

Romance has never been a category of storytelling I was fond of, and I long debated why. After much internal reflection and self-work, I determined my deterrence for the genre was related to childhood trauma. Go figure!

This same trauma led to many irresponsible relationship decisions in my twenties. It's been a wild ride, but writing romance and erotica has shaped my life in many unexpected ways. Not only have I developed a deep understanding of my needs and wants, but I've finally embraced my feminine sensuality in all its forms. We don't need to explain why we feel or want anything in life. We only answer to ourselves.

For years, I shoved aside desires because I thought they were socially unacceptable. The truth was that my reality was distorted by a childhood growing up in a society that shunned people for openly embracing the more primal displays of affection and love. Those same people probably think I've gone off the deep end—especially if they've read some of my more debaucherous work.

That being said, I could not be more grateful for the community writing has brought me. In a world full of billions of people and living things, it's easy to feel alone. As insane as that statement should be, I know it resonates with many. In my darkest and most loneliest moments, books have always been there for me. Stories have kept my heart aching and my mind swirling. They've given my life more meaning, and I hope my books do the same for others. I have much to learn and so much more to grow. As I do, I plan to write my challenges, successes, and lessons learned into the underlying plot of every book I write.

Guilty Pleasures was a culmination of short stories I put together based on fantasies that drifted into my head during lonely moments. Dom Daddy—one of these fantasies—became so much more than a few chapters. I expand this short into a full-length novel that explores the limits of embracing our deepest, darkest desires. It follows Lily, our main character, on a quest to discover her sensuality. She explores her boundaries, her fears, and her desires in ways that even she didn't know possible. Her mind is expanded by the willingness to be vulnerable and embrace new experiences.

As I wrote Dom Daddy, I experienced my own sort of sensual awakening. I mention sensual, not sexual, because they are two very different things. Becoming comfortable and confident in your body and mind is an entirely different experience that I hope everyone comes to understand one day. Dom Daddy was a delight to write as I worked through this awakening. I cannot wait for you all to get your hands on this next book. Be sure to join my newsletter and follow my socials to stay up-to-date on all my book releases.

XOXO

Sam

About the Author

Sam Marie is a contemporary fiction author who loves writing everything from spicy romances to science fiction. When she's not reading or writing, she walks her fur child along the beach, hosts dinner parties, and travels often.

Her love of storytelling started at a young age. Sam often entertained her family on road trips with long-winded stories about wild adventures in make-believe lands, and her love affair with writing only grew from there. She wrote her debut novel, Foreign Desires, in one month, publishing it on a popular online reading platform, Inkitt, as she completed chapters. The community engagement surrounding her stories led Sam to leave the corporate life behind and pursue her passion for writing full-time.

Sign up for her newsletter to stay current on Sam's book news. You can also follow her here:

Website: authorsammarie.com

Facebook: Sam Marie

Instagram: @author.sam.marie

Tiktok: @sammarieofficial

Linktree: linktr.ee/sammarie.author

Goodreads: Sam Marie